T.Torrest

REMEMBER
WHEN 3:

The Finale

For my sister, Diana.
She's waited for this longer than anyone.

T. Torrest
Remember When 3: The Finale

Cover Design: Dana Gollance
www.ateliergollance.com

Cover Design: Hang Le
www.byhangle.com

Printed in the United States of America
Third paperback edition ©2015

REMEMBER WHEN 3:

The Finale

Prologue
TRIP
OCTOBER 1st (well, 2nd), 2000

12:27 AM. What the ever-loving fuck.

I thought Layla would have been here hours ago. What the hell could be taking her so long?

My brain refuses to even consider that she won't come. I mean, that's not even an option, right? There is no possible way she won't show up. Maybe she just needs a little time to get her head in the right place, accept that this is happening.

Because it is *so* happening.

I keep waiting for the room phone to ring. The front desk has explicit instructions to call me the second she walks into the lobby, giving me a five-minute window to light all these stupid candles I put all over the place. I had the cabbie make a stop at the Duane Reade, where I bought every goddamned candle they had on the shelves. The suite is filled with them.

Who says guys aren't romantic?

12:49.

I've been sitting in this bed for hours, flipping through channels on the TV, trying to distract my mind from my wait.

And from the minibar.

I've needed a drink since I got back here, needed to take the edge off after that fight at her apartment. Jesus. What the hell are we even arguing for? Leave it to that girl to find a way to turn *I love you* into a standoff.

Well, maybe I didn't say those exact words, but I came damn near close enough. Besides, she already knows I love her. Practically told her as much.

Practically.

I mean, I sent that damned lunchbox, didn't I?

The first thing I did when I got back here was to interrogate the concierge. Veronica? Vanessa? Whoever she was, she swore it went out. I called down to the front desk about a million times since to confirm it, finally got smart and asked for the number of the messenger service she'd used. By that time, the place was already done for the day, a recording telling me they close at eight on Sundays, so at least I know it had to have been delivered no later than that.

So, Layla got the gift. And she's still not here.

1:10.

I actually restrained myself from banging her against the damned wall, actually forced myself to hold back, and not just… take. It was probably the most difficult thing I've ever done in my life. I mean, I had her *right there*. Right there in my arms, smashed up against the wall, her tongue in my mouth, her legs wrapped around my waist, her body pressed… *Shit*. What the hell am I doing? I'm getting myself all worked up and I can't even do anything about it. I will not jerk off. I will *not*. She'll be here any minute and I'm not seventeen anymore. Takes a few minutes to reboot these days, and I'm not waiting another minute longer than necessary to finally take her to bed. I plan on slamming into that girl the second she walks through that door. There's only one place I'm prepared to unload this thing, and it will *not* be in a tissue.

Great. So now I'm sober *and* hard.

I need a drink. I mean, I really, *really* need a drink. But I'm not going to cave. After my outburst Friday night at the diner, I'm not touching the hard stuff ever again. I scared the hell out of Layla. Scared my*self*. I haven't touched a drop since then.

This isn't the first time I've tried to dry out. Not the first time that I've gotten disgusted with myself, heard my old man's voice while I was speaking, saw his face when I looked in the mirror.

Not the first time I found myself picking a fight.

That night at The Westlake Pub was pretty freaking insane. I only went there hoping to run into Layla. It was a shot in the dark, but she wasn't taking any of my calls, and I had to see her again. I figured the chances were good that she probably dropped into the local watering hole from time to time. It's the only bar in our hometown. Well, the only one anybody ever went to, anyway. When she didn't show, I slammed down a few too many and the next thing I knew, I was provoking some 'roid rage guido and his entourage. And then I wound up in jail.

Kind of a wakeup call.

So, yeah. I try to lay off the booze from time to time.

Hell, I went to that club on the Lower East Side a couple weeks ago and spent the whole time drinking soda all night, for godsakes. Soda. At the Luna Lounge. Now that's commitment. But again, I was hoping to run into Layla and decided that this time I didn't want to be a drunken mess when I did.

She was the only reason I was even at a frigging bar at all. I mean, when I'm trying to curb my drinking, a bar isn't really the first place I want to find myself. But earlier that week, I'd just happened to strike up a conversation with one of the security guys on set. It's amazing what you can learn about a person after only a few minutes. And what I'd learned about that security guy was that his brother went to college at NYU. I asked him to give the guy a call, and holy shit, yeah, he's friends with Layla Warren. Not only that, but said brother was a bartender at the Luna, and mentioned that she came in pretty regularly on Saturday nights.

So, we went. Me and my new best friend, Mitch. And I waited. Feeling like a stalker.

And she never showed up.

But I didn't have a drink.

1:48. Dammit.

Nine years I went without seeing her. Nine. Fucking. Years. And then I walked into that room, and there she was. That beautiful smile, those gorgeous brown eyes. Looking at me like we were seventeen again. Looking at me like I was... me.

Where. Is. She?

I could call her. There's the phone. Right there. I could just call her and find out what the hell is going on in that brain of hers. I mean, we belong together. She has to know that. She knows that *I* know that. Were my intentions not clear?

No. I laid it all out there. She knows what I want.

She knows what *she* wants.

So, why the hell isn't she here right now?

I launch off the bed, throw the stupid remote onto the pillows, and head for the fridge. I swore I wasn't going to have a drink tonight. I swore I was going to be one-hundred-percent present when she got here. I pull out a mini bottle of Jack anyway and set it on the counter.

But I don't open it.

I stand there staring at it instead, even though I know that just one little drink will help to take the edge off. Calm my nerves. Keep me sane until she gets here. I'm standing here, talking to myself, the voice in my head telling me that it's okay to just have one.

Just. One. Little. Drink.

But I don't open it.

I grab the Toblerone instead, chomping on it as I pace around the living room.

I will not go back into that bedroom alone.

I will not go back in that bed without Layla.

Layla Effing Warren. The most beautiful girl I've ever known. The girl who makes me laugh. The girl who loved me.

Who *loves* me.

Right?

Shit. 2:34.

I flop onto the sofa, but that damn bottle on the counter is in my line of sight, calling my name. I switch position on the couch, resting my head on the other end so I don't have to look at it. But now I can see the phone on the side table, so I cover it with a pillow, resisting the urge to use it. But what if it rings, and I don't hear it? As if some stupid pillow is really going to muffle the sound of a ringing phone. But crap. I don't want to take the chance that I'll miss the call from the front desk letting me know Layla's here. *Fuck!* I get up and put the phone on the floor, out of sight.

The remote catches my attention, so I flick on the tube and channel surf aimlessly, my mind not even registering what I'm looking at until I come across *Sixteen Candles* on HBO. Classic.

And Layla's favorite movie.

Sonofabitch.

If she doesn't show up, I don't think I'll ever be able to watch this movie ever again. I don't think I'll ever be able to watch *my* movie ever again. It was hard enough just having to see myself onscreen, but it was even harder having her sitting right there next to me... where I could smell her, touch her. Sitting there with a boner like some thirteen-year-old just from holding her hand.

Sitting here with a boner *right now* just thinking about it. Dammit. I really need to take care of this thing.

Where the fuck is she?

3:02.

I don't think she's coming.

Holy shit. She's really not fucking coming.

Christ. My chest hurts. There's an actual, physical pain in my chest right now. She's killing me. And she's doing it slowly. She could have shown a little compassion and finished me off years ago, instead of letting me bleed out over ten whole years. Because this? This is merciless.

And completely unbearable.

I'm tired. I'm horny. I'm *pissed*. And I'm way, way too sober.

Fuck it.

I bound off the couch and crack that bottle of Jack, bringing it to my lips and downing it quickly, the scalding in my throat a familiar salve. I savor the burn for only a minute, because I've got some brain cells to obliterate and this little mini sampler-sized bottle isn't cutting it. I grab a tall glass from the cabinet and empty about a million of those little bottles into it, not even checking the labels before I do. And then I throw the whole thing back in one, magnificent, pathetic chug. I slam the empty glass on the counter, bracing my hands on either side of it.

And I wait.

Wait for the booze to do its work. Wait for the memories to blur, for the pain in my chest to slip away.

I stare at my cast for like the hundredth time since coming back to my room. She'd tattooed the entire thing, filled in every available space of white with fictional creatures and their fake little worlds. I check out every line she sketched, every inch she colored in while we talked. Talked about us. Talked about who we were to each other. Who we *are*.

I know now that it was all a lie.

She was just drawing out the myth.

Before I know it, I'm slamming my forearm against the edge of the counter, cracking the cast and breaking it into bits, tearing it from my skin. White powder is coating the dark blue surface, chunks of plaster are littering the floor, ribbons of gauze are trailing from my arm in tatters, and I look like a deranged mummy. My pale, pickled, smelly arm comes into view, the scars a deep pink from where the bone protruded through my skin.

And it hurts.

She actually did it. She chose him instead of me. It's over.

I can't do this. I can't play this game with her anymore. I'm completely annihilated, and this isn't the first time she's crushed me. I always knew I loved her, always made myself remember. I just never thought anything could come of it. We were kids, for chrissakes. But we're not kids anymore. I thought that would mean something, make it bigger somehow, give us the chance we'd denied ourselves all those years ago.

But she doesn't want me.

And I can't have her.

And there it is.

I allow myself to remember everything. Every moment we've shared since the first second I saw her sitting in that desk in English class, right on up to her lips on mine a few hours ago. Every look, every laugh, every kiss, every touch.

And then I make myself forget.

I sever her memory like a limb off a tree, like an arm from my body. It was a part of me, but not anymore. It's been cut off. Buried. Gone forever.

She is dead to me.

Layla Warren, you are no more.

I slam down another two bottles of whatever, and before my brain can step in, I whip one across the room. It bounces off an upholstered chair and pings against the TV. But it doesn't even cause a crack in the screen before dropping to the carpet and rolling under the coffee table.

The tiny snap isn't nearly big enough for the madness I'm feeling.

I'm feeling bigger. I'm feeling louder.

I stomp to the living room and rip a drawer from the side table, discus-throwing it at the television with a roar, where it connects with a spectacular crash, the wood splintering apart on its way to the carpet. It is quickly followed by the TV, which cracks face-first onto the floor, its descent causing the armoire that housed it to pull away from the wall in a *Smooth Criminal* lean, tethered to the studs by a vinyl safety restraint. I shove the remains of the TV out of the way, knocking over one of those fucking *Wilmington Blue* easy chairs. I grab hold of the top of the armoire, using my full weight to unleash the tether in a fantastic rip, pulling the massive thing down where it crashes and flattens almost completely to the ground. Surprisingly, the bulky piece of furniture hasn't broken apart upon its landing, but the coffee table hasn't fared as well.

I stand with my hands in fists at my hips, chest heaving, the alcohol and adrenaline coursing through me, taking in the whole demolition site. The throbbing in my broken arm has exploded into a sharp, stabbing pain that drowns the ache in my chest. It's an improvement.

The room is trashed. Such a beautiful disaster.

I head back to the mini fridge and slam down another bottle of whatever just as the knocking starts. For a second, I pathetically hope it's *her*, but then I hear the voice of Jeffrey, the hotel manager. *"Mr. Wiley? Is everything okay in there?"*

Yeah. Sure, buddy. Everything's peachy.

Fuck 'em. I crack open another bottle as Jeffrey pounds on the door again. *"Mr. Wiley!"*

"Go away!"

"Mr. Wiley, I'm sorry, but we've received a few phone calls about some excessive noise up here. Are you sure everything's alright?"

This guy.

I storm over to the door and whip it open clumsily, but violently enough that Jeffrey takes a step back. Or maybe I just look like enough of a maniac that I've scared him. Good.

"I told you I'm fine!"

Jeffrey peeks past me into the room. I know *it* isn't fine.

"Mr. Wiley… your room…"

"Thass right, pal. *My* room. My fugging hotel, actually. So I did a li'l remodeling. So what?"

I know I'm slurring, and I sound like a dick. I know I *am* a dick. And Jeffrey's taken care of every detail for me since the minute I checked into this place. He doesn't deserve this. He's not the one who stood me up tonight. I can always count on Jeffrey.

I lose the smarm and switch gears, offering casually, "Hey, I'm sorry, Jeffy. You wanna come in an' have a drink? Come on. Come on in."

I open the door fully, inviting him in with a sweep of my damaged arm, coated in white powder and the few remnants of gauze still sticking to my skin. Jeffrey doesn't look like he's in a sociable mood and doesn't make it past the threshold.

"Mr. Wiley, thank you, but no." He gives the mess in the living room another once over and says, "I trust you'll keep the noise level down for the rest of the night, yes?"

I'm calm as a cucumber. My tantrum has exhausted me. There will be no more hotel-room-trashing from me.

"Yes, Jeffy. I'll keep it down. You can count on me," I tell him, giving some sloppy, crazy-eyed, military salute. "G'night. I'll be quiet. Okay. G'night."

And then I close the door, grab a few more bottles, and head back into the bedroom.

Alone.

SEPTEMBER

2002

Prologue: Take Two
TRIP
SEPTEMBER 30, 2002

"You are *such* an asshole!"

Jenna's been screeching at me for over an hour now, but this is the first time she's resorted to name-calling.

"Yeah, well you were engaged to this asshole for two whole years, sweetheart!"

She stares me down for a moment before squinting her eyes and offering, "*Were.*"

I know she's waiting for me to take back my words, tell her I didn't really mean it when I said we were through. We've had lots of fights over the years but we've never broken up over one. In fact, it was when the fighting stopped that I realized we were in real trouble. Nothing signals the imminent death of a relationship quicker than indifference, and we've been indifferent for quite some time now.

And apparently, I'm an asshole. Jesus. Tell me something I *don't* know.

When I don't respond, Jenna throws her hands in the air and goes back to her packing. She's tearing her dresser apart, pulling out every stitch of designer clothing inside, and dumping everything into the suitcases at her feet. She's been rampaging around the room ever since we had our little talk, ever since I asked her kindly to move the fuck out of my house.

She looked at me as though I'd lost my mind, which, to tell you the truth, I kind of had. But one thing I did know was that it was way past time for us to end our relationship. She knew it, too, but that hasn't stopped her from putting on one hell of a performance, storming around my bedroom like a raving banshee. Best acting she's done in years.

Whatever. If she needs to stomp around this house and cause a big dramatic scene, I'll shut up and let her have at it. Besides, I've got one hell of a hangover going on, and I just don't have it in me to fight back. But watching her in full bitch mode makes me miss the person she used to be. When she was just a fairly sweet, extraordinarily pretty girl trying to get her acting career off the ground. But fame does funny things to a person. Some people just can't handle it.

"I can't believe you're doing this to me!" she pouts before moving into the closet and pulling her dresses off their hangers.

"Look, Jenna," I explain to the back of her head, "I'm not doing this *to you*. I'm going to rehab *for me*. Why can't you see that?"

Jenna stops flinging clothes out the door and turns to face me. She puts her hands on her bony hips and practically snarls, "Of course I see it, Trip. God forbid anything not be about *you*."

So uncool. But in spite of the fact that her comment was completely out of line, I find myself cringing at her words. The sad truth is that I *am* the center of attention a lot of the time, but it's not like I asked for it. All I want is to be an actor. The stupid fame part of it just happens to go along with that. I'm sure lots of people—like Jenna, for example—think that being famous is the goal in and of itself. It's not. It's an unfortunate byproduct of my chosen career. Hell, if I were just some Joe Nobody, all my bullshit would remain private. As it is, privacy isn't really a part of my life anymore. I don't get to do anything these days without the goddamn cameras in my face. It's not ideal, but I've had to get used to it. Comes with the territory.

Jenna double-checks the dresser, leaving the drawers gaping open and empty. She storms into the master bath and gives a sigh when she sees all her stuff scattered across the counter.

Trust me, it makes me sigh, too.

She picks up the wastebasket and shakes its contents upside down onto the bathroom floor, leaving a pile of used tissues and other assorted garbage in her wake. She braces the basket against the counter, and with a full arm-sweep, clears the space in one fell swoop. Shit. My razor was on there. Screw it. I'd rather get a new one than deal with asking for it back.

I'm already asking for enough, apparently.

I don't know where Jenna gets off being so pissed about the situation, though I suppose if she gave even one single crap about me, she'd have forced me to get some help a long time ago. Instead, she was too busy fucking her way up the Hollywood ladder to even notice that I was killing myself.

That's right, sweetheart. I know all about it.

I sit on the bed, causing her to give a huff. Goddammit, I'm not even doing anything, but I guess even *breathing* is going to be met with her venom right now.

We weren't always like this with each other. In fact, there was a time, not so long ago, that I thought we'd actually get married.

I eye her up, wondering how we got here. A boozy cut-rate actor and his estranged model fiancée.

Ex-fiancée.

Our association started off like any other normal relationship: We met. We liked each other. We started dating. But somewhere along the way, our true personalities came out. And yet I still proposed. And she still said yes.

I'm not proud for staying with her as long as I have, knowing I never loved her. Although, if I'm going to be honest here, it's not like I've ever led her to believe otherwise. I was always straightforward with her. Always told her the truth regarding our arrangement.

It's been a rapid decline since then, but like I said, it didn't start out that way.

"Jenna. I really don't want us to end like this."

Grappling with the zipper on her suitcase, she stops to meet my gaze. "Like what?"

"Like this. With us hating each other."

She brushes a hand through her hair and turns her attention back to her suitcase. "But you *do* want us to *end*."

"Yes, but... What happened to us? We used to..."

"Like each other?"

"Yeah."

Finally victorious in her battle with the zipper, she stands and crosses her arms. Her stance isn't one of defiance, but of resignation. It actually serves to make her look like the easy-going girl she used to be. The girl she was before she turned into this emaciated, pissed-off bag of Botox. *Jesus, Jenna. When the hell did you do that to your lips?*

Taking a deep breath, she says, "It's not like there's been much for either of us to like these days."

She's right.

When your life doesn't live up to your expectations, it's all too easy to take it out on the nearest person. When you're a kid, your whole life is ahead of you. No dream is too big and it feels as though the entire world is within your grasp. All you need to do is reach out and take it.

I did.

Just to fuck it all up and get caught in a bottle. The fucking world had been handed to me from the minute I was born. And what do I do? Ruin everything. Turn into my old man.

But instead of dwelling on it, I decide to save the philosophy for another day. Right now, Jenna needs help carrying all these bags downstairs, and I'm more than ready to assist in her departure. So, I grab what I can and leave the wastebasket and the duffle to her. As we head down the stairs, she grabs the vase off the nook in the wall.

"Do you mind?" she asks. "I always loved this piece."

"No. Take it. You're the one that picked it out, after all."

And I always hated it.

I load her stuff into her BMW out front and meet her back in the foyer. Our eyes meet awkwardly, the both of us trying to figure out the right way to say goodbye. Just when I think we'll actually be able to part ways on decent terms, she storms out, giving one final, "Asshole!" before slamming the door behind her. Real nice.

And suddenly, the house is dead silent.

I'm not used to silence.

Out of pure habit, I go over to the bar in my living room, and pull down the Jackie D to make a drink. I'm hungover as shit, and could use a little hair o' the dog.

Wait.

I can't do that anymore. I've got the car scheduled to take me to Shady Pines in... dammit. One hour.

How the fuck did it come to this? How did I end up turning into this pathetic mess of a human being? My career is in the shitter, my relationship—or lack thereof—is a complete farce, and oh man, my mother is going to completely flip out when I tell her there's not going to be a wedding. She's already been robbed of one with Claudia; she'll never let me live this down.

17

I put the Jack back on the shelf, wondering what the hell I should do about all this booze. Since I won't be drinking anymore, shouldn't I dismantle the bar and have it removed from the house? Can I stand having it here if I don't?

I already know I won't be strong enough. Sure, I'm determined right now, but my willpower never lasts long. Do they even let you check into the treatment center if you're plowed? Maybe I *should* toss back a few before I go, just so they'll believe that I have a problem.

Hell. I don't need visual proof. They could probably do a blood test on me now and find that I'm still drunk from *yesterday*.

I was always a drinker. I've made it a point *not* to abstain just because my old man was a complete alcoholic. I wanted to prove that I could handle it, not let it control me the way it has with him. I kept myself in check for years. Could have a drink or a few and then call it a night.

That was, until after... *her.*

Nope. I'm not going there. If I start thinking about *her*, there's no way I'll be able to stop myself from chugging that whole damned bottle. She's the reason I'm hung over right now anyway.

No. You know what? It's not fair to blame her. I did this to myself.

And now it's time to pay for it.

Despite my wishes to the contrary, a flash of her smiling brown eyes flitters across my brain. I grip the edge of the leather stool in front of me, trying to force the image from my mind. *Oh, God. Why can't I just forget?*

She was completely erased from my brain. Her memory was swiped. I was doing fine.

But then last week... I saw her.

I'd been back home a few times to visit my folks, but I never managed to run into her. I know she lives in the city, but I figured there was always the chance that she could be back home, visiting too. This last time, I was downtown, picking up some stuff for my mom... and there she was. Right there on the sidewalk out front of Norman Bakery.

Before I knew what I was doing, I pulled up onto the curb and practically jumped out of my truck. I was going to go over and say hello, kiss her, *something*, but I just stood there in the open door of my truck, frozen.

Because it wasn't her.

Just some random girl with the same color hair.

As soon as the vision appeared, it was gone. It got me thinking that I should just show up on her father's doorstep and demand that he tell me where I could find her, once and for all.

But then I remembered. She must be furious with me, and hell, the feeling was quite mutual. It had been a couple years since that day in her apartment, when I tried to get her to break up with her fiancé. She wouldn't do it. But where the hell did I get off? I had nothing to offer her then. I was a pathetic, empty shell of a man, well on my way to rock bottom. Even then, I knew I was fucked up.

And instead of being a man, instead of straightening my life out, I'd tried to fuck hers up. She had a good guy who wanted to take care of her. Give her a respectable life. Not this circus that I live in.

I stood there and told myself—again—what I already knew to be true: She's better off with him.

As bad as it hurts to admit that, it's the truth. No wonder she didn't pick me.

What would have happened if she had made a different choice that day? Would we still be together now? Would she have stuck around through this? The sleeping all day and the drinking all night? Would I have any reason to drink at all if she were with me?

I got back in my truck and drove away.

I came home and spent the following week on a bender, not that that was anything new. But then yesterday, I wound up face down in my pool.

Yeah.

It stopped being cute after that. Actually, I guess it stopped being cute well *before* that.

I finally woke up and realized there was no way I could keep going like this. I'm a mess. I've got to work on myself before I can give anything to anyone else. My career, my family, my friends... *her*. It's too easy to believe that if she had just stuck by my side, I could've been the man I always thought I'd be.

Goddammit. It's too unfair to put any of this on her. It's pathetic. I'm done looking for excuses. Fact is, this is all my doing. I'm ready to own that now.

And even if she won't have me, I have to do this. I need to be the man she thought I was. Live up to her assessment in order to have any sort of life at all. Maybe it won't be for her, but I can do it for me.

Time to man up.

Take responsibility.

Then I might be worthy of her.

Even though she married someone else.

PART THREE

2005

Chapter 1
WINTER PASSING

Do you ever have psychic premonitions? I'm not talking about foreseeing world events in your crystal ball or being able to read someone's mind. But do you ever get that little tingle along your skin, that little whisper in a forgotten corner of your brain that makes the hair on the back of your neck stand up?

It doesn't happen often, but when it does, I know it. So, I wasn't quite as surprised as I should have been when the phone rang one otherwise uneventful afternoon. I was pretty sure I already knew who was calling.

I grabbed it off its base on the first ring, and I don't even think I said hello before being met with, "My father died."

I gripped the phone in my hand, not quite believing what I was hearing. Not just the startling news being disseminated, but the voice of the person delivering it.

It's strange how there are people in your life that never seem to leave it. Those friends that you may not talk to regularly, but whom you still very much consider a part of your life. You may go months, even years without seeing one another or speaking. But once you wind up together again, it's as if not a single day has gone by.

I have lots of friends like that. I don't know what the formula is, but I'm like Fry's dog. Once I bond with someone, even someone new, it's for life. Most of the people in my inner circle are the ones who have steadily been a part of it, however. My father has always been there for me, and my best friend Lisa is my rock. Even my little brother Bruce and I managed to form a decent friendship during our twenties.

But what is it about high school? Is it just the fact that you spend every single day with those people? Every single day over the course of four very formative years that bonds you forever? At the age of thirty-one, I had friends through work and around the neighborhood. I had lots of buddies from college. But for some reason, it wasn't the same. Sure, I kept in touch. But I always found myself coming back to my center, my core. The tightest bond I ever maintained was with the group from St. Norman's graduating class of '91.

Lisa was my go-to, my partner-in-crime, my touchstone. Her husband Pickford was like the big brother I never had. Cooper Benedict was a childhood friend, and even though he lived down in Maryland, we still talked occasionally and made a point to get together at least once a year. Even Greg Rymer still lived right in town, and I managed to toss him some work every now and again.

Fourteen years after high school, and I was still surrounded by the people from my youth. Hell, it was like I was still *living* my youth. Years ago, I'd moved back to the town I'd grown up in. Not only that, but I was living in my childhood home as well. I was sitting in my old bedroom, staring at the same white-painted furniture that lined the walls, the same pink princess phone in my hand.

I twirled the cord around my finger as my eyes landed on the back of my bedroom door. I noticed the tiny drawing near the bottom, saw the small heart sketched in red Sharpie years before, registered the initials lovingly drawn inside. I'd scribbled it there a lifetime ago and had completely forgotten about it in all the years since… until the phone rang.

Because at that moment, I found my eyes zeroing in on the silly little spot as I spoke to my high school sweetheart.

"Oh, Trip. I'm so sorry."

Chapter 2
AN UNFINISHED LIFE

Fighting down my nausea, I pulled my car into the driveway of the Malachi Bros. Funeral Home and parked near the back of the lot. I figured there was every chance that I'd be there for the entire day. I took a deep breath, checked the clock on my dashboard, and found that it was 1:05. The wake started at one, but I wanted to allow a little time for Trip and his family to have a few private moments before the mourners arrived. It would be the only peace they'd have for a while, once the steady stream of friends and family started running roughshod through their lives. My plan was to sit and wait it out for a few minutes in my car.

But then I saw the van.

Parked around the corner of the building was a white truck with a satellite jobby on top, so there was no mistaking the fact that it was a news van. I should have expected it, but I couldn't believe the press was staking out the place on such a personal day. I was busy shooting scathing death-looks in its general direction, so I didn't notice the photographer approaching my car until he was already at my window with a clacking camera poised between us.

Seriously, dude?

I opened the car door into his hip, but he continued snapping away, asking a barrage of stupid, nosy questions. "Are you family? Are you Trip Wiley's girlfriend? Hey, over here! C'mon, lemme just get one shot! Who are you?"

I put my pocketbook in front of my face and shuffled toward the front door to the funeral home. I stopped with my fingers on the handle, just long enough to shoot back from behind my purse, "You should be ashamed of yourself! His father just died, asshole! Get a real job."

Okay, not necessarily graceful, but my God. What a bunch of bloodsuckers.

Since my plan to wait it out had been thwarted, I had no choice but to head inside. The overwhelming smell of funeral flowers immediately smacked me in the face. It was too fragrant, and it made me feel even more nauseated than before. The lobby was quiet, save for some soft music playing. It was not new age or classical. It was doo-wop. I smiled to myself, quite sure that Trip had been the one to arrange for the unconventional selection of fifties tunes to be played in honor of his father. Very nice.

The director made his way out of a door located just off the lobby. He had mastered the sympathetic smile after so many years and aimed one at me now. "Wilmington?" he asked unnecessarily. Malachi's is a large home, but there would be no other deceased laid out that day. Terrence Chester Wilmington II was a very successful hotelier, with a chain of establishments dotted across the country. Aside from family and friends, there would be many business associates coming to pay their respects. But right then, I knew I would probably only find his immediate family and the occasional straggler like me.

Before I could make my way into the viewing room, I encountered Sandy Carron, Trip's publicist, whom I had met briefly four-and-a-half years prior. It seemed like a lifetime ago when I'd interviewed Trip for my job at the time. I also registered that the last time Sandy and I spoke, she'd basically told me to go fornicate myself. But we both put that aside for the time being. There were more important things to deal with at the moment.

I wondered if I should reintroduce myself to her, but she came right over and hugged me hello. "Layla. Thank God you're here. Trip's been waiting for you."

Trip's been waiting for me?

I tried not to sound too startled, and asked, "Is he okay?"

It truly was the only thing I wanted to know. The only thing I could allow myself to care about right then.

Sandy pulled back, swiping a tear from her eye. "I wish I could tell you yes, but…."

Shit. The poor guy was a mess. He always had a tumultuous relationship with his father; a lifelong love/hate situation going on. I couldn't even imagine what he must have been feeling.

"Hey, umm… am I intruding? I wasn't planning on getting here so early, but I was accosted by a damned photographer." Sandy rolled her eyes in understanding as I added, "I feel kind of awkward about being here right now. Maybe I should come back later."

I started to hitch my purse higher onto my shoulder, but hadn't even turned on my heel before Sandy grabbed my wrist. "No. Please stay. It would mean so much to him."

I tried not to read too deeply into her statement. Surely, she was just trying to make me feel comfortable.

Sandy led me to a set of doors at the back of the nearly empty room. It was unnaturally quiet, save for the non-sequitur doo-wop playing softly in the background. My eyes grazed the rows of empty chairs until they landed on the two women sitting in the front. Even from the back of her head, I was pretty sure I recognized Trip's sister Claudia, and next to her was Mrs. Wilmington, whom I would have known anywhere.

And kneeling in front of his father's casket, shoulders slumped and defeated, I saw Trip.

My heart wrenched at his beaten posture, the pain evident in his grieving form. This was not the invincible hero people saw on the movie screens. This was a fragmented human being. This was my old friend Trip; the boy I had loved and the man who had broken my heart.

He stood and swiped a hand down his face as he turned away from his father's body. His mother murmured something to him, and he nodded absently as his eyes scanned the room...

...and landed on mine.

His brows creased and he tilted his head, almost as though he thought I would disappear if he viewed me from a different angle. A myriad of emotions flitted across his face: Shock. Anger. Pain.

And then I watched, mesmerized, as his blue eyes gentled, their red rims soft with tears. His chest rose and fell with an audible *huff,* and the corner of his mouth tipped up ever, ever so slightly.

Gratitude.

He strode his way across the room, his eyes never straying from mine until he stopped, inches from me, the toes of his shiny black shoes just touching my own black pumps.

We stood there, staring at one another, for several minutes.

Four years and four months.

I had not seen this man in four years and four months. The last time we were in the same room together, he was begging me to take a chance with him. I had refused, thinking I was making the mature, "adult" decision, and wound up breaking both of our hearts in the process.

I was unsure where that left us.

My arms itched to reach up and wrap around him, and I had to fist my fingers at my side to stop myself from cupping his jaw. But I was determined to wait it out, to put his needs before my own wants.

After what felt like forever, his arm stretched toward me, and I felt his pinky finger curl around mine.

"You're here."

His voice was coarse and lacked the usual levity that I adored, but it washed over me nonetheless, soothing all of my nerves.

I offered him a shy smile, then twisted my hand to lace *all* our fingers together, my heart almost bursting from the familiar touch and the sweet, welcoming look on his beautiful face.

"I'm exactly where I'm supposed to be, Trip."

Chapter 3
AT LAST

Trip released his hold on me to plant his hands on either side of my face. He swiped the tears from my cheeks with his thumbs as the smallest of smiles escaped from his lips. "You're really here."

I gripped his wrists in my hands, smoothing them with my palms. "I'm here."

He tucked a strand of hair behind my ear, kissing the spot near my temple. "You ready for this?" he asked, as his hand slid down to grasp mine again.

I've been ready for fifteen years, pal.

But as it turned out, the "this" he was referring to was our immediate situation, because he led me over to his mother. I could see that Mrs. Wilmington had hardly aged at all. What little age I could see on her face could probably be more attributed to the immediate stress of the situation rather than the passage of time.

I gave her a quick hug and offered my condolences as Claudia reclaimed her jaw from where it had fallen to the floor. I guessed her brother and I had made quite the scene. "So, this is the infamous Layla Warren. You were right, Drip. I actually do remember her." Then she directed her next comments to me. "Let me ask you something. Is this Rymer character an actual person?"

I had to remember where I was and stifled the laugh at Claudia's question and her nickname for her little brother. (I logged it away for future torture.) But her jab had lightened the tone in the room, enough that by the time the first mourners filed in, we found ourselves chatting casually with them. Well, as casually as possible with a dead body in the vicinity. I've always been amazed at the lengths people will go to just to avoid talking about the real reason why they're in that room in the first place. It seems borderline disrespectful to the person in the box. Maybe when someone had been dying for years, it made for an easier time once it finally became official.

Trip kept me glued to his side on the receiving line, introducing me to every family member and business associate as "*my Layla.*" It was almost as if he were treating me like I was his long-time girlfriend.

Which, I guess, in a way, I kinda was.

There were a few times Trip would crack and start tearing up again, normally at the sight of a particularly close friend of his dad's or a family member he hadn't seen in years.

But when Lisa and Pickford strolled through the door, he positively broke.

The boys didn't hesitate to throw their arms around each other, Trip just crumbling against his old buddy Pickford. The two of them used to have quite the bromance back in the day, and the passage of time obviously hadn't done anything to break that bond.

Lisa and I held hands as the tears ran down our cheeks. It was so amazing to have the four of us in the same room again, even if the circumstances weren't quite so ideal. But having us all there was exactly what Trip needed in that moment. What he'd needed for years.

I was lost in that thought as a familiar voice behind me said, "Aww. You two faggots finally making it official?"

We all stopped for a beat and turned to find Rymer standing there, giving us the finger and wearing a wide grin. At a wake.

Trip was the first to crack up. "Rymer, you compassionate bastard!"

We all laughed as those two hugged hello, breaking the serious vibe of the moment.

Rymer and his filterless mouth. Thank God for him.

After the last mourner left the building, Trip escorted me out the door and walked me over to my car. It was dark out, but I could see the smirk that cracked his features once his eyes landed on my Mustang, surely humored by the fact that I still owned the thing.

He swiped a hand through his hair with a chuckle as he turned toward me. "Hey. Thanks for staying all day. I know it wasn't easy."

I rubbed my hands together, trying to ward off the February cold. My breath came out in a cloud of smoke as I answered, "No thanks necessary. You'd do the same for me."

"You're coming back to my Mom's, right?"

"If you need me, yes."

"I do. I always do."

His eyes met mine at that, and I saw the heartbreak playing across his face; something beyond the exhaustion, beyond the sorrow of the day. An understanding passed between us just then, the excruciatingly obvious truth of our past suddenly making itself clear:

We loved one another.

We belonged together.

And yet, we'd torn each other apart.

There were so many things between us that needed saying, so many reasons we shouldn't have been standing across from one another right then. Nevertheless, there we were just the same.

Every choice we'd ever made, every road we'd ever travelled brought us to this place.

Every bad decision, every stupid screwup, every bit of drama.

Every beautiful second together, every miserable hour apart... led us here.

We hadn't seen each other in over four years, but that didn't mean a thing right then. The time apart almost visibly shed as we stood there, looking into each other's eyes. For all our heartache and yearning and our many, many mistakes... it was simply the past. We were bound by it... but what we were really seeing was our *future*.

It was there, in that spot, in the goddamned parking lot of the Malachi Bros. Funeral Parlor on Colfax Avenue in Norman, New Jersey... that we finally recognized our forever.

His reserve cracked as a shaky breath escaped from his chest, I swallowed past the lump in my throat, and suddenly, there we were, falling into each other all over again. He grabbed me, his arms like a vice around my middle, gathering me to his crumpled form, just bawling into my neck. My arms clamped around his shoulders, holding him to me, the tears streaming down my face as well.

Trip cried like he did everything else: *completely*. His body racked with trembling sobs, and I joined him, shivering so hard I thought I'd never stop.

There were no words that needed to be spoken, but I whispered, "I'm so sorry, Trip. I'm so sorry," and I was apologizing as much for his father's death as I was about ever letting him go.

He pulled back, not even trying to hide his pain, peering at me through a haze of tears. "Oh, God, Layla. Oh, God, how I've missed you."

My heart positively stopped, but even still, I tried to explain. "I didn't even know... I never really thought..."

He shook his head, cutting off my words, trying to pull himself together. "No. We're not doing this here. We'll talk later, but right now, I just want to hold you."

So I let him.

We held each other and we cried and there was no one outside the two of us, there, in that moment.

It did not matter that we hadn't been in the same room together for over four years. It did not matter that we both almost married other people. It did not matter that he was an insanely famous actor and known the world over. It did not matter that I was not.

He was simply Chester and I was Lay-Lay.

We were *us* again.

* * *

The repast was at the Wilmingtons' house. The burial was set for the following day, but the cemetery was way out on Long Island, so Mrs. W., Claudia, and Trip intended to make it a private affair. Originally, they'd planned to have the dinner at the country club one town over, but that idea was squelched once they realized the press had caught wind of the news. The club sent all the food over to the private estate instead, escorted by their entire waitstaff.

Mrs. Wilmington entertained everyone in the solarium at the back of the house. It was a large room with floor to ceiling windows that looked out over the rolling, snow-covered lawn of the backyard. I'd only been to the house twice in my life, and both times, I'd never made it past the foyer. It was interesting to finally get to see the full layout of the place. But even from my incomplete glimpse, the house turned out to be just as huge and imposing as my memories. I had a stab of guilt at how comfortable I felt, knowing Mr. Wilmington wouldn't be lurking in some darkened hallway with a jab at the ready.

Trip refused to let me leave his side, and if I wasn't so thrilled about it, I would have felt a little smothered. But after all those years apart, I was anxious to make up for all the time we'd lost. I guessed he was, too.

34

Eventually, he led the five of us into a parlor off the main room, ditching his jacket over the back of a couch before slumping to sit down on it. Just the simple act of watching Trip unbuttoning his cuffs and rolling his black shirt up to his elbows was enough to liquefy my insides. I knew I was supposed to be focusing on the solemnity of the day, but my stomach wasn't cooperating, flipping uncontrollably at the sight of Trip lounged out on the sofa. He was pure, unadulterated *male* sitting there.

He was wearing his hair a bit longer than usual; still perfectly golden, artfully mussed, and practically begging me to run my hands through it. There were some new crinkles at the corners of his fathomless blue eyes, and the dimple in his left cheek had become more pronounced, but the new lines only added an effective ruggedness to his almost-pretty features.

His feet were crossed at the ankles on an ottoman, his elbow propped casually on the arm of the couch, his fingers at his temple. The emotional upheaval of the day played out on his face, his eyes taking on a smoldering squint, making him look a little sleepy. He flexed his fingers together and gave a yawn against an outstretched bicep.

Yeah. You're right, Chester. Let's go to bed.

He pulled me to sit down next to him, practically on his lap, throwing an arm around my shoulders. I caught Lisa's eye and bit my lip. It was like not a single day had gone by. Right there were Lisa and Pick, sitting on the sofa across from us. And there was Rymer, occupying the easy chair in between. If Cooper and Sargento were there, I would have sworn it was 1991.

Pick slung himself onto the couch and settled in at his wife's back, his stretched form leaning into the sofa, his mile-long legs taking over the floor space. He waggled a finger between Trip and me and said, "So... I see *this* is happening again."

Lisa elbowed him in the ribs, and I could have cheerfully strangled him, but Trip just chuckled. He met my eyes, gave my shoulder a squeeze, and answered, "Hell yeah it is."

I melted at the satisfied grin he aimed at me.

"Took you long enough," Pick jeered.

I was smiling into Trip's eyes, but directed my reply to Pickford, "Some of us weren't as smart right out of high school."

At that, Lisa and Pick shared a knowing look.

Rymer was taking in the scene, his head darting back and forth between the four of us. "For chrissakes! I think I just threw up in my mouth a little." That made us chuckle as he hauled himself off the chair and added, "Alright. I'm getting a drink. Who needs? Ladies? Pick? Trip?"

There was a moment of unease before Lisa and I answered that we were fine, Pick put in an order for a Coke, and Trip cleared his throat. "I'll take a water, thanks."

Rymer started to navigate around the coffee table, shaking his head. "Coke? Water? Jesus. Be careful you don't spill any on your skirts. C'mon you pansies. Let's do a shot or something."

The smile suddenly dropped from his face, realizing what he'd just said. I mean, we were all there because Trip's father had just lost his battle with alcohol. Trip had just recently kicked the habit himself. "Oh, Trip. Man. I'm sorry. I wasn't even—"

"Dude, no. It's alright. Don't worry about it." Trip offered a genuine grin to his friend, who nodded his head before exiting the room.

Trip's drinking was an unavoidable piece of knowledge. In the years since I'd seen him last, he'd gone swiftly downhill, bottomed out, cleaned up, and set his star back on the rise. He'd actually won an Oscar for his role in *Swayed*, and it was well-deserved. But by that time, he'd also won a spot as cover boy for numerous entertainment magazines, his downfall documented at every turn. Hollywood must be a very forgiving town, because only a few years later, those same magazines were lauding him as an unparalleled talent.

However, *The Backlot,* in particular, wasn't as kind. I couldn't check out at the supermarket without seeing Trip's face splashed across their cover, scathing headlines blaring out "Binging Bad Boy In Bar Brawl" or "Another TRIP To The Bottom Of A Bottle?" I knew that most of the stuff in those stupid tabloids was simply made up in order to sell magazines. But when they attacked a person I actually *knew*—one who'd been to Hell and back in order to set his life straight—it seemed extraordinarily cruel.

I mean, he wasn't that same party boy anymore. He'd battled his demons and clawed his way back to the world of the living, taking it entirely by storm. He'd taken all that energy he'd put into drinking and channeled it into philanthropy. He'd started his own charity, and from all accounts, it was a fruitful venture. That circumstance had turned him into a media darling, which completely negated the previously held image of him as a drunken playboy.

His work was never better; his family life never more secure.

Claudia was walking around with her new baby, introducing Skylar to the room. When she came in by us, Trip grabbed his niece out of his sister's clutches and gave her a soft nuzzle, completely smitten with the little bundle in his arms. Seeing him holding a baby just about made me melt. She really was an adorable little thing. Six months old, a little tuft of black hair on her head, those exotic, heavily-lashed, almond-shaped eyes smiling through her gurgling. Plus, she had that perfect amount of baby fat just made for biting. I wanted to put that kid on a plate and eat her.

Sandy came into the room just then, put an arm around Claudia's shoulders and kissed her full on the mouth.

Oh.

Trip never mentioned that Sandy was family. Although, the trust he placed in her and the way she looked out for him suddenly made perfect sense. She commandeered Skylar from her uncle's grasp, Trip giving an, "Aww. You stealing her away so soon?"

Claudia shot back, "*You* get to see her all the time. Don't hog the baby, Uncle Drip."

That made us chuckle, Rymer expressing his regret at not having come up with the nickname himself years ago. "What a waste," he lamented, shaking his head.

Trip actually laughed at that, a full, side-splitting guffaw, and it was as if all the tension of the day was finally draining from his body. Rymer was always good for some comic relief, but that day, he helped to turn the glum occasion into more of a reunion and less of a funeral.

Trip's mood continued to lighten all evening as the guys swapped stories and reminisced. "Hey," he said to Rymer. "You remember that time in the locker room when we were playing *Pa-ting!* and you got hit in the eye with that bar of soap?"

Rymer shook his head laughing. "That wasn't me. That was Sargento."

Pick piped in. "No, man. That was *you.*"

I watched the exchange, finally cutting in with, "Hold up. What's *Pa-ting?*"

The guys all exchanged a glance, waiting for someone else to speak up. Pickford finally took the honors. "Okay, fine. So, there was this doorway that led from the locker room to the showers, right. And we'd all decide who was gonna be the target, and then we'd shove them into the showers, you know?"

"No. I don't know. But continue."

"Well, the target would have to walk back and forth in front of the doorway, and the rest of us would find random stuff to throw at them as they passed."

"Wait," I said. "Like what kind of stuff?"

"I don't know, man. Like shoes and balls or tape or whatever. Anyway, if the target got hit, he had to yell, 'pa-*TING!*', and then change direction. You know, like a carnival game."

I asked, "And the point of this was?"

The guys all looked at each other and started laughing, Rymer snorting out, "Who the fuck knows? It was fun!"

"So… You just all stood around naked and threw stuff at each other?"

That made them bust up even harder, Trip explaining, "No! What the hell, Lay?"

"He said it was in the shower!" I defended.

Lisa backed me up. "I was thinking you were naked, too."

"You would," shot Pick, before continuing with his story. "Anyway, this one day we had Rymer in there—and dude, it was totally you—and he's strutting back and forth, pa-tinging away. And Aetine whips this bar of soap at him and *bam!* Right in the eye!"

"Ow!" Lisa and I squealed in unison.

Pick was practically crying as he reenacted the scene, holding a hand over his eye and yelling, "*I'm blind! I'm blind!*"

The guys started cracking up again as Lisa and I exchanged an eyeroll.

Boys were so weird.

"Oh shit," Rymer said. "You're right. It *was* me."

That had us *all* laughing that time.

"When was this?" I asked.

Trip pulled himself together and said, "I don't know. One day during gym."

"I never heard that story!"

"Why would we tell you? You're a *girl*."

I shoved him for that.

Chapter 4
INTO THE BLUE

A few guests made their leave, stopping in to shake Trip's hand, offer their final condolences, say their goodbyes. Eventually, Lisa, Pick, and Rymer cut out too, but the house was still crawling with Mrs. Wilmington's people. I figured the party wouldn't end until very, very late.

I stifled a yawn, and Trip clamped his palm over my knee, asking, "Want the nickel tour?"

Before I could answer, he pulled me in the direction of the stairwell, leading me to the second floor.

I chuckled when he turned the corner and smirked out, "This is the hallway," as he backed me up against a wall and closed his smiling mouth over mine.

I was pretty sure this tour was going to be worth way more than my five cents.

Those lips against mine once again. It was hard to breathe, but who cared about something stupid like breathing when I had Trip in my arms? His hand slid around my neck, pulling my face closer to his, a slight groan escaping from his lips as they parted and consumed mine. My heart was beating in that familiar cadence, my racing pulse threatening a full-on faint. I ran my hands along the linen shirt at his back, up to his shoulder blades, involuntarily sliding to tangle in his hair, my mouth opening to take him in.

Last time he had me up against a wall, we both practically combusted, and this time looked as though it wasn't going to be any different.

Only, back then, I ruined everything by being an insecure idiot. *But not this time, pal.*

Trip's palm was smoothing against my waist, grasping at the material of my dress, his hardened length pressing against my midsection. The familiar humming in his throat melted me down to my core, and I felt my hands slipping down to grasp his backside, pulling him tighter against me.

Trip braced his palms against the wall on either side of my shoulders, dropped his face, and spat out, "*Christ.*"

He gave a shake to his head, trying to pull himself together. His smoldering cobalt eyes met mine in wonder as he asked, "Are you trying to kill me?"

I giggled as he backed me through a doorway, but I positively squealed in delight when I realized we were in his childhood room. "Your room! Oh my God. I waited fifteen years to see this!"

Trip chuckled. "Well, I've always wanted to bring a girl up here, so I guess the wait is over for both of us."

He crammed his fists into his pockets, standing there smiling at me as I checked out all his stuff. I looked around at the Trip Museum: the navy plaid comforter on the bed, the tan walls covered in sports pennants from every city he'd ever lived in, the shelf of hockey trophies.

I pulled a "Trip" and made a big show of checking out every little knick-knack on every surface, from the Michael Jordan figurine to the signed Gordie Howe puck to the vintage Nintendo console, eventually grabbing the Magic 8-ball off his dresser, giving it a good shake.

"Will I hit the lottery?" I asked, checking the answer in the little plastic window. "See there? *All signs point to yes!* Whoohoo!"

The warm smirk he shot me made my knees go weak.

I noticed some high school textbooks still sitting on a corner of his desk, saw his St. Norman's letterman jacket hanging from a hook on the back of his door. It was as though his room had been sealed off with caution tape, frozen in time since the day he'd left the house.

"Holy crap. It's like a shrine in here!"

I turned to see Trip staring at me, that lazy, lopsided grin still plastered on his gorgeous face. "What?" I asked, trying not to melt from the sweet, familiar smile he was aiming into my eyes.

"Nothing's changed at all."

I smiled back, knowing his comment applied to more than just the room we were standing in.

I put the 8-ball back down on the dresser and stepped closer to him, laid my hand over his heart. God. It was so amazing to be able to touch him whenever and however I wanted. Finally. "No. I guess it hasn't."

At that, his hands slipped out of his pockets and wrapped around me, pulling my head against his chest, a palm smoothing my hair. I hugged him back, allowed myself a deep breath, taking in that beautifully sweet, clean scent that was his and his alone. One of these days, I was going to find out what kind of soap he used so I could put it through a cheese grater and snort it like it was coke. Someday, my body would be found in a dirty alley somewhere, OD'd on the stuff.

I'd woken up that morning feeling sad and anxious, but only a few hours later, my life had begun. Trip and I had torn each other apart, and there were still so many unspoken questions between us. All those years of hurt and anguish wouldn't just disappear in a day. But right then, I was just grateful that we were standing there wrapped up in each other's arms. Feeling him against me, his heartbeat drumming under my ear, the only thought in my brain at that moment was getting his lips back on mine again.

He kissed the top of my head and said, "We probably need to have that talk at some point."

He was right. We had a lot of baggage to sort through. Hell, we had an entire *airport* of baggage. But right then, I wasn't really thinking about *talking*, if you catch my drift.

"Trip? Do we really have to do that *now*?"

His shoulders shook as he laughed, and I knew victory was within my grasp.

He tipped my chin toward his face and dipped his head for a sweet, soft kiss against my welcoming lips. "Okay, fine. You're right. But I just want to say one thing." He put his hands on my shoulders, bracing me for his words. "I know you didn't marry that guy, but you need to understand that I wouldn't care even if you did. You need to know that it wouldn't stop me from taking you, right here, right now. I wouldn't even feel badly about it. If that makes me an asshole, so be it. But you're *mine*, Lay. You always have been." His hands moved to cup my face, fixing my eyes to his. "The thing is, though, is that I'm yours. You own me. You always did. This is happening. And we're making it work this time."

I thought I was going to melt into the carpet from his words before he'd be able to take me to his bed. But take me he did.

I will not go into detail here. I'm sorry, and I know it might seem strange after everything else I've shared about our sex lives. But we didn't have sex that day. We made love. As corny and as sappy as that might sound, it's the truth. I will share the gritty details about our sexual encounters, because that is fun and sometimes funny and most of the time, it's just hot. But when the man I love is so deep inside me it's as though we share a soul, when I don't know where I end and he begins, when he is looking into my eyes and whispering the sweetest things this side of Shakespeare... that is simply between *us* and no one else.

Chapter 5
FUNNY HA HA

Oh my God, I'm totally messing with you. *Of course* I'm going to tell you every detail! Can you freaking imagine if I didn't?

Chapter 6
NEVER BEEN THAWED

After Trip's little speech, I couldn't breathe. *You're mine. I'm yours.* What could I possibly say that could even compare to that?

I bypassed any attempt at speaking, and just grabbed his head, pulling it to mine in a shattering kiss.

He *was* mine. Mine for the taking. And I planned on taking all I could get from that man.

I slid my tongue against the seam of his lips until they opened for me, our breath mingling with one another's, the rapid gasps exchanged in frantic bursts of pure, unapologetic need.

My body thrummed in his grasp, his hands smoothing over my back, across my hips, pulling me tightly to him, afraid to let go. His low moans reverberated throughout my insides, turning me to mush. He wanted me. He *needed* me.

And there it was. That inevitable, electric pull we'd always shared. That all-consuming, obsessive attraction we'd never been able to deny, try as we might. It was always there. Even when *he* wasn't.

He stepped slightly out of my grasp, a wicked expression on his face, holding my gaze prisoner as he rolled down his sleeves, starting to get himself undressed right before my very eyes. But I stopped him when his hands went to his throat.

"No. I want to do it."

That made him smile a shit-eating grin, and his eyebrows raised as my hands worked the buttons down his chest.

"Trip? Could you do me a favor and try not to look so damn pleased with yourself?"

That made him chuckle. "I can't help it. I'm about to bang my old girlfriend in my old room. You know how many times I jerked off right there just thinking about it? And now you're here. And I totally get to nail your ass."

"Yeah, um, you go anywhere near my ass and you'll be whacking off alone again."

"Don't knock it 'til you've tried it, sweetheart."

He cracked up as he pulled me toward him, reaching around my back to lower the zipper of my dress, his breath tickling against my ear as he whispered, "Don't worry, Lay. I'm gonna fuck you *just right.*"

Yep. I hear ya. That line did it for me, too.

I shivered at his words, the feel of his breath on my skin. He grabbed at the neckline of my dress and pulled one side down my shoulder, kissing the bared skin there before sliding the fabric down my body.

As it pooled into a heap on the floor at my feet, I stood there feeling a bit insecure in just my bra and panties. I mean, the last time Trip had seen me naked, I was in the body of a seventeen-year-old, toned to the bejeezus. To be honest, at the age of thirty-one, things had kind of shifted, filled out, and well, *dropped* since then. To add insult to injury, I rarely worked out over the winter months, and being that it was the middle of February, I was also ass-pale as well.

But Trip didn't seem to notice as he cupped my breast over my bra, testing its new weight, running his other hand over my curved hip, pulling me toward him for a kiss. Tongues entwined, I slid my palms over his bare chest to his shoulders, dropping his shirt to the floor as I kicked my dress away from my feet.

He suddenly turned me in his arms, pulling my back against his front as he shoved my hair away and attacked my neck. I leaned into him, raising my arms to his hair, pulling his face in tighter against my skin as his hands went to my front, groping at my breasts and pressing himself against the small of my back. I did what any sane woman would do in that situation, which was to rise up on tiptoes so I could press my backside against the steel rod poking me from behind. He let out a groan and playfully shoved me over the footboard of his bed, my hands splaying out on the mattress to stop my fall as he pulled down my undies and gave me a slap on my ass.

We both laughed when he smacked me, and I stood up, shooting him a look. "Be nice, Chester."

He pulled me to him, unhooking my bra and replying, "I *will* be nice. But only for so long."

The wicked smile he aimed at me shot an electric charge down my entire length—my entire *naked* length—as I stood there, trying to not fidget while he looked me up and down.

He was entirely way too clothed for my liking. It wasn't fair.

I went to unbutton his slacks when I noticed his abs, and stopped short. I mean, I had just stripped off his shirt, but I hadn't yet really *looked* at him, you know?

I took a step back and appraised the sight of the naked torso in front of me. He'd always had an amazing body, but Christ. Trip had gotten freaking ripped.

I put my hands to my hips and asked, "Are you kidding me? What the hell is this?"

My anger probably missed its mark, considering I was standing there totally nude. It's hard to be taken seriously when you're not wearing any clothes.

He knew exactly what I was talking about and was trying to contain a smile as he asked, "What?"

I rolled my eyes. "When did this happen? Jesus. Look at you! Give a girl a heads up about such a thing, huh?"

That made the smile crack his features. "What? So I've been hitting it a little harder lately. I just came off a gladiator film and I'm starting a hockey flick in a few weeks. Occupational hazard, I guess."

"Yeah. A hazard to *me*, maybe! Here I am with my saggy ass and you're standing there looking like Michelangelo's *David*, you jagweed!"

He stepped closer, grabbing my butt and pulling me into direct contact with what was assuredly going to be revealed as his perfect dick. He probably lifted weights with that thing, too. His cock probably possessed its own set of washboard abs.

"Your ass," he stated firmly, "along with the rest of you, is *perfect*."

I gave him a *"yeah right"* look.

"It's true," he said. "If I was lying, then why haven't I been able to take my eyes off you since you dropped the dress? I don't think I ever want to see you wearing clothes again. I've been standing here plotting how to keep you naked twenty-four hours a day."

"Might be kinda hard to go back down to the party. Or the supermarket. Or church."

That made him chuckle. "Oh, it'll be hard alright. In fact..." he pulled me against his hips again, "I'd say it already is."

"Wow, that was bad."

"I'll show you bad."

"Stop talking, you retard! Just take off your damned pants already."

"I'll show you retard."

"Oh my God."

His hands went to the belt at his waist, and then he slid his zipper down. Slowly. The move would have been sexy as hell if he hadn't thrown out this line along with it:

"Want me to dance for you?"

"Oh my God! Just shut up!" I chastised as we both laughed. I gave his shoulder a shove before diving into his bed and sliding under the sheets. I laid on my side, propping a hand up under my head to watch him strip.

Trip didn't disappoint.

His thumbs hooked into the waistband of his boxer-briefs and he gave a little eyebrow wiggle before dropping his drawers. I will swear to my dying day that the sound that accompanied this action was: *Boioioioioing!*

Hello, my old friend.

I was lying there, taking in his perfect body, watching as he climbed onto the bed and crawled over me slowly, feeling stunned and excited that he was mine for the taking.

Mine. Holy shit. After all these years, Trip was finally *mine.*

I shivered as he kissed his way up my body, felt his soft, hot lips grazing over the thin sheet that separated him from my bare skin. He pulled it away to plant a quick suction-kiss on my breast *which better not leave a hickey* before reaching into his nightstand drawer. He pulled out like a freaking magician's scarf of condoms, tearing one off and tossing the rest back into the drawer.

"Hey. I thought you said you've never brought a girl up here. What's with the Trojan army?"

"A boy can dream, can't he?"

"Whoa. Wait. How old are those things?"

Trip's brows furrowed, focused on the packet in his hand. "I don't know. Why? Do they go bad?"

Jane, you ignorant slut.

My eyes practically rolled out of my head. "I'm guessing that's never been a problem for you, as I'm quite sure you've managed to tear through a gross of these puppies at a clip, but yeah. They have expiration dates."

He ignored my jab and checked the stamp on the packaging. Before I could get confirmation that the date was from the Clinton administration, I said, "Just forget it. I'm on the pill anyway. Unless, you know... I mean... you're... *okay*, right?"

He pursed his lips in a scowl before answering. "Babe. Yes. I know you won't believe me, but it's been... a while. I've been tested since then."

Ugh. I hated the clinical conversation we were having. But after all those years apart, there was no way we were waiting another minute to sleep together. We'd waited long enough. But the fact was, Trip was a bit of a... *popular guy* during his twenties. And even though he'd recently professed himself to be a one-woman-man... well, sometimes what happens in Vegas doesn't always *stay* in Vegas, you know what I'm saying?

But thank God for small favors, because it seemed the extracurricular activities of his past weren't about to affect our present.

I gave him the wide eyes and tossed out, "Looks like we're going bareback, baby."

"Yippee-ki-yay, motherfucker."

I laughed at that, until his expression turned serious. He brushed a sweet, soft kiss against my lips, then said, "Hey Lay?"

"Yeah?"

"A lot of women... they, uh... they expect me to be some sort of sexual dynamo between the sheets."

"Kinda tacky bringing up other women right now, don't you think?"

"Sorry."

"Besides. I'm not a lot of women."

"Oh, I know that. I'm just trying to give you a heads up about what to expect here. Because I totally am."

The kiss he planted on me was enough to stop our laughter, as I felt his hot, sweet lips slanting fiercely across my own. His tongue invaded my mouth, the taste of him sweeter than ever. His scent assaulted my inhales, the same crisp, clean smell that had always been a part of him.

I ran my hands up his sides, making him flinch and causing me to shudder. There were new planes of his body to explore, this foreign land of bulges and bumps along his arms, his chest, his stomach. I was taken aback by the feel of him, the firmness at my fingertips, the smooth skin covering the solid knots of muscle under my palms.

Trip was doing some exploring of his own.

His hands roved over my breasts, between my legs, his breathing coming out in ragged moans against my neck as he pressed his hardened length into my thigh. I grabbed his hair in my fists, directing his mouth to mine once again, writhing underneath his touch, groaning with stinging need, reveling in the staccato beats of my quickening heart.

He positioned his body between my legs and pushed himself against me, just the tip of him teasing at my entrance, his face buried in my neck, his voice rasping, "Oh God, Lay. I've only got so much restraint, here. I need to be inside you."

Chapter 7
ASSISTED LIVING

The ache in his voice caused the tremors to start, made my heart race with anticipation. He was always able to do this to me. Always able to drive me over the brink with just a few spoken words, a few well-executed touches. Oh, please. Who am I kidding? He could *look* at me the right way and it was enough to make me fall to pieces.

I know it may seem odd that we were hooking up while the repast was still happening downstairs. But I didn't let myself feel too guilty. Trip was entitled to a little happiness after all he'd been through. We were allowed to embrace *life*.

I ran my fingers over the pale scars at his forearm, the remnants from when he broke it years before, a faint reminder of the self-destructive boy he once was. It was at total odds with the reformed man in my arms, the generous, thriving person he'd become. It wasn't an easy transition to make, and he'd worked really hard to come so far.

So, I knew Trip needed this. He needed to know he was still breathing. Needed to know that he'd kicked his habit—when his father couldn't—and that he wouldn't end up on a slab before the age of sixty. At least not from drinking, anyway. He needed to feel alive. He needed to feel loved. Hell, *I* needed it.

It was amazing, knowing this man loved me. That was a fact. Our timing may have sucked, but the feelings had already been confirmed. Years ago.

At least his were.

He didn't know that I had chosen to love him back. I needed to rectify that right now. I took a deep breath and said the words I thought I'd never get the chance to say to him, the words I'd never *allowed* myself to say. Well, not on purpose anyway.

52

"I love you."

He lifted his head and looked at me in disbelief. "What?"

Oh God. Too soon? Is this just supposed to be sex right now?

I wanted to die. I wanted to stuff the words back into my mouth, wishing I'd never said them. Maybe I could laugh and play it off like a joke, like I didn't really mean it.

No. I immediately shook the negative thoughts aside. I would not go down this road again. I would never fail to put my heart on the line when it came to Trip ever again. We'd lost too much time because of my insecurities and our inability to communicate properly.

Never. Again.

I put my hands on either side of his neck, my thumbs brushing along his jaw. I was scared, but I looked directly into his eyes and said it again. "I'm in love with you, Trip. I love you. I always have."

It looked as though he'd been slapped in the face by my words. Pain drifted across his features as he dropped his head and shook it. "I know."

Not the words I was imagining, and the unexpectedness made me laugh.

"You *know*? Oh my God. Did you just Han Solo me?"

I felt him shaking with laughter against my body before any sound came out of his mouth. When it did, it sent us both into a fit of giggles, as I jokingly tried to shove the big galoot off of me.

"Okay. Where's my dress? This was a big mistake. I take it back. I meant to say '*Up yours, Chester*'."

He pinned me to the mattress with his heavy body, settling himself between my legs again, explaining, "You didn't let me finish! I was trying to say *I know* you love me. I know, and it's incredible." He looked down at me, his eyes a shifting pool of blue, the corner of his lip quirked into a lopsided smile as he gently swiped my hair behind my ear. He buried his face against my neck, his breath tickling against my skin as he whispered softly, "Because I am *completely* in love with you right back."

It only took fifteen freaking years, but we managed to finally recite our lines properly. *I love you. Well, I love you, too.* Jesus. Isn't that how normal people do it?

He raised his head and smiled into my eyes as he requested, "Say it again."

"What? Han Solo? Does that turn you on, nerd? Should I Leia my hair and throw on a gold bikini?" God, he was so cute. Just look at that face.

His grin was infectious. "Yes. Eventually. But right now I just want to hear you say it. Say it again."

I stopped laughing and met his eyes. "I love y—"

My words were cut off with a gasp as he slid into me with a groan; proudly, confidently, holding himself still, letting my body get used to the feel of him inside me. Again.

It was as if he'd never left me, as if the two of us had always been joined together, as if we were always meant to be.

He didn't. We had. We were.

"Say it again."

"I love you."

He pulled out almost fully, then slid back in—*slowly*—full-length this time, which was almost my undoing. *Oh God yes.* I twined my fingers in his hair and arched toward him as he repeated the movement, his arm wrapped around my middle, holding me fixed to him, gliding in and out of me leisurely, as if we had all the time in the world. Each time he entered me, he plunged just a little harder, a little faster, picking up the pace ever so slightly until he was rocking against me in an unhurried, steady rhythm, a never-ending slow-dance that threatened to completely shatter my heart.

This man in my arms. This beautiful man who was capable of beautiful things, in as well as out of the bedroom. The exquisiteness of his touch, the weight of his words, the tender care he took to make me feel loved, cherished… unbelievably turned on. It was too much emotion. Bittersweet and wonderful, being in the bed of the man I loved deep down to my core; my heart, my soul. The man I had loved—and would continue to love—forever.

Trip's voice cracked on a rough whisper. "Open your eyes."

When I did, I saw him looking into my eyes, heavy-lidded, full of adoration and wanting. Making sure I knew he was with me. Only me.

"I love you, Lay."

His words brought the fresh sting of tears, and my eyes began to leak even as my heart swelled.

"Hey… hey, why are you crying?" He gave a little chuckle in understanding, swiping the moisture from my cheeks and saying, "It's okay, babe. We're okay now."

It was hard to believe, even though I knew he was right. It was just that we had a million unsaid things between us, a million hurts to heal. It was scary to think that our chance for happiness could be ruined again by misunderstandings. I didn't think I'd survive if things didn't work out for us this time.

Jeebus. I needed to turn my brain off. Why was I allowing myself to worry about tomorrow and the unlikely demise of us when I finally had him exactly where I wanted right then?

"Trip?" I said through tear-blurred eyes. "I'm just so happy right now."

That made him laugh. "You sure have a weird way of showing it, babe." He lowered his mouth toward mine again. "Luckily, I know the right way."

His kiss was sweet, but heated, his lips brushing against mine in waves. I felt the current stirring, this beautiful man holding my gaze locked to his, his incredible body rocking against mine, bringing me right to the edge of the cliff, willing me to fall.

I allowed the electric charges to overtake me, looking right into his face for as long as I could, until I came, unashamed, the tears slinking from my eyes and down my cheeks. It made a small smile appear across his gorgeous face as he quickened his pace to match the tremors cascading along my insides, finally growling into the air as his every muscle tensed and his movements stilled.

He collapsed on top of my body, still joined with me, and rolled us to our sides, the both of us breathless. I thought it would be nice to stay like that for a few days, just lounge around with him inside me indefinitely, but I guessed it would've been kind of hard to do stuff like drive a car or go to the bathroom. But for now, it was nice.

It was insane to think it had been so many years since we'd done this. At least I knew it wouldn't be another fourteen years before the next time. How did we survive without each other all that time? We were always meant to be together. Always would be.

Trip felt it, too. He was actually tearing up himself as he said, "My God, every time, it never fails. You happen to me all over again." He swiped a palm across my cheek and added, "I never stopped loving you, Lay. You were always with me. *Everywhere.*"

* * *

We did a quick cleanup in his bathroom and got dressed again. My heart always broke a little whenever I had to watch Trip put his clothes back on. It was just such a crying shame.

He grabbed my hand and led me around the hall, pointing out the framed pictures from his life. I may have been biased, but Trip was absolutely the most adorable little boy you'd ever want to see in your life. His hair was a much lighter shade of blond, and he looked like a filthy mess in most of the shots. Too freaking cute.

I was laughing about that when I turned to see Trip staring at a framed portrait of his father. He had his hands jammed into his pockets and was shooting daggers at the image of the man whose life was being celebrated downstairs.

"Trip?" I asked warily. He was wound too tightly, a mousetrap that could snap with the slightest provocation. I didn't want to set him off.

Too late.

"Asshole!" he spat, throwing a fist at the wall next to his father's head, denting the sheetrock. It wasn't a satisfying jab, I guess, because he threw another punch, this one harder, cracking the wall. And then he took another. I stepped backwards as he continued thrashing the wall, eventually going for his real target, landing a punch against the man's smiling jaw, splintering the glass. "Son of a bitch!" He ripped the picture fully off the wall and threw it to the floor.

At that, his angry rage quickly turned to collapsed sobbing as he buried his face and elbows against the damaged wall, his arms wrapped over his head, his right hand a bloody mess. "I hate him *so much.*"

I didn't know the right way to console him, and I was hesitant to do so when he was in the middle of such a tirade. I decided to try out a rational angle when I said, "Trip. You don't mean that."

He whirled on me then, his eyes chips of ice as he answered, "Yes, I do! He died a long time ago, Lay." He pointed to the ruined picture on the ground. "That man who was my father died years ago."

I am the poster child for stubbornness during my anger, so I decided to let Trip have his. I smoothed some hair off of his forehead and kissed him there, soothing the raging beast. I slipped a hand down his arm and gripped his wrist, saying, "Okay. But let's get you cleaned up, alright?"

57

He looked down at his hand in confusion, as if the appendage attached to his body wasn't his own, finally realizing that it was bleeding. I took him into the bathroom and ran his hand under the water, picking out the occasional shard of glass imbedded in his skin. I worked in silence, not knowing what to say. He was angry, and I wasn't used to seeing him like that.

But of course he was angry. He had every right to be.

I Bactined and Band-Aided his knuckles, then dug out a dustpan and broom from the same closet where I'd found the first-aid kit.

"You don't need to do that," Trip said as I ignored him.

I swept up the glass and drywall debris while he gathered the remains of the portrait, depositing it in a spare bedroom, a sheepish expression on his face. We worked in silence, Trip in no mood to talk and me not wanting to say the wrong thing. The mess had been taken care of, but there wasn't much we could do about the wall at that moment.

He pulled a new picture down from the spare room, and I used my heel to hammer its nail in the appropriate spot. That must have been enough to break the last of Trip's anguish, because he kind of laughed as he looked on.

I held the shoe up and gave it a wiggle. "Girl hammer."

When I was done, I slipped it back onto my foot, hung the picture over the hole, and dusted off my hands. "Well, that's that."

He had his hands jammed into his pockets as he nodded his head toward the wall. "Remind me to get someone over here to fix that tomorrow."

"Don't sweat it. I'll give Rymer a call in the morning."

"Rymer's a contractor?"

"Rymer's a little bit of everything these days."

Trip was silent at that, letting the new information sink in. He stood there for a beat, looking embarrassed, his tail between his legs.

"Look. I'm sorry, Lay. I'm sorry you saw that."

I could have used the opportunity for some big psychoanalytic development, some it-wasn't-your-fault, *Good Will Hunting*-type breakthrough. But it's not what he needed from me at that moment. I knew we'd get through it eventually; it just didn't have to be right then. So, instead of opening my big mouth, I shut up and slipped my arms around his waist for a hug.

He sighed, running the fingertips of his damaged hand along my back, lowering his lips to the top of my head. "I really am sorry."

It had been an emotional day. Nauseated to trepidatious, heart-swelling to heart-breaking. Sad to happy to silly to sexy to contented to furious to remorseful.

What can I say? It was the Trip Wilmington roller coaster ride all over again. I wouldn't have had it any other way.

I squeezed his waist and gave him a shy smile. "I know."

Chapter 8
YOURS, MINE AND OURS

I took a break from the computer when I heard the troops heading up the stairs. I tended to get lost in a zone whenever I was writing and didn't even hear the doorbell ring. But nothing could ever distract me from the sound of Lisa in the vicinity.

My beautiful goddaughter reached my office first, however, rushing into the room with a squeal, so I spun around in my chair and scooped her up in a big hug. "How's my sunshine?" I asked, getting a giggle in answer. She tried squirming out of my grasp almost immediately, and I knew that snuggle time would be over almost as soon as it had begun. She was such a little perpetual motion machine. I held her tighter, though, my hand raised in The Claw, threatening a massive tickle. "You know what I want to hear. Don't make me use this."

Julia's eyes opened wide and her mouth gaped open, pretending to recoil with fear.

Just then, her twin brother came bounding into the room, appraising the scene and saying, "Uh-oh, Jooya."

I gave Caleb a wink and flinched my hand at the stubborn little monkey on my lap, psyching her out. But it was enough to make her scream, "Auntie Layla is my favorite aunt!"

She squirmed again, so I released her from my clutches and opened my arms to Caleb for a hug. He was dirty and sticky—like all good little boys are supposed to be—and I buried my face at his shoulder to blow razzberries into his neck. He smelled like watermelon Jolly Ranchers.

"Did Grampa Kenny give you candy already?" I asked.

They both nodded their heads as Caleb said, "Are you gonna cwaw me now?"

I raised my hand in The Claw. "Do I need to?"

He giggled and yelled, "Auntie Waywa is my favewit aunt!"

Caleb could hit decibel levels that didn't exist on this planet. He'd totally inherited Lisa's loudness gene. Burn.

"I have trained you well, young patawan."

I set him back down as Lisa came into the room. "You have to stop teaching them to say that. They have another aunt besides you, you know."

I shrugged and said, "Yes, but Aunt Penny's not their *favorite* aunt," giving my two favorite tiny humans a conspiratorial look, which made them break into a new fit of giggles.

Lisa just shook her head and said, "You guys know that you should never ever say that in front of Aunt Penny, right?"

They both nodded their heads reverently before running off to destroy my bedroom.

Lisa plopped herself down on my old, padded futon across from my old, well-worn desk. I'd moved back home over four years before and used some of the stuff from my New York apartment to convert Bruce's room into an office.

I know it seems kind of pathetic that I was thirty-one and living in my father's house. Not only should I have wanted a bit more privacy for myself, but Dad had a girlfriend, so you'd think that he'd want a little privacy, too.

But we were used to living together. Heck, we'd done it for the first eighteen years of my life. And the fact was, he was spending a lot of his time at Sylvia's anyway. He actually liked the idea that I was there taking care of things while he was gone. Plus, he knew I was saving every penny for a down payment on a house of my own and didn't want me wasting my hard-earned cash by paying rent on some random place.

Hard-earned might be an exaggeration, however. I definitely put everything I had into my writing, but I could scarcely consider it "hard work" when it could be done in my PJs.

I was presently, officially, and blissfully a not-so-starving artist. I'd given up on a career in journalism to become an author. I wrote books for a living—mostly fiction—and I actually got paid to do so. It was awesome. I was living out a dream I never knew I always had.

Funny that it coincided with the only *other* dream I'd ever had (but I'm pretty sure I always knew I had that one).

Back in 2000, I'd called that agent who left me a message the day I was fired from *Now! Magazine*. Diana Cavanaugh and I just clicked from the get go, and I spent the entirety of that following year writing my first book. It wasn't quite the factual exposé she'd originally been campaigning for, but it was a good story and managed to find an audience. For my second novel, I actually received an advance, so I took my sweet old time getting that baby out. There were a couple novellas and a few short stories sprinkled in there, but I was currently dabbling with some ideas for my third full-length book.

Lisa was on her third baby, too.

She gave a rub to her lower back, and I could see her baby bump straining against her DKNY sweatshirt. "Ow. Four months in and this one's already killing me."

"Don't complain to me, sister. You're the psycho that decided to have another kid after a set of *twins*."

She ignored my jab and got down to brass tacks. "So, you know what I came here to hear. Tell me about Trip! This is really happening, huh?"

We were both smiling like a couple of loons. "Yeah. Finally."

An unspoken understanding passed between us at the situation. Lisa knew better than anyone what a long road it had been. She was there from the first minute and had been there for every moment since. She was the one who helped me survive in those first weeks after Trip announced his engagement. She was the one who helped me stay sane. She was the one who got me through that very long winter, kept me focused on the many good things I had to look forward to, didn't allow me to sink into the crazed depression my mind was begging for.

That's the thing about Lisa. She's always up for some good times, but she doesn't run away during the bad ones.

A huge, contented sigh came from my best friend. "I'd love to give you a big lecture here. I should probably feel compelled to warn you about everything that could go wrong again." She looked up at me, and she actually had tears in her smiling eyes. "But I just can't. Seeing you two together... It's like... like it's..." she trailed off, a dreamy expression on her dazed face.

"I know. And it is."

"'Bout time."

"Tell me about it."

She shook her head, laughing. "A freaking movie star. Leave it to you."

I had a flash of that freaking movie star's beautiful body poised above me, reducing me to a heaving pile of useless flesh the night before, and a delightful shiver made its way down my spine. I tried to contain my smile. I really did. But Lisa saw my battle and her eyes went wide. "You already had sex with him!"

I let my smile turn into a huge grin. "I did."

"You slut!"

"Shh! Your kids are in the next room!"

"Well, I think it's best that they know something like this now. Hey kids! Your aunt is a tramp!"

I leapt onto the couch and stifled her stupid, loud mouth with my hand. She was trying to squirm out of my grasp, but I held firm until she pinched my arm. "Ow!" I yelped as we both cracked up.

She was just looking at me, shaking her head. "This is like, so weird."

I rubbed my forearm and answered, "I know. But Lis... I can't even tell you. Trip and me... we're like, even better than we ever were. It's as if every stupid thing we've ever done to each other was worth it just to get us here, you know?"

"There were a lot of stupid things."

"I'm quite aware of that, thank you."

"So, this is it, then. You guys are really doing it this time."

"Holy shit. Yeah, I guess we are."

Lis smiled, and I was just getting ready to spill all the sordid details when Caleb came tearing into the room. "Mommy? When will Daddy be home?"

She shook her head and directed her commentary to me. "Every flipping day with this question," she lamented before answering Caleb, "No game tonight. Daddy will be home at the regular time, baby."

"Will he do fwips wif me?"

Pickford was an insanely amazing father. He doted on those kids every minute he got. His coaching job wiped him out every day, yet he still found the energy to roughhouse with the twins when he got home at night. I can't tell you the number of times he'd start a sentence with, "You can't believe what those two did the other day," before regaling me with prideful stories about the latest adorableness to ooze from his precious children.

"Yes, baby, he'll do flips with you. Hey. Auntie Layla has to get back to work. Why don't you find your sister and we'll walk down to Gramma and Pop Pop's. Then we can hit Chuck E. Cheese."

"I don't wanna hit Chuckie. I wike him."

We cracked up at that as Lisa explained what she really meant.

"Oh. Okay! Wet's go now! JOO-YA!" he shouted at the top of his lungs.

I laughed. "Don't yell, monkey! Go in the other room and get her, you wacko."

He skipped out of the room as I whispered to Lisa, "Oh my God. Please reconsider your decision to send that kid for speech. I freaking love hearing him talk."

"Yeah. I'm sure it'll be real cute when he's president or something." She rolled her eyes, admitting that she agreed with me, however, as Caleb stuck his head back around the door.

"Mommy?"

"Yes, baby?"

"What's a twamp?"

Chapter 9
THE TALENT GIVEN US

A couple days later, I was back at my desk, attempting—again—to get some actual writing done. My head was still spinning from the sudden reemergence of Trip in my life, and we'd spent practically every minute together since then. I needed a day just to concentrate on my *pre*-Trip persona. At least for a few hours.

I wasn't on any sort of imposed deadline for the next book, but I normally liked to set some timeline goals for myself just the same. The problem was that I hadn't really nailed down exactly what I'd be writing about yet. I had pages of outlined ideas, just waiting for one of them to spark, catch fire, and suck me into its world.

My mind was wandering, and I found myself pulling out an old file, some of the research I'd done while writing my first book. Originally, *Beachlight Publishing* had used Diana as their middle man, asking if she'd sign me as her client. They were expecting her to convince me to submit a memoir about my high school days with Trip and actually thought it would have more teeth if I used real names. They soon found out that there was no way I'd ever agree to write such a thing. Instead, I'd offered up a fictional retelling of my life. They didn't go for it.

Thankfully, however, Diana did. She put out her feelers to a few different publishing houses, and eventually, it managed to find a home.

Nevertheless, I still had tons of leftover notes from that time; random scraps of paper or envelopes or napkins, thoughts jotted down on whatever writing surfaces were at hand whenever a memory struck. Most of the compilation read more like diary entries as opposed to an outline for a book. Once I sat down to actually write, however, I hardly had any need to consult my factual notes while getting lost in the fabricated story.

But that day, I dug it all back out and revisited it. I suddenly had the inexplicable urge to tell Trip's and my story in all its many details, get it all down on paper. Not to publish, of course, but I was thinking that it would be a special gift for him. I wasn't much of a scrapbooker, but I could document our life with words. It's not like I didn't have the time.

I got pretty lucky when that first book took off as well as it did. Because of that, Diana was pretty understanding about letting me work at my own pace. I'd made a few friends in the book world, and from the sound of it, some other literary agents weren't quite so lax. It helped that Diana was not only a pit bull, but on my side. She was a champion for all the "artists" under her tutelage and didn't take kindly to being told how to manage her talent.

So, it was pretty phenomenal that I was afforded a fairly long leash in regards to my career. Essentially, I was self-employed, a circumstance I'd never had during my working life and one in which I found an unexpected discipline.

Not so disciplined that I couldn't take some time to swim through some writer's block every now and again, however.

I had a membership at a nearby full-service gym just so I could use their indoor pool. I knew it would be a great way to keep fit over the winter, but I hadn't been there more than a few times. Now that Trip and his marble-carved muscles were back in the picture, I figured it was high time I got myself back into shape. Over the seventy-two hours he'd been back in my life, I made it a point to hit the pool every day since the wake. I could already feel my body coming back to me, which was a good thing, because I refused to let my boyfriend be prettier than me.

Who am I kidding? Even if I were in top form, he'd still be prettier than me, dammit.

So, there I was, back in my office after my morning swim, a big, fat, personal folder screaming for attention and an entire as-yet-to-be-determined novel waiting to be written… and what was I doing?

Organizing my desk drawer.

Granted, with my obsessive tendencies, such a task was a weekly undertaking, but with two huge projects hanging over my head, it wasn't the most pressing matter at the moment.

The one thing that stole the *highest* priority in my mind finally took precedence as I allowed myself to dial the phone.

Trip's mom answered.

"Hi, Mrs. Wilmington. It's Layla. May I speak to Trip please?"

Oh my God. I'm seventeen.

"Sure, honey. Hey, I'm sorry we didn't get much chance to talk the other day."

The woman was a bit preoccupied dealing with the death of her husband of almost forty years. It's not like I blamed her for not taking time away from that to catch up on our gossip. "Umm. You were a *little* busy."

"It was still good to see you. I'd like to catch up."

It was a sweet thing to say. She and I had always gotten along pretty well back in the day, and I guess I didn't realize how much I'd been missing her until she said that. "Well, don't worry. I'll be around from now on."

I could hear her smile on the other end of the phone. "Well, I'm glad to hear that. Hang on, I'll get him. *Terrence!*"

There was a fumbling on the other line, then I heard Trip's voice. "Hello?"

"Hi!"

"Hi there."

"What's up?"

"Hang on." He held the phone away from his mouth and yelled, "Ma! I got it! Hang up!"

Click!

"I can't believe I just had to say that."

68

I laughed. "Well, if you'd just join the rest of us in this millennium, you'd get yourself a cell phone."

"Never."

"What's the matter? Big strong guy like you afraid of a little brain cancer?"

"No. Big strong guy like me is afraid of an even bigger and stronger Big Brother."

"You can't be serious."

"As a brain tumor."

I rolled my eyes at that one. "So... Guess what?"

"What?"

I wrapped the cord around my finger and sing-songed, "My father's going out tonight... I have the house to myself..." I was only half-kidding. It was getting ridiculous with the both of us living at our parents' houses. We came this close to screwing in his truck in my driveway the other day. But then my father started flicking the porch lights to bust our chops and we just died laughing. Kinda broke the mood.

He chuckled at my invitation. "Should I bring the keg? Call the football team?"

With that, I had a quick flashback of that beautiful man as the beautiful teenager he once was. Jeez. We really did do a lot of partying back in the day. "No keg. Just bring that sweet little ass of yours over here. I wanna squeeze it while we make out on the couch."

There was a distinct pause before he breathed out, "Christ, that was hot."

I laughed. "See you later."

* * *

I was really looking forward to my "date" with Trip. It was going to be weirdly awesome to have him sitting on my family room couch again, watching a movie just like we used to do as teenagers. I very carefully chose a few DVDs for our viewing selection and figured I'd give Trip the ultimate vote on what we watched. After dismissing nearly my entire collection, I was confident that I'd come up with a handful of films that would meet with his approval, ensuring that I wouldn't have to listen to his tireless critique all night.

When I heard the doorbell ring, my heart actually leapt into my throat. I was almost as nervous as the first time he'd ever come over.

Get it together, Warren!

Dad had answered the door, and as I came up the stairs, I saw the two of them reuniting. Trip turned and smiled as I shyly said hello. I didn't know what my deal was. I went into the kitchen to grab him a soda as Dad invited him into the living room to meet Sylvia.

It was surreal, having him there in the house once again, chatting it up with my father as if fifteen years hadn't passed since their last conversation. I braced my hands on the counter and tried to steady my breathing. I didn't know why I was feeling so freaked out about everything. Maybe just having him there in my house again brought up all the old insecurities. I mean, the first time he'd ever come over, we were just a couple of stupid kids. Just two friends who didn't know how to change that status. Now... Well, now we were "adults." Having him there suddenly seemed like a much bigger deal.

Trip, Dad, and Sylvia were in the living room chatting when I came in to join them. Neither of the men acknowledged my presence, but I saw Dad smirk before he asked, "So, Trip. Just exactly what are your intentions toward my daughter?"

"Oh my God! Dad!"

That had him laughing and made Sylvia almost spit out her club soda.

"Would you rather I lecture him about being responsible?" He turned toward Trip again and said, "I hope you plan on using protection, son."

I almost leapt across the living room and strangled him.

Trip took the digs with the humor they were intended, but answered just the same. "Sir, I learned years ago that there's no protecting me from *that*." He pointed in my direction and all eyes turned toward me as he added, "Believe me. Lord knows I've tried."

I pursed my lips together, trying to contain my smile. Was he not just the cutest thing? I handed him his drink and sat down next to him on the couch. He didn't take his smiling eyes off me the entire time. Oh, God. We were turning into two big sappy idiots all over again.

He turned back to my dad and changed the subject. "Hey, you'll never guess who I ran into at the Super Bowl last month. Your nephew, Jack."

"No kidding! Loo, did you know that?"

Obviously, I did not. I was going to have to remember to murder my cousin the next time I saw him. How could he just forget to tell me something like that? "No, I didn't. I just talked to him last week and he never mentioned it!"

Dad chuckled and said, "Well, maybe he just didn't want to look like he was bragging about hanging out with powerful movie stars."

From anyone else, a line like that would seem pretty cheesy, but the way my father said it, it came across as funny. I got the impression that Dad found it amusing that the carefree teenager he once knew had just been named to TIME's Most Influential list. I couldn't say as I blamed him. I'm sure he still saw Trip as that

71

same punky young kid, as opposed to the world-famous actor presently sitting in his living room.

Trip just smiled and took the hit with his usual charm. "Trust me, I wasn't the most powerful guy in that skybox. He was there with Lutz Hamburg."

"Lutz Hamburg? Who's that?" I asked.

Trip grabbed my hand casually, and I could tell by Sylvia's expression that the little move hadn't gone unnoticed. But I didn't think Trip was even aware that he'd done it. I loved that.

"He's a music producer. The guy's a pretty big deal, and Jack was his guest. I was there with the director for my next film, and I was introduced to them both. Turned out, Carlos had invited them to talk about working on a soundtrack for the movie."

Jack used to be in a band that found some moderate fame back in the mid-nineties, but he gave up the rock star lifestyle when he got married and had kids. He still played some local bars just for fun nowadays, but how the heck did he wind up in a skybox in Jacksonville with Lutz Hamburg? I wondered just exactly what was going on there.

Dad shot me a smile as he announced it was time to go. Trip stood and shook his hand, but he gave Sylvia a kiss on her cheek. She actually blushed and was flustered and stammering just the slightest bit as she offered, "It was very nice to meet you."

I realized that Sylvia had been sucked into the Trip charm, maybe even a little blown away by it. She didn't have the advantage of knowing him as the goofy teenager he once was like my father and I did. I could barely handle him at full capacity, but at least I was able to ease into it over the years. Poor Sylvia was getting smacked with the overwhelming force of *Movie Star Trip* right out of the gate. And let me tell you, that guy's presence was intense enough as it was, even when he wasn't being *him*. He had that effect on people. It's what made him so famous.

Chapter 10
WHERE THE TRUTH LIES

We said our goodbyes to Dad and Sylvia, and as the door closed behind them, Trip said, "She's really great!"

I nodded my head in agreement. "She really is. I told you. And she makes my father happy. He deserves that."

Trip winked and shot back, "Doesn't everybody?"

I sure as heck hoped so.

I led him downstairs into the family room, where I'd lain out some snacks and sodas. Trip flopped onto his old spot on the couch and grabbed the bowl of Cool Ranch, munching away as I rattled off our movie choices for the evening.

We settled on *Boogie Nights*, and I snuggled into his side, that crook in his body that was always pre-destined for me and me alone. It was only slightly bizarre to be sitting in my house next to America's Biggest Movie Star. It was actually stranger to have my ex-now-current boyfriend there with me.

It was a miracle that we were able to watch the movie and have him shut up through the thing. He only offered commentary at a few spots, but I guessed it was easier for him to watch a film in which he had no personal investment. It's not like I would have suggested watching one of his anyway.

Trip must have been thinking along the same lines, because out of nowhere, he said, "I see you didn't offer any of *my* movies as choices for the evening."

He sounded almost hurt, and I didn't really think that that situation was one that would need explaining. "I thought it might be awkward. Why? Did you actually want to watch one of yours?"

"Never. I guess I kind of just expected you to throw on *Swayed* or something. You know, finish what we started and all that."

We never did get to see the end of his movie. At least *I* hadn't. "I don't have that one." His face sort of fell at that, and I thought there was a chance he'd taken my statement as an insult. "I have all the others, though."

I hoped he understood what I was getting at.

"Oh. Thanks," he offered, before getting lost in thought for a minute. "But not *Swayed*?"

Guess not.

It was probably his greatest role to date. He'd been nominated for Academy Awards before and since, but actually took the statue home for that one. But for obvious reasons, I could never bring myself to watch that movie ever again.

I opened the TV cabinet and pulled out a stack of DVDs, showing him the pile of his movies that we owned. What I didn't tell him is that my father was the one to buy them all. A couple even still had the plastic on them. After what had happened between us in New York, there was no way I could stomach seeing him onscreen. I hadn't seen any of his movies since then.

"No. Not *Swayed*," I answered.

An uncomfortable silence hung in the air between us. I grabbed the remote off the table and hit pause.

He massaged the back of his neck and said, "I guess we're doing this now, huh?"

"Yeah. I think we need to."

The past days had been a whirlwind. We were just so happy to be back in each other's lives that we'd avoided having The Talk. But we couldn't bury our problems forever. May as well get it over with so we could move on.

I settled my back against his chest again and his arm twined around my waist as he offered, "You're right. We do. Okay. Let's fill in the blanks."

"I'm not going to hold back," I said. "You should prepare yourself for the new and improved brain-vomit version of me." I absently played with his hand around my middle. "I don't even know where we should start."

"Well, let's start at the beginning. Why didn't you come to the hotel?"

I was startled by his question, and Trip could feel me tense against his body. He tried to calm me, rubbing a palm along my shoulders.

"Oh, Trip. It was truly the biggest mistake I've ever made in my life. I just... I don't even know if I'll be able to talk about this."

"We have to. C'mon. Brain vomit away."

He was right. We had to do this. It was time to just lay everything out on the table. I took a deep breath and launched in. "I was scared. You need to understand that I'd spent ten years living my life in a daze, and I didn't even realize it. I pushed myself to do well in college, then I pushed myself to get a good job. The job I ended up with wasn't a good one, but it had promise, and I kept waiting for it to get better. I had this blinders-on focus just to keep moving forward, live my life like a real adult. A very powerful man asked me to be his wife, and I thought marrying him was what I was expected to do."

Trip winced at the reference to my ex-fiancé, but I had no words of comfort for him. If we were going to get through this, we both needed to hear things we might not like.

"I was finally on the verge of achieving everything I'd worked for, everything I'd ever wanted. Or so I thought." I smoothed a hand over his to continue, "I'd finally gotten a shot to prove myself as a reporter—interviewing *you*—and I figured my life was really beginning. It was, of course, but not because of my job and my fiancé, like I'd thought."

"What do you mean?"

"My life had started because of *you*. Because you'd come back into it. Only I was too stupid to realize it. I didn't know... until *after*."

Trip repositioned himself on the couch, settling me between his legs and leaning me back against his torso. I could sense his reluctance to speak as an uneasy silence crept between us. Finally, he asked, "How long after?"

"Not long." I hesitated for a second, but decided to just forge on. "I may not have gone to the hotel that night, but I went the next day, you know. I went there for you. But you were already gone."

"Is that why you tried to call? Because you didn't get to say goodbye?"

Oh, holy Jesus. I knew we had to do this. But he really had no clue.

"Not exactly. But you wouldn't even speak to me."

He let out with a heavy breath. "I was hung-over and heartbroken, babe. When I realized you weren't coming that night, I got stinking drunk. That next day, I woke up Hunter and had him bump up my flight. I didn't want to be in that city an extra second. I was at the airport when Sandy called to tell me you wanted my number. I poured out the whole pathetic story, told her to call you back, but then to pull the battery from her phone the second she hung up with you. I set her up with a new number so you couldn't get in touch with me." He sounded guilty about all that, but he had no idea what sort of chain-reaction he was *truly* responsible for.

"I tried everything I could think of to contact you. You didn't even give me a chance to explain."

"I didn't want to hear you say it. I didn't want to hear you say you picked the other guy."

Hearing him lay that right out there caused a fracture to form, right down the middle of my heart; I could feel *his* being broken. God. I really hoped we were done causing each other so much grief. "You really spent the whole night drinking?" It was ludicrous to feel relieved at his admission. But the drinking, I could handle. Sex with a replacement, I could not.

"Drinking doesn't cover it. I got completely polluted." He chuckled, but it was just a cover. "What about you? What did you do with your night after you kicked me out of your apartment with a raging hard-on?"

It was so difficult to talk about, even after all those years, even with him sitting right there, back in my life, the idea that our future together was an established probability.

"Well, I didn't sleep much, for starters. At all, actually. The next morning, I went into work, only to find I didn't have a job waiting for me. Devin had fired me so casually, and I got offended enough to break off our engagement. But it was more than that. I realized he wasn't... He wasn't nearly the right man for me. That's when I went back to the hotel to find you, but you had already gone. I already knew I'd made a huge mistake by not showing up the night before, but I didn't realize *how* huge until I saw the package waiting for me when I got home."

Trip's face fell. "Wait. You didn't get it until..."

"Right. That next day."

His hand clamped into a fist and a muscle was working furiously in his jaw.

"I died, Trip. I swear. I had no idea that you were trying to do anything other than take me to bed the day before. When I saw that lunchbox..."

He grabbed me and pulled me to him, crushing his arms around me, trying to hug the pain from us both. The tears slipped down my cheeks.

"And that's when you tried to call Sandy... to tell me..." There I was, in his arms, and he still didn't want to believe that I had really wanted him. I couldn't blame him. We'd screwed this up so many times before.

"To tell you I loved you, too."

He let out a breath that was part relief, part agony. We were both in tears, but he still didn't know the whole story.

"You haven't heard the worst of it," I said into his shirt.

"It gets *worse*?"

"Exponentially."

"I don't know if I can take it."

"Well," I started in, hesitantly, "I wasn't exactly thinking rationally at the time. I mean, I moved back here but—"

"I see that."

"It uh… it wasn't really part of the plan."

"Then why'd you do it?"

"Well, I had already packed everything. I had no job and didn't have much of a choice. The landlord already had new tenants lined up. I thought… I figured I'd be moving somewhere new. Hopefully, with a roommate."

I turned in his arms to face him, but wimped out and kept my face buried against his chest instead. My eyes were gathering tears again and my voice had begun to shake. "I rolled the dice and I lost. I'd gambled on you. I was coming to California to be with you."

"You came out to California? You were there?"

"No, I… I never made it."

His hand stilled. "Wait. When was this?"

"A few days after I got your present."

I raised my head to gauge his reaction and could see the understanding dawning across his features, putting the timeline into perspective, realizing what prevented me from coming to find him. But the martyr in him wanted to hear me say it. "What… stopped you?"

"I'd have to say it was the fact that you'd just announced your engagement to Jenna Barnes." I put a hand against his neck, buried my face in his chest again, and added, "When she got out of that limo… God, Trip. I thought I'd die. It killed me."

He wrapped his arms around me tightly, and I could feel his jaw clenching under my palm. "You loved me."

"I did. I do."

"You should have come anyway."

"Ha! That would have gone over well."

"You could have saved me from myself."

I tensed at his words. I'd suffered years of guilt for his downward decline. And there he was, confirming that it was my fault.

Trip felt me stiffen in his arms and pulled back. His brows were furrowed in confusion. He had no idea what he'd just said.

"Trip... I've completely beaten myself up over that very thing. How could you—"

"Oh my God. No. Babe, no one could have saved me from the bottle, let's just get that straight right now. Yes, I fell hard after you, but it was only the excuse I needed. I was sinking on my own long before you destroyed me. Those were *my* choices, and mine alone. If you don't hear anything else I say, hear that." He paused and turned my face to him, his eyes solemn. "My choices, Lay. Don't you dare put that burden on yourself." He held my gaze until I nodded slightly, relenting. He gave me a brief smile, then continued. "I meant you could have saved me from the years of pining for you. All these years we wasted, loving each other and not doing anything about it. It was supposed to be a joke."

"Good one."

"It was a bad one. I'm sorry."

"Why didn't *you*?" I asked.

"Why didn't I what?"

"Why didn't you come for me? If you loved me so much... why—"

"Lay. I was stuck in a bottle for years. Even after I broke it off with Jenna and cleaned up... I never thought I could contact you. I thought I'd made it very clear that I was in love with you, and you just... turned me down. I thought I was saving face by announcing my engagement, running in another direction, thinking it would ease my pain. It didn't. I was trying to destroy you, and I hoped that I did. Wanted to hurt you even if I wasn't sure you'd even care. I couldn't very well just call you up to say 'hey' after that. Look at it from my side. Why would I have thought you even wanted me to? I always thought you'd chosen the other guy. I figured I was long out of the running."

"But I didn't choose him. I was in love with *you*." That earned me a sweet kiss against my knuckles and a shy smile across that gorgeous mug. There we were, together again. I couldn't even imagine what my life would be like had I actually married Devin. I couldn't believe I almost did. I couldn't believe *Trip* thought that I actually *had*. "How did you find out I didn't marry him?"

"I have my sources."

I looked at him, eyebrows raised, waiting for him to continue.

"I had Sandy do some digging last week. The first thing I did when I found out my father died was to ask her to find you. Turns out, she'd been keeping tabs on you all these years. She told me about your books. More importantly, told me you were single."

"So, this whole time, you thought that I…"

"Married him. Yes."

"You really didn't know?"

"Babe. I didn't *want* to know. I was shredded. So, I cut you off. You were dead to me. It was the only way I could keep myself breathing every day."

I thought on that for a moment. I'd spent most of my time during the past years wandering around in a daze. He didn't need to imagine it; I *was* dead. "Then why'd you think to call me when your dad died?"

"Why *wouldn't* I think to call you? I was coming back home. I realized you were the only one who really knew the whole story with him. There wasn't anyone else in the world I wanted at that moment. I needed you." He smoothed my hair and added, "I also realized I was done waiting around for this. I hoped we'd have a second chance."

"Third chance."

"Who's counting?" He gave a nervous chuckle, but the situation was far from funny. "Thanks for making it easy on me by not being married, by the way. I don't know too many hit men out on the west coast."

I elbowed him for such a lame dig.

I started thinking about Trip's father, and an unexpected guilt crept into my brain. I realized I'd never get the chance to let him know how grateful I was to him. I may not have ever liked the guy, but it was time to give credit where credit was due. "You know... You can say what you want about the guy being a dick, but he's the one that brought us together. Twice."

"Well, this time, yeah, but...?"

"Our first kiss. Remember?"

His eyes softened at that, reliving the memory along with me. His arm tightened protectively around my waist as he said, "Your sad brown eyes looking at me like I was the only one who could make your world right is what brought us together for that first kiss. That, and the fact that I was crazy about you."

Chapter 11
PEACE, PROPAGANDA AND THE PROMISED LAND

The windows of my Mustang were actually steamed over as Trip and I made out in the backseat.

It was freezing outside, but inside the car... well, let's just say it was much hotter (and not just because of the cramped quarters). I'd just dislodged my foot from under the passenger seat as Trip wrapped my newly-freed leg around his waist, grinding his hips into mine.

There was something so indescribably sexy about being fully clothed and hooking up like a couple of teenagers in the back of my old car. We thought the Mustang would have afforded us a bit more room after the make-out session in his truck a few nights back, but we'd started to realize car sex isn't what it used to be. Don't get me wrong, it was hot. Just not the most comfortable place.

He had his face in my cleavage as his hand started to slide down the front of my jeans. He was revving up to round third when he slammed against me roughly, causing my head to knock against the window.

"Ow!" I laughed out.

That stopped his motion as he started laughing, too. "Fuck. We're too old for this."

That might have been true, but in my eyes, he'd always be a seventeen-year-old boy. Wait. Is that weird?

We untangled ourselves from each other's limbs and found a more comfortable position, Trip sitting normally, while I lounged out sideways along the backseat, my legs across his lap.

I'd picked up some take-out from *Thyme*—Norman's only five-star restaurant—and brought it over to his house for dinner with his mom, sister, and Sandy. After we ate, he and I went out to find a secluded place to have *dessert*. We were parked behind the abandoned strip mall at the edge of town, and it wasn't until that moment that I realized how ridiculous that was. I'd suggested getting a room at The Norman Inn, but Trip thought the place was a dive (he was right), and he was hesitant to be seen anywhere out in public. The paparazzi knew he was home and had been practically camped out on the street out front of his mother's all week. I didn't know how he managed to get to my house without being followed on the other days, but that night, he had to scrunch down on the floor of the backseat with a blanket over him just so we could get out of the driveway.

If things continued like this, however, we were both going to explode.

He rubbed his palms along my legs, a mysterious, guilty smile cracking his features. "Hey, uh… I know it's short notice, but I'm heading back tomorrow night."

What? He'd just gotten back here. It was like he was trying to beat it out of Dodge. I didn't expect him to stay in Jersey indefinitely, but I was crushed that he was heading back so soon.

He must have seen my face fall, and explained, "I just got the call this afternoon. Gotta get back to work. The show must go on."

Dammit. I felt like he'd only been back in my life for a minute, and now we already had to confront the long-distance relationship we were setting up for. *Six days? That's all I get? Really, God?*

I played his fingers with my hands, and said more casually than I felt, "Oh. Yeah, I know. I mean, I don't have to like it, but I understand."

At that, his mysterious smile turned into a full-force grin. "Why don't you come back out with me for a while? You'll love L.A."

My heart just about leapt into my throat. "Are you serious?"

I don't know why I was so surprised by the invitation. I mean, we'd pretty much solidified the decision that this thing was happening for us, that we were going to be together. I guess things had just happened so fast—well, after a decade-and-a-half, I guess the word *fast* doesn't really apply—that I hadn't really thought about the logistics of it all. But hell. I'd been in limbo since the night I packed up my apartment in New York. It was finally time to put the California Plan back into effect. It was almost as if I'd sub-consciously set up my life to be able to take off at a moment's notice. No apartment to deal with, no nine-to-five to keep me tied in town.

Yet… he'd only asked me to come out to L.A. for "a while."

I followed my new lay-it-all-out-there rule and confronted him, flat out. "Trip… I want to go with you. I do. But just exactly how long is… '*a while*'?"

His head fell as his shoulders started shaking. "You know, this new brain-vomit version of you is going to be a real pain in the ass sometimes."

"Thanks a lot!"

"Look. You're coming to California with me, end of story. I'm not letting you out of my sight. Last time I left here without you, I ended up engaged to the wrong girl." He gave my hand a good squeeze and added, "I'd like to think the *right* one will be sitting next to me on that plane tomorrow."

My stomach dropped out from inside me, my brain in a full-on panic. What he'd just said almost sounded like… a *proposal.* Almost.

He must have seen me go pale, because he tried to lighten the proposition. "It's just that I don't expect you to pick up and start a whole new life at a moment's notice. That's all I meant by 'a while.' I figure you'll *want* to come back to Jersey at some point." He grabbed both my hands in his again, smiling into my eyes, throwing away that whole "lightened proposition" thing when he said, "You know, so you'll have time to plan for the arrangement to become more… *permanent.*"

Cue the marching band.

Screw it. How could I say no to that man? Why would I want to ever again?

I had a big, doofy grin on my face when I answered, "Okay. Yes. Of course I'll come to California with you! I lost you twice already. I'm not stupid enough to do it again."

Trip actually let out a breath, and I was startled to find that he thought there was a chance I would have answered otherwise. I decided to press my advantage.

"But... I have a condition." I twined my fingers in his and bit my lip. He knew I was going for it. I expelled my request on a hasty breath. "I want to go to the Oscars."

Trip's posture slumped and he dropped his chin to his chest. I didn't know what that meant, but I could see the smile playing at his lips.

"What?" I asked.

He shook his head and raised his eyes to mine. "I thought you were going to ask for something else."

Before I could inquire about that, he said, "Which is the only reason I'm even considering this. You know I don't do the award-ceremony thing."

That I did. For all the years he'd been out in Hollywood, for all the Golden Globes and Oscars and MTV and People's Choice Awards... he'd never made an appearance at a single one. He'd been nominated a bunch of times, even won quite a few little statues, but they were always accepted in absentia.

So, no. Trip didn't do the award-ceremony thing.

"Why is that, exactly?" I asked. I'd always wondered, but could only come up with my own answers over the years. Stage fright? Too nerve-wracking?

He leaned back and swiped a hand over his face. "Shit, Lay. I don't know. I didn't even go to our *prom* because I heard I was a shoo-in to get King."

I literally did a double-take as I stared at him in open-mouthed shock. "Whaaat?"

"You never knew?"

"Well, I heard the same rumors, I knew you were at the top of the list, but you never told me that's why you didn't go. But what does that have to do with going to an awards show?"

His lip curled into a snarl as he blurted out, "Because it's the same thing? Because it's stupid? Because it's a big popularity contest?"

"You seem to have fared okay in that department. You've got an Oscar, for godsakes!"

"Amongst others."

"Bragging now, are we?"

He sighed. "A little. Okay, yes. I'm bragging. I'd be lying if I said it didn't feel great to win those things."

I gave him a *see?* face.

"*But*, I don't really think they mean anything. They're just... They're just nice to have, I guess. I mean, really. In the grand scheme of the universe, who really cares about some stupid actor winning an award?"

I grabbed his hand again. "Understood. But in *your* little universe, the universe in which you make your living, I think it happens to be pretty phenomenal. It's nice to be acknowledged for all that hard work. Besides, you're not even nominated for anything this year. You won't have to suffer the indignity of actually getting up on that stage."

That made him chuckle. "You're right. I'm not nominated. But I will have to get on that stage."

"What do you mean?"

"They've been bugging me for years to be a presenter. I always declined because I wasn't ever going to even be there. If I go, there's no way I'll be able to get out of it."

I weighed that for a moment. "If?"

He sighed heavily, rolling his neck from side to side. If it weren't for his twitching lip, I would have been duped into believing he was trying to come up with a way to let me down easily. His gorgeous face turned in my direction as he gave me a sham dirty look out of the corner of his eyes. God. I freaking died every time he did that. "Okay, fine. You win. *When.*"

I gave a yelp and threw my arms around him for a hug. "Thank you! We're going to have so much fun. Just you wait!"

He couldn't contain his laughter.

* * *

The next morning, I called my agent, Diana. She was based out of the main office located in New York, but I tried to schedule my visits on the days when she'd be in the New Jersey branch. The city wasn't a far ride from Norman, but Paramus was a hell of a lot closer. For days like this, the phone was even more convenient.

I wasn't much looking forward to reporting on my non-progress on Book Three. I had a few half-assed ideas to pitch, though, and I figured she'd be able to help me nail down the one I should dive into first. But forty minutes into our call, we hadn't even touched on the subject of my next work of fiction. Diana was more interested in my *real* life.

Of course I had to let her know I was going to be out of town. She was my agent, after all. But I guess I was so excited about *where* I'd be going, that I managed to slip the name Trip Wiley into the conversation. What followed was a solid half-hour of Diana gushing about my boyfriend's movies, peppered with the occasional plea for me to bring him by the office and introduce them.

God. Even the straitlaced, ball-busting Diana Cavanaugh wasn't immune to The Great and Powerful Trip Wiley.

Then she said something even more shocking. "So, does this mean I'm finally going to get the real story between you and the movie star?"

It was only surprising because I'd really thought we'd gotten past that in the almost five years since I'd been working with her. But in my life, I've learned to never say never.

More importantly, I've learned to never say no to Diana Cavanaugh.

"I don't know, Dee. *That* story doesn't have an ending yet."

Chapter 12
JUST LIKE HEAVEN

We scheduled a late afternoon flight out to L.A., and I tried to forget how much I hated to fly. It truly scared the hell out of me, but I figured I'd better get used to a bi-coastal lifestyle. Flying first-class made it just a tad easier to change my opinion on airplanes, however. Actually, it made it *hugely* easier. I was pleasantly surprised to find that most of my aerophobia was caused by *claustro*phobia, and not so much the whole winging through the sky thing. I wished I had discovered first class years ago.

A few photographers were lurking at the gate, and got off a bunch of shots as Trip and I were getting off the plane. I was tired from the flight, but took Trip's cue and smiled as we walked past briskly, but not rudely. It was strange to be smacked with his world within only the first few seconds of entering it. I was still getting used to the idea that he even lived like that, when *BAM!* Welcome to Hollywood.

I figured after six hours crammed onto an airplane, I probably didn't look my best. I hoped the pictures were boring enough that they'd never turn up in some magazine or something. What was the story there? "Trip Wiley And Some Random Chick Get Off An Airplane"? Fascinating journalism, kids. I'll be sure to frame your article and hang it on the wall next to my LIFE cover of the Kennedy assassination.

Stepping out of the airport was like stepping out onto a different planet. After suffering through yet another long winter in Jersey, arriving in Los Angeles was like going from black and white to full-on Technicolor. With the time change, it was still fairly light out, and I was so invigorated to see all the green of southern California.

Swimmin' pools. Movie stars. Beach Boys music piped in on every corner.

Not really, but it felt like it should have been.

Our driver pulled the towncar in front of the *Beverly Hills TRU,* parked in a spot reserved for registration, and I breathed a sigh of relief that we hadn't been followed by any of those pesky photographers from the airport. As we got out, Trip asked, "Are you seriously planning on staying here?"

It had been a much-discussed topic on the plane. Trip wanted me to stay at his house, but I insisted on staying at a hotel. The whole week had been such a whirlwind and I wanted to give him time to get used to the idea that I'd be invading his life.

We made our way through the lobby, and I swear, every eye in the place turned our way. Trip pasted his movie-star-smile onto his face and ignored all of them, save for the concierge behind the desk who welcomed him by name. "Mr. Wiley. Welcome back. We were all very sorry to hear about your father. How did everything go back home?"

Trip had turned into *him* by this time, so he was able to answer appropriately, "Thank you, Jim. Everything went very well. Of course we're all saddened by the loss of a good man, and I'm sure the *TRU* won't be the same without him. But I see everything's in order here?"

Jim puffed up a bit with pride as he answered, "Of course, Mr. Wiley. Miss Wilmington is making sure of that."

When Mr. Wilmington's health had finally taken its ultimate turn for the worse, Claudia had stepped into his vacated role as Chairman of the Board. I thought it was more of a figurehead-type position—you know, keeping with the family name and all—but apparently, she was actively running the show. Good for her.

Trip introduced me to Jim, then checked me in under the name Mrs. Martin Bishop. Still with the freaking Redford characters. He smiled cheerfully at his name choice, but he wasn't very happy about having to kiss me goodbye. He pulled me behind a potted tree and planted his lips on mine. What started out as a simple goodbye kiss quickly picked up a bit of steam. I hoped none of the tourists in the lobby could see us, or worse, pull out their cameras and start snapping photos.

We were both a bit jetlagged from the flight, so while half of me wanted nothing more than to drag him upstairs with me, the other half just wanted to crash for the next twelve hours.

But there we were, right there in the lobby, our goodbye kiss turning heated.

Screw sleep. Some things were more important. I needed this man between my thighs more than sleep. More than food. More than *air*.

He slipped an arm around my waist and we followed the bellboy to the elevators along with the baggage cart that held all my stuff. Once the doors closed, Trip didn't waste any time. He slid a hand right down my spine, teasing his fingers under the waistband at the back of my jeans. I stood perfectly still, even though I wanted to slap his hand away. I could've killed him for playing games with the bellboy right there in the cramped elevator. Either that, or jumped his bones. I wasn't sure which. In any case, the ride to the penthouse took forever.

We were shown to our room, and Trip promptly tipped the bellboy. As soon as he was out the door, we started tearing at each other, our clothes strewn all over the floor. Trip shoved me onto the bed and pounced on top of me, kissing his way along every inch of my body.

"No way, pal. It's *my* turn," I teased, as I rolled him to his back and straddled him, kissing his neck and running my hands along his smooth, hard chest.

The light from outside had started to dim, and I was reminded of a dream I once had, during a time when the mere thought of having this gorgeous man back in my life was an abstract idea at best. And yet, there he was, *right there*, his hands clasped behind his head, his eyes closed, a contented smile pasted to his beautiful face, lying right there underneath my naked body, the reality far better than any dream could ever be.

I kissed him, brushing my mouth along those full, sensual lips of his, savoring the taste of him, the feel of his heart rushing under my palms. A possessiveness overtook me as I pushed back against his torso, trying to brand myself into his skin. I had waited for this, longer than any woman should have been asked to wait. And now, he was mine.

I earned him.

Trip wasn't feeling very patient at that moment either. He released his hands from behind his head and grasped my hips, pulling me toward him and spearing himself into my body. I gasped as I rocked against him, feeling the fullness of his hardened length plunging inside of me, claiming me as his own.

He was smiling as he had his way with me, his free hands running over every inch of exposed skin within his reach, his hips thrusting to meet my movements, again and again and again, eventually causing the both of us to explode, leaving us sated and out of breath.

What is it about a hotel room that turns people into sex-crazed lunatics?

We settled into the heavenly mattress, our limbs tangled together under the bedsheets as I ran my hand along the soft skin on the inside of his arm.

He was staring at me, his face half-buried in the pillow. "I can't believe you're really going to stay here. Isn't there anything I can say to change your mind?"

My chest was still heaving as I tried to catch my breath. I nuzzled into his neck, shivering at the brush of stubble that tickled my lips. The truth was, all I really wanted was to curl up in that man's bed and stay there forever.

I slowly pushed myself up and straddled his lap, peering down at him while he offered me his most lethally persuasive glare with those potent blue eyes of his—eyes that I was virtually powerless to deny.

I shifted my attention to take in the room we had all but ignored in our frantic dance to make it to the bed.

My jaw dropped.

The room was ginormous. That bedroom alone was probably two times larger than my entire apartment in the city, and decorated a hundred times better. The Wilmingtons' Beverly Hills hotel was way more relaxed and inviting than their über-hip Times Square property. Less mod; more island. Rustic wood furnishings contrasted against pale cream walls with the perfect kisses of *Wilmington Blue* in the patterned fabric of the upholstered furniture, pillows, and curtains. Along one wall, floor to ceiling windows showcased the Los Angeles skyline at night, a breathtaking array of bright lights in darkened skyscrapers against an almost amethyst sky.

I looked down at Trip. "I'm in L.A.," I said in awe.

He grinned cautiously and nodded.

I glanced back up, scanned the room again, then collapsed on top of him. "Holy shit! I'm in L.A. I'm really here."

Trip's arms wrapped around me, his hands gently stroking up and down my back. His voice rumbled through his chest. "You're where you're supposed to be, Lay."

I buried my face in his chest and fought the wave of disbelief washing over me. "A week ago, I was Layla Warren, self-employed writer, living in her childhood bedroom in Norman, New Jersey. You were nothing more than a late-night fantasy, and a crazy day was a visit from Lisa and the kids."

I rested my chin on his chest and looked up at him. "Now I'm in the penthouse suite of the *Beverly Hills TRU*. Naked, mind you, in

93

one of the most comfortable beds I've ever felt, with one of the biggest movie stars the world has ever seen."

I hesitated, mentally reminding myself of my new pledge to verbally vomit, then went for it. "*Also* one of the world's biggest playboys."

His mouth opened, then closed. I squeezed my eyes shut and burrowed into him, wishing I could ignore the insecurity I had thus far managed to keep at bay.

It was impossible to avoid the numerous reports about the many, many women who had been "guests" at his home over the years. Not to mention an ex-fiancée who had actually *lived* there. I could only assume that Trip had seen more action in that house than Hef did in the Playboy Mansion.

Okay, maybe not more than Hef.

It had better not be more than Hef.

His arms tightened, and he whispered against my hair. "You know they meant nothing to me. You know I've spent the last fifteen years pining away for some infuriating chick I met back in high school."

I smiled slightly. "But you were engaged. To a freaking *Victoria's Secret Angel*, Trip. *She* had to mean something."

He pressed soft kisses along my hair and jaw. "She was just a placeholder until you were finally able to figure out how awesome I was."

I sputtered out a laugh, then slapped his chest. He grabbed my arm and slid his hand to my cheek, tilting my face to look at him. "She wasn't you, Lay. Do you understand what I'm saying?"

I stared into his blue eyes, taking in the devotion brimming from their depths. I swallowed past the lump in my throat and nodded.

He brushed a soft kiss against my lips, but I soon pulled away. "Give me a few days, okay? Let's catch our breath. You've just come back from your father's funeral. I'm twenty-five-hundred miles away from the only home I've ever known, with a man I never thought I'd ever see again. I just need a minute to wrap my head around all of this. A few days, and then I'll gladly stay with you."

He nodded, giving me a deep, toe-curling kiss to let me know he understood, no hard feelings. Then he shifted my body off of him and got out of the bed.

"Hey! That didn't mean you had to leave *now*!"

A grin spread across his lips. "Yes, it does. Otherwise certain body parts are going to get way too happy to have a naked you against them, and then it will start all over again, and the next thing you know, it's morning." He gestured below his waist to my favorite body part. Sure enough, it was waking up and taking notice.

I brazenly watched him pull on his jeans and yank his T-shirt over his head, shamelessly ogling what was finally mine to ogle. He smirked, then stalked to the bed and flattened me with another searing kiss.

I gasped for breath as he pulled away and said, "See you tomorrow, babe. This is good. Now I have time to make sure there are no lingering thongs under my mattress."

I shrieked and grabbed one of the dozens of pillows from behind my head, launching it at his retreating form.

"*Kidding!* You know I'm only kidding." He flashed a huge smile, kissed the air between us, and ducked out the door.

I fell to the bed, the giggles escaping despite my efforts. About thirty seconds after he left, I passed out and slept forever.

* * *

The next day Trip had some errands to run, but he set a time to come get me later in the evening. My room was a beautiful suite that took over the entire top floor of the hotel. I thought it was a bit excessive, but I decided to shake off my misgivings and just enjoy it. How often would I ever get a chance to stay in a room like that? I didn't date too many heirs to hotel fortunes.

I took a look out the front windows and checked out the view of Beverly Hills' main drag. It was lively and bustling; not quite at New York City levels, but busy nonetheless. It was strange to be in such a populated city and hardly see any pedestrians. The opposite windows looked out over the pool in back. It was a known social gathering place for the young and beautiful set of Los Angeles; *the* place to see and be seen. And my God. Even the tourists were beautiful.

I threw on a bathing suit and decided to check out the action poolside. When I headed outside, a young man came up to me and introduced himself as Philippe. He explained that he was my personal cabana boy for the day, which almost made me crack up laughing. A personal cabana boy? What exactly was I supposed to *do* with him?

There were blue and white striped tents bordering one side of the property, and Philippe escorted me toward one of them, letting me know that it was reserved exclusively for me during my stay. I peeked inside briefly, took note of the pile of spare towels stacked on the white Adirondack chairs inside, but opted to head out near the pool instead. I needed some *color*. Not only just because my skin was practically blinding white in February, but because I especially wanted to get some sun-kissed glow before the Academy Awards the following week.

I settled into a poolside lounger, and whipped out my cell phone to call Lisa. She answered with her usual tact. "How's the sunshine, bitch?"

I laughed. "How did you ever leave this place? It's incredible!"

"Well, if you'd ever come out to visit during the *four years* we lived there, you would have known that already, dipwit."

"You know I don't fly. But after travelling first class, my opinion may have changed on the matter."

"Nice, isn't it?"

"Mmm hmm. You know what else is nice?"

"What's that?"

"This fricking hotel! I'm poolside right now on the comfiest lounge chair ever created, a cabana boy at my disposal."

"Mmm. Cabana boy. Is he hot?"

"He's adorable. But he's probably nineteen. Get your head out of the gutter."

"Can't. Pregnant, remember?"

"Obviously. Lord knows you never let anyone forget it."

"Shut up, you turd. Oh, hey! Make sure you get their avocado salad. It's delicious."

My jaw gaped open at her unwitting revelation. "Wait. You've eaten here? *Here?*"

"Uh, no. I just heard that it's really good."

I wasn't buying it for a second. "You traitor! You've been to this hotel before, haven't you?"

Lis finally copped to her crime. "Just once, I swear! Pick had some UCLA event and it was held at the *TRU*. We had to go."

When I didn't speak, she was forced to fill in the empty space.

"Trip hadn't even moved out there at the time! This was back in like '92 or '93. I would have told you if we saw him."

Still, I remained silent.

"Fine! I'm a traitorous whore! Happy now?"

That made me laugh. "Very. Now put one of your kids on the phone."

Chapter 13
THE PERFECT MAN

At seven o'clock, the front desk rang my room to let me know that *Mr. Bishop* had arrived. I grabbed my handbag and made my way downstairs. But when the elevator doors opened, Trip wasn't there waiting for me. I took a lap around the lobby, but I still didn't see him. I figured he was using the bathroom or something and took a seat on one of the sofas, figuring he'd find me eventually. But after five whole minutes, he was still nowhere to be found.

I approached the front desk and asked, "I received a call that Mr. Bishop was here?"

The attendant behind the desk offered a knowing smile as he said, "Ah, yes, *Mrs. Bishop.* He requested that you meet him out front."

I thanked him and headed out the front entryway.

And right there at the curb was my gorgeous boyfriend, wearing cuffed jeans, arms crossed over his chest... and leaning against a red Porsche.

Sixteen Candles! I positively melted. I put my hand over my heart and said, "Jake Ryan! You Jake Ryaned to pick me up tonight!"

The scene would have been perfect if Trip didn't look so annoyed. "Christ! What took you so long? I've only been standing out here like a jackass, holding this pose for like an hour."

I bounded down the few steps and crossed the sidewalk that separated us, sidling up to his chest and slipping a hand around his neck. His "anger" broke at that, and I watched his lips twitch, trying to contain a smile as I slid my fingers into the back of his hair and said, "Oh my God please just whisper *yeah you* for me. I think I'll die."

He lost the battle with his smile as his face cracked into a wide grin. *"Yeah, you* have way too big a crush on that guy. *Yeah, you* are really making me jealous right about now."

I pecked him on the cheek and said, *"Yeah, you* are like the cutest thing ever. Even if you forgot the sweater vest."

"I drew the line at the sweater vest."

"Well, now my night is just completely ruined!" I joked.

He just rolled his eyes and opened the car door for me.

I slipped into the passenger seat and sank into the soft, white leather as Trip made his way to the driver's side. I ran my hand over the dash, asking, "Is this your car?"

Trip started the engine with a glorious, retro rumble. "Nope. Borrowed it from a friend."

I looked at him questioningly. "You happen to have a friend that just happens to own an antique Porsche?"

"Yep." He buckled his seatbelt and slid on a pair of shades. "It's Paul Newman's."

My mouth gaped open as he put the car in gear and we took off down Wilshire Boulevard.

The restaurant Trip chose was not at all what I was expecting. I'd thought we were going to go to some fancy-schmancy eatery where there'd be celebrities at every other table. Where he took me instead was an off-the-beaten-path Mexican place out in Encino. I don't know why I was surprised. It was such a Trip thing to do.

He surrendered the keys to the valet, along with a fifty dollar bill. He saw the look I shot him at that, put his hand at the small of my back, and escorted me into the restaurant, explaining, "I'm not taking any chances with that thing," which just made me laugh.

As soon as we were in the front door, I fell in love with the place. Every cheesy, Mexican cliché was on full display, from the sombreros hanging on the wall, to the piñatas suspended from the high ceiling, to the mariachi band playing on the small stage along the far wall.

I absolutely loved it.

Trip gauged the expression on my face, and it made a wide grin split his features. He took my hand as the hostess led us through the dining room, but when she started to put the menus down at a booth near the stage, Trip whispered something to her I couldn't hear as he slipped a bill in her hand. She changed direction and led us to a private table in a darkened corner instead.

Once we were alone, I said, "Hey. Henry Hill. How come we didn't come in through the kitchen?"

He got my *Goodfellas* reference and started to chuckle. "What am I, a clown? Do I *amuse* you?"

Before I could tell him what a *funny guy* he was, he said, "I've learned it's best to tip *beforehand*. You get better service that way."

"Fair enough, Mr. Wiley."

He looked at me then, frozen in the act of placing his napkin across his lap. "You know, you've only called me that once before."

I took a sip of my water. "What? Mr. Wiley?"

"Yeah. During our interview. You said that exact same thing to me. You never... You never call me by that name."

"Because it's *not* your name."

"Yeah. But even people who knew me growing up can accept that I changed it."

"Not legally, though, right?"

He leaned back in his seat and shot me a sham dirty look. "No. Not legally. What's your point?"

"That it's just... all for show. Trip *Wiley* is all just smoke and mirrors. Trip *Wilmington*'s the guy I fell in love with."

I'd never seen him smile quite so big. "And that's why you'll always be my rosebud."

That was a new one. "Well, you'll always be my... tulip... *Dear*."

100

He cracked up at that. "Not my rosebud. My *Rosebud*. Citizen Kane, remember? You're my happy thing before the fame, before the money."

How adorable was that? I gave him a shy smile, touched that he thought of me in such an endearing way. I was sure, however, that he was just talking about who I *used* to be for him. After the past few days, I hoped I was coming to mean even more to him *now* than I did *then*.

Our waiter came over with some chips and salsa, asking if we'd like something to drink. I was thinking that I should probably just order a soda and was startled when Trip ordered a bottle of house wine instead. But I waited for our server to leave before making a stink about it.

I had just opened my mouth to question him when Trip put a hand up. "It's for you, not me. You had that look."

"What look?"

"That look like you didn't know whether or not to order a drink. That look like you didn't know whether or not to even ask me about it. For future reference—and trust me, you'll encounter plenty of recovering alcoholics out here—you don't need to curb your drinking just because we can't control ours."

"Is that the general consensus?"

"Pretty much. One of the first things you learn is that you can't control other people's behavior. You can only control your own. Even some guys at the treatment center were classified as *problem drinkers*, not alcoholics. They take their recovery hats off on the weekends and think just because they're only having a few beers means they're handling the situation. They're not. It's a recipe for disaster."

"There's a difference between the two? Which one are you?"

"For me personally, it doesn't matter. The way I see it, a problem's a problem. If I felt like I could drink, but still had to constantly monitor every drop, I figure I shouldn't be drinking at all, you know? Believe me. I've done lots of trial and error over the years. I'm not about to tempt fate. It's easier just to avoid all of it."

I accepted his assessment. He was a smart guy and been through hell and back. I had both trust and precedent to know that he wasn't going to go out of his way to screw up his life again.

"Well, I don't have to have wine, either."

He snickered out, "Yes you do. I plan on getting you drunk tonight and taking full advantage of you."

I reached under the table and ran my fingertips down his thigh. "You don't need to get me drunk for that."

He snarled at me across our bowl of chips, took a sip of his water. "You are going to be the death of me, woman."

I was still laughing as I said, "So… I was trying to be cool about this, but I can't just pretend I'm not blown away, here. Just exactly how do you know Paul Newman well enough that he let you borrow his car?"

"I told you I'm starting a hockey movie in the next couple of weeks. What I didn't tell you was that it's a remake of *Slap Shot*."

"I love that movie!"

"Exactly."

He didn't look pleased.

"Why do I get the impression that you're not happy about this?"

"No, I am. Now, anyway. But think about it. *Everyone* loves that movie. It's awesome exactly the way it is. A remake might be a really bad idea. I'd been completely paranoid about it, and decided to consult the source before committing to do it. Paul's doing a cameo, so I was able to finagle his info and get in touch with him."

"Membership has its privileges."

"That it does. Anyway, after talking to him a few times, we kind of hit it off. For all the dicky characters he plays onscreen, he's really a great guy. And for some reason, he likes me."

"You like him, too."

He gave a sheepish smile at that. "Yeah. I admire him. I mean, the guy has had a career that spans six decades, and yet he doesn't even live here most of the time. He's been married to the same woman for fifty years, with not even a hint of scandal. The bastard just turned eighty and he still looks great, still racing cars." I smiled at that, envisioning Trip as a hell-raising octogenarian. He totally would be. "But I think most of all, I admire the work he does with those kids at that camp. Oh. And he created an entire food company just to donate the profits to charity."

I loved that he idolized the man, not just because he'd hoped to emulate his successful career, but because he'd hoped to emulate his successful *life*. "You want to be him when you grow up?"

He chuckled as he answered, "Yeah. I guess I do."

"Well, taking on one of his most beloved roles might be a step in the right direction."

"Or a step in the really wrong one."

"You'll make it work. I know it. You haven't filmed a stinker yet."

"Which one was your favorite?"

I knew he was probably digging for a compliment, but I didn't mind. I hadn't seen any of his newer films, but there would never be a movie that took the place of the one we'd seen *together*. "I think I'm gonna have to go with *Swayed*. For obvious reasons. I've never watched a movie that brought out such... *emotion* in me." Things had gotten so tense between us while viewing that film, that I still get shivers just from thinking about it. Not only because he'd brought me to near-orgasm just from holding my hand in the theater that night, but because he'd nearly brought me to tears with his flawless execution of that role. From what little I'd seen of it, I knew that Oscar was well-deserved. "I never did see the ending, however."

Trip looked at me with a quirked brow. Dammit, he was hot. "Me neither."

"What? I mean, I know why *I* couldn't watch it, but it's *your* movie. You won an academy award for it! And you never even saw the ending?"

"No. I only saw it that one time with you. Just that once."

"Twice."

"*Once*. I didn't stay that night at the premiere. I had to leave early because I was sure I was coming down with the flu."

"The flu."

"Je—My *date* for the evening went to hold my hand, and for *some reason*, my stomach decided to object. I got all sweaty and my head started pounding. We had to leave."

"That may be the sweetest thing you've ever said to me."

We cracked open our menus as Trip tried to contain a smile. I was zeroing in on the chicken fajitas, but I still couldn't shake the Paul Newman thing from my mind. "So. You think Paul will be at the Oscars?" I asked.

His smile broke out full-force at that. "Nah. He doesn't go to those things anymore."

"Darn. Now I won't get a chance to hit on him. I might have to slip my phone number in the glovebox or something when we get back in his car. You're okay with that, right?"

Trip didn't even raise his eyes from the menu as he shot back, "Sweetheart, he might be the only guy I'd let you dump me for."

Chapter 14
HEIGHTS

After dinner, Trip was intent on showing me his favorite place in Hollywood, so we took the scenic route up Western Canyon and found ourselves at Griffith Observatory. It was after hours, so it's not like we could have gone inside, but Trip only wanted to wander around the grounds anyway.

He took my hand and excitedly pulled me in the direction of the domed building, explaining how, "Parts of *Rebel Without a Cause* were filmed here. *'I've got the bullets'?* Yeah right there by the front doors. C'mon. I'll show you where they filmed the knife fight. And there's a statue here somewhere of Dean, but I don't remember exactly where it is. We'll find it."

We made our way up the white concrete ramp to a walled patio on the second floor. Trip peeked over the side and pointed. "Knife fight. Right there."

I took a look and was surprised that the spot actually looked familiar. "Oh yeah! You're right. It looks smaller than I thought it would be."

"Everything looks bigger on the screen. Except me. I'm just as huge in real life. So's my dick."

I rolled my eyes on that one.

He hopped up to walk along the concrete knee-wall, gave a scan across the grounds, and changed the subject. "I haven't been here in a while, but I came here a lot back in the old days."

He was making me nervous, balancing up on that partition like a Flying Wallenda. I hauled myself up to sit on the edge, waving my hand out to him to get down. "Trip, you're causing me to panic, here. Please come sit with me so I don't have to worry about your brains splattering out all over the concrete."

He chuckled as he jumped down, then sprawled out along the top of the wall with his head in my lap.

I ran my fingers through his golden hair, saying, "You need a haircut."

He closed his eyes and just gave a contented, "Hmmm," smiling and practically purring at my touch.

I breathed in the night air, registered its balmy warmth. Even at night, everything in southern California seemed so *green*. I was happy to have escaped the winter doldrums of Jersey for a little while. Happier still because I had Trip at my fingertips. I looked down at the smiling, contented man in my lap and nearly sighed. He always looked so young with his eyes closed like that. Always looked like the boy I had fallen in love with all those many years ago. The boy who never stopped loving me.

I tore my gaze from the god within my grasp and checked out the view. From our vantage point, I could see the Hollywood sign lit off in the distance, and wished I'd thought to bring my camera. It really was a beautiful place. The domes of the planetarium were illuminated by flood lamps, the white, concrete walls surrounding it virtually glowing from the deflection. The grounds of the observatory were abandoned at such a late hour, the flat, green lawns quietly breathing in the faint moonlight. It was peaceful, there. I could see why Trip chose the place as his sanctuary.

I ran a fingertip along his temple, saying, "I get why you come here to escape. It's... *quiet*." I'd lived in New York for nine years. Trip had been in L.A. for eleven. Quiet was a luxury.

He laced his fingers across his chest and took a deep, contented breath. "Quiet's not that easy to come by these days."

I knew he was talking about more than just the noise level of his city. The guy had been living in a circus for the past five years. I couldn't even imagine. I'd found a bit of "fame" with my line of work, too. But author-fame was completely different from actor-fame. I'd gotten my share of fan letters and notoriety, but I could still live my life without intrusion. I could still go to the supermarket, unshowered and no makeup, without having to worry about some paparazzo jumping out from behind the lima beans. Well, I *used* to, anyway.

"How do you do it?" I asked. "How do you deal with every detail of your life being so public?"

He shrugged. "Believe it or not, I don't really think about it. 'There's no such thing as bad publicity' and all that. It keeps me working. You always hear celebs bitching about the latest pictures of them splashed all over the tabloids. But believe me, they get even bitchier when they *don't* appear in those things. I mean, most of those articles paint me in a decent light. These days, anyway."

I thought about his tumultuous past. "That must have been difficult."

"I was drunk through most of it. I hardly even realized people had noticed me."

"They did. Trust me. It's like one day, you were just Trip Wiley: Actor, and the next, you were Trip Wiley: *Superstar*. Did *you* notice the difference?"

He huffed at that. "I don't know. I came back here in... what? October of two-thousand, right? I was at the top of my game career-wise, but feeling lower than I had in my entire life."

I winced at his admission. No matter what he said the other day, I knew *I* was the reason he'd gotten so depressed.

"*Swayed* hit the theaters and it hit *big*."

"I remember."

"Well, the offers kept pouring in. I was already working on *Red Nevada* and I had already signed on for *The Sanction* by the time I won the Oscar. I spent Academy Award night in a bar, by the way. I didn't even know I'd won until the next day when my agent, David brought the thing over to my house."

"I spent it in a bar, too. I knew you were going to win, and I couldn't even think about hearing your name get called, much less watch you walk up onto that stage to accept it. Having to see you thank... *her*."

"There wouldn't have been anything to thank her for." He gave a squeeze to my knee at that admission, but didn't dwell on it.

I knew he was only trying to downplay his relationship for my benefit. But he was *engaged* to that woman, for godsakes. I knew Trip better than that to believe he took such a thing so lightly.

His voice was anything but light when he said, "My mother was a wreck. When I think about how selfish I was, drinking like that... God. She was already dealing with my alchy father, and then her son goes and hits the booze. I'll never forgive myself for doing that to her. To Claudia. They were the ones who got me through that time, you should know. I left you in New York, came back here, and couldn't talk about it for months. I was an absolute wrecked mess. Mom came out to L.A. for a 'visit', but I knew Claudia had tipped her off, and what she was actually doing was checking up on me. She surprised me at my house one day, telling me she came out to help with the wedding planning. Just hearing the word 'wedding' made me sick. I threw up. Right there on the patio, at her feet."

"You did not!"

He smiled, knowing I was such a twisted witch that I actually found the scenario entertaining.

"I did."

"Why did you take the engagement as far as you did? It doesn't really seem very fair to Jenna."

He practically snorted. "Oh, please. Jenna didn't care about anything but looking pretty in her wedding gown. She couldn't even see I was a mess. She just kept making plans, and I just kept avoiding setting a date. Two years she turned a blind eye. Two years of bloodshot eyes and slurred speech and whiskey dick. It's like she didn't *want* to see. I finally hit rock bottom and she was forced to face the truth. She couldn't really ignore the fact that I was moving into the treatment center, for godsakes. I did that on my own, by the way."

I'd read about a few of Trip's drunken shenanigans in the tabloids. They were mostly treated as entertaining little stories about America's new favorite bad boy, relaying the tales of the amusing stunts he had pulled at some prominent club or Hollywood party. But then… rehab.

"We were engaged for two years and she was screwing around the whole time, I think. Not like I can blame her. I couldn't really see it through the bottom of a bottle, or maybe I just didn't care. Even still, I used rehab as the excuse to make the break. She didn't fight me on it."

"What made you finally go?"

"What was my rock bottom, you mean?"

"Yeah, I guess."

He took a deep breath and shook his head in disbelief. "I just… Oh Jesus. What *wasn't* my rock bottom? I was out at the bars almost every night, and managed to pick a fight almost every time. A few times, I'd show up to the set of *Red Nevada* with bruises so dark, the makeup girl was paid overtime. Once, my face was so puffed out that shooting had to be put on hold until the swelling could go down. Biker guy. Real big bastard." He chuckled dejectedly at the memory. "We got that movie finished by the skin of our teeth, and God. It really sucked when we did. I can't normally watch *any* of my movies, but that one? Holy shit. I can barely even say the *title*. It really fucked with my career. Miramax heard all about my bullshit on—and *off*—the set, and that, combined with it bombing was enough for them to cancel my contract for *Sanction*. Instead of waking me up, it just allowed more time for drinking."

I stayed quiet through his rambling. Not only was his monologue enlightening, but it was just too damned shocking for words. I couldn't believe he was ever that broken person. It sounded nothing like the Trip I thought I knew; the sweet boy he was as a teenager, the confident man he was now. I smoothed a palm over the hair above his ear and just let him talk.

"I gotta say, though, the thing that really clinched it for me, the thing that truly woke me up... It wasn't the fighting or the bruises or the threat to my career. It was Claudia."

"Your sister was your rock bottom?"

He gave a chuckle and explained. "No. It was something she said. She'd stopped by unexpectedly one day—she does that a lot by the way, be prepared—and I was floating in the pool on a raft, passed out, *fully clothed*, just a complete disaster as usual. She thought she was being cute when she tossed a snorkel at me to wake me up. I did, for about a second, long enough to roll face first into the water. I didn't come back up."

My fingers had been twirling his hair, but at that, my hand stilled.

"She told me afterward that she had to jump in and drag me over to the stairs. All I know is that one minute, I thought going for a swim seemed like a great idea, and the next, I'm waking up to my sister shaking me, just screaming in my face. I'd pretty much tuned her out the whole time. But then... then she said, '*You look like shit, Terrence! You look just like Dad!*' And if you don't think that fucking got to me, you'd be wrong. And I *knew* it. I *knew* I was turning into the old man. The one asshole in the world I never wanted to turn into. I checked into rehab the following day. Second best move I ever made."

"What was the first?" I asked, smiling, knowing full-well what he was going to say.

"Taking your virginity in that tent."

I smacked him for that. "Asshole."

He laughed, then sat up to face me. "Okay, fine. The *best* move was from Indiana to New Jersey. Because that's when I met *you*. Happy?" He ran a palm across my jaw and kissed me on the corner of my mouth, my skin shivering from the sweet words and gentle touch. There I was, with Trip Effing Wilmington by my side once again.

"But that virginity thing is a pretty close third."

"Shut up, you creep!" I snickered as I gave him a shove.

He smiled and grabbed my hand, looking down at our twined fingers as he said, "I got that letter you sent after I got out. It meant a lot. Thank you."

When I'd heard Trip was in rehab, I kind of lost it a little bit. I was happy that he'd decided to get help, but I was stunned that his drinking problem had gotten so bad. That one letter was the only time I'd ever reached out to him over our four-and-a-half year separation. I wrote about ten different drafts before finally putting the tamest one in an envelope and shooting it off to his agent's office. I was relieved to find out it actually found its way into his hands. "I wished I'd explained things to you then, but... as far as I knew, you were still engaged, and I didn't even know how to tell you what I was feeling without..."

"No. The words of encouragement were enough. I wasn't in the right place back then to hear anything more than that. I didn't read it right away—I should confess that to you right now. It took me a few weeks to even open the envelope. Then a few more to actually read the letter. I was glad once I finally did. I was proud that I was able to resist getting drunk in order to do it. It was the first real test after I got out. So... thanks."

It seemed like a strange thing to be thanked for, but I knew what he meant. "You're welcome."

He swiped his free hand through his hair and said, "I channeled all of my focus into getting back into shape after that. I figured if I was going to come back, I was going to come back stronger than ever. Any time I had the urge for a drink, I worked out instead."

I slid a hand up his arm and gave a squeeze against his rock-hard bicep. "You must have wanted to drink all the time."

That made him snicker, but I was feeling a bit swoony from the bulging muscle under my palm. Jesus. I wouldn't have ever thought it was possible for Trip to get any more gorgeous. Goes to show you never know. I hoped he'd maxed out on his hotness level. I didn't think I could take it if he kicked it up another notch.

I was knocked out of my wandering thoughts when he said, "I had to *audition* for *Unleaded*, you know."

The way he said it made me think that he was embarrassed. I'd heard *Unleaded* was an incredible film, and of course I knew that Trip was a member of the cast. But I guessed it was hard for him not only to take on a mere supporting role, but to have to audition just to get the part. He'd already long surpassed that point in his career. It probably sucked to have to take such a huge step backwards. "Well, whatever you had to do to get the part, it was worth it. You were nominated for that one."

He let out a heavy breath. "Yeah, I know. And thank God for that. I mean, I put it all out there. If it bombed, I don't know where I'd be right now."

I suddenly felt really awful that I hadn't seen it. It was his comeback film, and from all reports, he was amazing in it. I realized I suddenly had a lot of movies to watch in the following days. Time to catch up.

"Well," I started in, leaning against his side, "I'd *like* to think you'd be sitting on a wall with the love of your life."

That made his face split into a wide grin, the dimple in his left cheek more prominent than ever. He kissed me then, those sweet lips brushing softly against mine, his hand under the hair at my nape. My stomach actually flipped at the contact. God. Would I ever get *used* to kissing this man? Would there ever be a day when I wouldn't fall apart from his touch?

He pulled his lips back, but pressed his forehead against mine. "Hey Lay? I hate to cut our evening short, but I've got a meeting tomorrow with the pre-prod for a new movie."

I'd hardly call midnight "cutting the evening short," but maybe that's just because I wasn't in my twenties anymore. I reluctantly pulled out of his grasp and let him help me down from the wall.

* * *

Trip pulled the Porsche into the lot at the *TRU* and cut the engine. I was pretty impatient during the ride down from the observatory. It wasn't an incredibly long trek, but if I didn't get that man in bed soon, I thought I'd pass out from wanting.

Trip must have been feeling it, too. He turned to me and said, "This is ridiculous, Lay. I'm checking you out of here. I know you said a few days, but I want you with me *now*. You're staying with me." He put a hand at my neck and pulled my lips to his. In between kisses, he said, "I want to keep my eye on you. And my hands. I want to keep my hands on you, too. And my mouth. Yeah, that too."

Who was I to argue?

I packed up all my stuff from the suite as Trip stayed downstairs to check me out of the hotel. I was only slightly saddened at having to leave such a beautiful room, but I was more curious and excited to see the home of my beautiful *man*. I was confident that it—that *he*—was ready for me.

We hopped back into the Porsche and drove through Benedict Canyon, then wound our way up Mulholland Drive. I could only catch the tiniest glimpses of the houses from the road. Most were completely hidden by large gates or trees. The few homes I could see were pretty freaking impressive, let me tell you.

We finally pulled in front of a large, black, iron gate, and Trip hit a button on the sun visor to open it. He cruised the car up a narrow, winding driveway and suddenly, his house came into view. It was a sprawling stucco ranch with those curved clay tiles on the roof— a California version of an "authentic" Spanish villa—painted tiles around the archways, forged iron fixtures on the heavy wooden doors.

He pulled the Porsche into the huge garage, where I could see a black Jeep, a black pickup truck, and a black... something that I didn't recognize. "What is that?" I asked. "It's pretty."

He got out of the car and came around to my side. "Layla. You don't call a Maserati 'pretty.' It's a beautiful piece of machinery."

I was well aware of another beautiful piece of machinery in the garage at that moment. But I put that out of my mind long enough to respond, "It looks like the Batmobile."

He snickered at that as he closed the garage door and led me into the house. "Wow," I said. "If your house is as nice as the garage, I think I'm officially astounded."

He backed me against the closed door and pressed his body full-length against mine. "Oh yeah? Well, wait until I get you to my bedroom, sweetheart. That'll astound the hell out of you."

Chapter 15
GIRL PLAY

I woke up, gave a good stretch, and rolled over to look out the window. I hadn't noticed it previously, but the entire second floor of his house looked out over the city of Los Angeles. Kinda goes to show you where my focus was the night before, because that view was hard to miss; two entire walls of his bedroom were made of glass.

I could see the impressive setup out back—cypress trees bordering two edges of the lawn, obscuring the iron fencing that I knew surrounded the property on three sides. The back line of his yard was nothing more than a drop-off, creating the desired effect for his infinity pool. There was no need for a fence along the rear border; Spiderman himself wouldn't be able to scale the cliff leading up to it.

Trip had reached a point in his notoriety where he needed such safeguards from the outside world. As he'd explained during the tour, he wasn't going to be made to feel unsafe in his own home.

He lived in a veritable fortress, but it was a gilded cage, at least. The house was absolutely incredible. It wasn't what I had expected, but it suited him somehow.

I let out with an exaggerated yawn, then settled myself under the cool, white, gazillion-thread-count sheets. Everything at Trip's house was just so much nicer than in an average home, and I was definitely more than a little freaked out about it. I wasn't used to such extravagance. It even smelled better. I reached over to his empty side of the bed, curled his pillow into my arms, and took a whiff. It smelled like him.

I finally made myself get out of bed and start my day. I cleaned up in his million-jet shower, then dried off with the fluffiest towel known to man. I swiped the steam off the mirror and took a look at the middle-class Jersey girl in the reflection, trying to reconcile that image with the opulence presently surrounding me.

Toto, I have a feeling we're not in Kansas anymore.

By the time I made my way downstairs to the kitchen, Trip's housekeeper had arrived. I introduced myself to Mrs. Elena, who very sweetly offered to make me breakfast. I declined, however, seeing as I was going dress shopping and didn't want a food baby popping out while I tried on designer gowns.

Trip left directions for me to his friend's boutique downtown. He also left me the keys to the Jeep and a black American Express card with a post-it note advising me to *"USE THIS! NO arguments."*

Well, if you insist...

I had to fiddle with the garage door openers until I found the right one, then slipped behind the wheel of Trip's Wrangler Sport. Nice. Thank God he didn't expect me to drive that Batmobile. The finer things with which he'd surrounded himself were overwhelming enough. I didn't need to be *responsible* for one of them on top of it.

I assumed navigating the roads of Los Angeles wouldn't be very difficult. The place is pretty much laid out like a grid, not unlike New York, sans the conveniently numbered streets. But hell. I figured since my driving chops had been tempered in the city from the time I was a teenager, L.A. would be a piece of cake.

I only lost my bearings once on my way out of the Hollywood Hills, but a very nice homeless man directed me to La Cienega. I tossed him a fiver and made it the rest of the way without incident.

Siobhan's was an elegant but quirky shop right in the heart of Melrose. I was expecting more of a Rodeo Drive snob-fest, and I loved that Trip had sent me to this place instead. It wasn't far from the hotel in Beverly Hills, but the neighborhood looked like a completely different world. Way less snooty, way more hip.

116

The parking gods were smiling down upon me that day, because I managed to find a spot right out front of the building.

When I walked through the door, Siobhan herself greeted me. She was tall and beautiful, with perfectly highlighted, wavy hair that fell almost to her skinny waist.

"Hello, Miss Warren! I've been expecting you." I looked down at my shirt to see if I had a nametag on or something, and Siobhan gave a knowing smile as she clarified, "Trip called earlier to let me know you were coming."

I suddenly became cognizant of two things:

1. I was an uncultured dork. And

2. This gorgeous woman had just referred to my boyfriend as "Trip" instead of "Mr. Wiley."

Friend my arse.

Ex sex-slave, maybe. But there was no way this chick was just a "friend." It was like being in a bad, real-life version of *Pretty Woman*. Only *I* was not the hooker in this scenario.

She showed me around the store, asking questions about my likes and dislikes in regards to fashion. When she asked me who my favorite designer was, I scrambled through my mental inventory, trying to come up with a name. Drawing a blank, I joked, "Umm, *Macy's*?"

She laughed jovially at my complete fashion-impairment and threw me into a dressing room, telling me to strip down so she could take my measurements. She logged them on a yellow legal pad that smelled like lavender, then darted out into the store while I stood there, passing the time by staring at the walls while hanging out in my underwear. I had just started to wonder if I should get dressed and go pick out some stuff to try on when she came barging back into the room carrying half a dozen dresses over her arm. I guessed she'd be deciding for me.

Gown after gown was flung in my direction, while my modesty was forced out the window. I was surprised at how quickly I got over it. She was incredibly professional, and thank God, never once acknowledged that my bra and undies didn't match. I started to feel guilty for my initial evil thoughts about the woman, considering she was going out of her way to be perfectly accommodating and wonderful.

She was very sweet and attentive and obviously knew her stuff. After I nixed the first three selections, she'd narrowed down my taste enough to zero in on a few beautiful dresses. I'd really liked almost all of them, but it wasn't until I tried on a shimmery cream ball gown that I finally fell in love.

Siobhan heard the gasp and immediately stopped fiddling with the hangers to put her hand to her heart, looking at me as if her baby had just taken its first steps.

The gown was exquisite; Grecian-styled bustier that cinched my waist and pushed my boobs up in an almost obscene, yet still tasteful way, with gathered folds of bunched fabric that billowed down to my ankles, a scandalous slit up one leg. It practically screamed "Oscar." It was a bit out of my comfort zone, but it really was a fabulous gown.

But then I checked the price tag.

Nope. Nuh-uh. No way.

I shook my head, explaining that while the dress was beautiful, there was no way I was spending that kind of cash on an item of clothing I was only going to wear once. I mean, the thing cost more than Lisa's wedding gown! I didn't even care if I looked like a pathetic rube. My conscience would just never let me indulge in such an extravagance, especially while shopping with Trip's money. Maybe I should have checked out some of the prices before trying on a dozen gowns. My poor, clueless boyfriend obviously had no idea where he'd sent me.

I put my clothes back on, apologized to Siobhan and thanked her for her time. She looked disheartened, and I felt bad about that, but there was just no way.

She said a graceful goodbye, and I zipped around the corner to the Beverly Center. I managed to find a beautiful, copper-colored dress at Nordstrom that was almost as nice as the one at Siobhan's for about a third of the price. It was still expensive, but compared to the cream one, it was a bargain. I bought some awesome coordinating heels that cost more than my first car and a small, clutch handbag to match (both with my own money) and was really proud of myself that I'd managed to find an appropriate ensemble. I had to pay extra for rush alterations on the dress, but the cost was still coming in way under Siobhan's, so I practically skipped out of the store.

I took advantage of my newfound free time and drove around the city like a big fat tourist. I was scoping the streets for a surgically-enhanced, California blonde walking a pair of Afghan doggies or some other clichéd movie scene I could find. No luck. I did see a little girl wearing a tiara, but without the Jon Benet frou-frou dress to go with it, she didn't look that different from my goddaughter, Julia.

Denied.

I made a few extra stops, took care of a few errands, and decided to head back to Trip's.

His backyard, aside from being a covert fortress, was also designed for entertaining. Not only was it private, but it was totally cool. He had this fabulous outdoor kitchen area; a stone and granite workspace with a monstrous grill, covered under a roof eave that jutted out over the six or so stools surrounding the adjoining snack bar.

That area abutted the massive patio which sported a few tables and chairs that looked brand, spanking new. It's as if they were placed there, not for their function, but because the patio called for them. I wondered if they'd ever been sat on.

I was in the pool when Trip came home. He walked outside, looking beautifully professional in his dark slacks and white button-down shirt. Just another day at the office.

"Honey, I'm home!" he called out playfully, thumbing through the mail and asking, "How'd it go at Siobhan's?"

I resisted the urge to pull him into the pool and attack him. "Okay. She was really nice."*And pretty.*

"Did you find a dress?"

I decided not to tell him about my cheapskate mentality. "No. Not at Siobhan's. But it wasn't for lack of trying. She really gave it her all. I found something at Nordstrom's, though."

"Great. Can't wait to see it. Hey. What do you want to do for dinner?"

"Already covered. I cooked."

He tossed the mail onto a nearby patio table. "Oh, you did, huh? Hmm. In that case, lemme just change into a bathing suit and I'll meet you in the pool."

"Please do."

I managed a few laps before Trip made his way out of the house and onto the diving board. It was hard to take my eyes off him when he was practically naked, strutting around the yard with that damned body of his. I mean, it was hard to keep my eyes off him *normally.* But in nothing but a pair of board shorts? I wanted to lay more than my sights on that man.

He dove in, emerging near me in the low end, wrapping his arms around me and backing me against the pool's wall. He planted one hell of a kiss on me, and I couldn't stop myself from smiling through it. It was sickeningly adorable, just being able to hang around Trip's house, waiting there for him after he came home from a long, hard day of work.

When we finally came up for air, I saw the huge grin he was wearing on his face. I was sure I looked just as dorky, smiling back at him. There was a huge part of me that still couldn't quite believe

I was there with him, playing house, tangled in his arms. But I didn't question it. For the first time in my life, I'd gone for it. And the payoff had been even greater than I could've ever imagined. More importantly, Trip was happy, too.

Most importantly, we were happy *together*.

I looped my arms over his shoulders and asked, "How was your day?"

His perfect, white teeth were still grinning at me, his eyes squinting from the sun. "It was good. Except that I missed you."

"Awww."

"The meeting took *forever*. Man, that guy can *talk*."

I knew his meeting was with some industry people that had been wooing him to be a part of their next production, but Trip didn't tell me much more beyond that. He was trying to focus more on his upcoming hockey film, and he was more irritated than flattered that they required his attention in the days leading up to it. Guess they wanted to nail him down as early as possible.

I knew the feeling.

"How'd it go?"

"Alright, I guess. I'm not the biggest fan of the director they've got lined up, but the script is pretty phenomenal. It could be big. I don't know." He released his hold on me to lounge out on the steps, his elbows thrown over the edge of the pool. "I told them I'd think about it in any case."

He seemed almost embarrassed talking about it. I guessed he was still getting used to the idea that he was so actively pursued by people other than horny women.

Although, I was one such horny woman at the moment. He wasn't quite out of those woods yet.

I sluiced through the water to where he was sitting and straddled him against the steps. "I'm guessing you've got time on this. You still have an entire movie to film before you could even commit to starting it, right? Did they say they'd wait for you?"

I lowered my lips to his neck. I couldn't help it.

I felt his throat vibrate against my mouth as he answered with a contented, "Hmmm."

"Was that a yes?"

He put his hands at my hips and squirmed a little underneath me. "Babe? You really think I've got my mind on work right now?"

Before I knew it, he'd wrapped an arm under my backside as he grabbed for the railing and hauled us both out of the water. I was giggling, my legs locked around his waist as he walked the few steps over to a chaise and laid me down on it, settling himself between my knees and lowering himself on top of me.

He kissed his way down my body and back up to my neck again, pulling my wet bikini top to the side of my breasts.

Release the hounds!

He kissed me there, too, before trailing a line of kisses down my stomach, over my sides, his hair trickling droplets across my skin. He hooked his fingers into my bikini bottoms and slid them off... and then stopped dead in his tracks.

Oh, yeah. I'd forgotten about the wax job on the way home.

His jaw gaped slightly as he stared at my nether regions, ironing a palm across the smooth skin at my pelvis. His eyes met mine in wonder. "Holy shit."

I laughed, but Trip looked rather serious, immediately pushing my thighs apart and closing his mouth over the space in between, as if he couldn't wait another second to lick me into oblivion.

Which he did.

Twice.

After a considerable amount of time spent making beautiful mouth-love to me on my pinkest parts, I lay there, my legs shaking, begging for him to stop. One more Tripgasm, and I was sure the neighbors would call the cops on us for disturbing the peace.

Because pieces of me were rather disturbed, let me tell you.

Ba-dum-dum. Tsss.

He was rather pleased with himself, sliding his body back up the length of mine, a wide, proud grin on his face. He raised an eyebrow and noted, "You were speaking Swahili there for a second." He sat back on his feet, cupping the front of his shorts with an expectant smirk. "Now what are we gonna do about this thing?"

I didn't wait to be asked twice. I threw him onto his back and barely made with the preliminaries. I may have landed a few kisses down his torso on the way to his shorts, reaching in and pulling him out. I know the typical Blowjob 101 Handbook recommends starting with some ice-cream-cone maneuvers, but I didn't bother with such trivialities. I opened my jaw over that thing and took him as far as my mouth would allow, sliding my lips back up as I suctioned my cheeks, gripping him with my hand at the base.

"What the… *Wha-* Fuck! Lay!"

Ha! I repeated the motion, and Trip almost floundered off the chaise. I saw his fingers in a white-knuckle grip against the cushion, felt his hips rising to match the movements of my mouth. He was hard as a rock, that beautiful, magical limb of his pointing north like a sundial. I estimated it to be close to six o'clock.

My body was still Jell-O, but I guess I had some strength left in my mouth. I worked that thing with more determination than a shop-vac on *Tool Time*.

Every downstroke of my hand was closely followed by my lips; every suck on the way up had him begging for mercy. My other hand wrapped around to mind the stepchildren—*You. Must. Mind. The Stepchildren*—and the groan he let out just then made me want to high-five myself.

He clenched his teeth, sputtering out a string of half-words and addressing our Lord and savior in a most sacrilegious way before letting out with a booming growl as he lurched, practically folding in half over me as he shot to the back of my throat, his throbbing cock pulsing against my tongue.

That's when I remembered I wasn't a swallower and had to pull a Blink 182 naked run for the outdoor bar sink. Classy.

I washed up and rinsed out, then wrapped myself in a towel. I darted into the house to get dressed and check on dinner, then came back outside to Trip, who'd managed to pull up his shorts before passing out in the sun. I took a moment to appreciate the dazzling god lying there. He was so beautiful and perfect, even while practically snoring away like an actual mortal. It was hard to remember that he was, in fact, human. That gorgeous crop of golden hair, that chiseled body, those inviting, full lips just begging to be kissed... Damn. I'm so wrong. Please disregard what I just said about him being human.

I went in the house to get dinner finished and plated. By the time I brought everything out, he was awake and doing laps in the pool. You'd think by looking at him that he was just born that beautiful. And he was. Genes definitely were very generous to that man. But the truth was, he worked really hard to look that good. A body like that doesn't come naturally. Even back in high school, hockey kept him in shape during the winter and jogging kept him fit the rest of the year. I stood there for a moment and watched him, pushing himself to go faster, harder. Testing his body to its limit. I knew he must've spent a fair amount of time in his private gym downstairs—so I apologize if I'm shattering any myths about him right here—because no one looks that good by accident.

He hauled himself out of the water, gave a shake to his head, and dried off with a towel before throwing on an Atari T-shirt and meeting me at the table. I'd made a London broil and a mesclun salad with some new potatoes dressed in a dill vinaigrette and a side basket of "homemade" biscuits to round it out. (Okay, fine. They were from a can.)

He appraised the spread on the table and gave me an enthusiastic, "Wow, this looks great!"

Then the sick bastard announced that he was heading inside to grab the ketchup.

He came out, the bottle swinging triumphantly from his fingers as I warned, "You are *not* putting ketchup on that meat."

He just ignored me, singing "You're So Vain" as he slathered a dollop on the side of his plate.

"Ummm... wrong song, fucktard."

I was stunned, watching as he sliced off a hunk of London Broil and dipped it into the glob before looking right into my eyes—a victorious gleam in his—as he chewed.

"I don't know if we can stay together anymore," I busted. "Ketchup on steak? That just might be a dealbreaker."

Chapter 16
SHOW ME

The next morning, I had barely opened my eyes when Trip came busting through the door whistling some unrecognizable tune, and I couldn't quite find it in me to raise my head yet. Even though I rarely slept-in, it still normally took me a few minutes to ease into my morning. But it looked as though Trip was apparently an even earlier riser than me.

Based on that circumstance, our future together did not look promising.

"'Morning."

I rolled over at his greeting and saw him grinning ear to ear, holding a mug of coffee and wearing nothing but a pair of cotton PJ bottoms. Yum.

I supposed I could overlook the morning person problem.

"Mmm. Good morning," I answered back, fluffing the pillows and sitting up in his bed.

He put the coffee on the nightstand. "I guessed cream and sugar. 'Suppose I should find stuff like this out."

I was touched by his thoughtfulness. "Cream and sugar is perfect. So are you."

He gave a shy smile and then pulled something out from behind his back. "Hey. Check this out. I'm going full-on John Lennon with the peace crusade, baby. I just had this made." He snapped a T-shirt out toward me and I saw the motto for his *Earthling Rights Foundation* across the front:

LOVE
WILL WIN♥

It was a song from the band Slanker Knox, and Trip had adopted it as the theme for his charity. What started out as a crusade for human rights had soon evolved into an all-encompassing organization, benefitting not just people in need, but animals, communities, and the environment as well. ERF helped military families, assisted children's groups, and aided in disaster recovery. It gave tons of money to the ASPCA and funded various movements directed toward improving education and medical research.

It was really pretty amazing.

He flipped the shirt around to the side, and I saw the extra hit he'd had customized on the sleeve:

earthlingrights.org

It looked really good. So did he. "Nice."

"You'd better get up. CNN will be here in about an hour."

There was a camera crew on its way over to set up for a taped interview. Trip was excited to have a chance to plug his philanthropic venture to such a large audience. He'd founded the organization soon after he'd gotten out of rehab, but it took a couple years before it grew legs.

After reports came back about our under-protected soldiers in Iraq, ERF sent over a shipment of bullet-proof vests. After that tsunami ravaged the Asian coast, Trip's people hand-delivered a shipment of goods and helped to care for the displaced citizens of Indonesia.

His charity was basically a group of real-life superheroes, coming to the rescue of any fellow humans that were in need. I was really proud of him for the time and money he devoted to it.

I stopped daydreaming and hauled myself out of bed, slammed down the coffee, and got my butt in the shower. By the time I made my way into the den, Trip was pacing the room. I watched as he futzed with the pillows on the couch, changed the angle of the side chair, and picked a non-existent piece of debris off the floor. I swear, he was being even more OCD than me.

"Trip! Stop. The place looks perfect." And it did. I'd seen with my own eyes the considerable amount of time Mrs. Elena had spent in that very room, readying it for the day's filming.

He stopped his pacing to look at me and say, "I don't know. You think we should do this outside instead? This room is too... serious."

I'd already taken note of the framed artwork Trip had chosen for his walls. Most were enlarged photographs or prints of various landscapes. But upon closer inspection, I realized they were tagged with the names of some of the places he'd visited over his lifetime: *Lagos, Nigeria. Cairo, Egypt. Antananarivo, Madagascar.* It was as though he were trying to constantly remind himself of all the people who didn't live in such grandeur.

"Your *charity* is serious. Stop second-guessing yourself. Once your face shows up onscreen, no one will be looking at the room, anyhow, studmuffin."

He gave me a *durr-hurr* face and threw one of the couch pillows at me.

I laughed and put it back on the sofa.

And then Trip rearranged it.

The film crew finally showed up then, taking over the house. Sandy was there, greeting everyone and directing the setup. I was panicked at the thought that the beautiful tile floors would be scratched by the wobbly wheels of the equipment dollies. I was too preoccupied with that spectacle to be nervous for Trip, who spent his time vacillating between gracious host and nervous wreck. This was, by far, not the *first* interview he'd ever conducted, but I guessed he was a little freaked out because it was the most *important.* Of course his charity was reported on and he was normally asked a few questions about it on talk shows, but this was the first time ERF was going to be the main focus of a full-length interview on a major news network.

After everyone had bagels (I will refrain from tearing California bagels a new asshole here) and coffee, it was time to film the interview. Perry Kingston settled himself in the chair, while Trip took a seat on the couch. A tech got them mic'd up as Sandy went over the line of questions, schmoozing just a bit with Perry. The man was a known egomaniac, and Sandy made sure to give him the proper attention to which he felt he was due.

Another tech checked the lighting with some hand-held electronic gizmo, readjusted the umbrella things, and checked the lighting again. It was pretty interesting, watching the behind-the-scenes production of a TV show.

Sandy finally made her way over by me, and the two of us claimed our spot out of the way, but with a good line-of-sight to Trip. He looked adorable with his hair all combed and lying flatter against his head than usual. I guessed he was going for a more respectable look. He'd even paired his rockin' tee with a black sportcoat, the lapels of which he was picking invisible lint from.

The crew did a few test takes before they were ready for the real interview, and soon enough, it was underway.

Perry debriefed the audience, starting out by asking Trip about his latest film projects. After a few minutes of friendly chitchat, he directed the conversation toward Trip's foundation.

"So, Trip, *Earthling Rights Foundation* has recently been recognized by Charity-Navigator-dot-org as a four-star organization, and it ranks in the top ten on their 'Celebrity Related Charities' list. Have the accolades brought any new attention to ERF?"

Trip had turned into *him*, but managed to answer with genuine humility. "It certainly has, Perry. The success of an organization like ours depends on making the public aware that we even exist.

Catching the eye of the preeminent not-for-profit analysts over at Charity Navigator has given a huge boost to our exposure."

"I suppose having the name of an Oscar-winning celebrity at the helm didn't hurt matters, either."

Damn. Perry was good. Watching him smooth his way from one question to the next was pretty impressive. I had a brief pang of longing, thinking about my abandoned journalism career.

Trip gave a chuckle. "I like to think so, yes. Only because I have a built-in audience to speak to. But it's not about celebrity. It's not about me. It's about a group of individuals helping as many people as we can. We have hundreds of in-house volunteers; kind, generous people who just want to spread a little love where they can. *They* make ERF happen." He turned his eyes toward the camera and added, "*You* do."

Perry took note of Trip's tee, acknowledging it with a nod of his head. "You mentioned that ERF is all about 'spreading the love,' and I'm guessing that's where your T-shirt comes in."

"Yes, Perry. Slanker Knox kindly let me steal their song title for ERF. They've generously agreed to donate a portion of the profits from sales of their album *Patched Soul,* so make sure you buy it, kids." At that last part, he smiled that spellbinding grin directly into the cameras which, I was sure, would have everyone running for the nearest music store.

All glory to the hypnotoad.

Perry chuckled jovially at Trip's blatant plug, asking casually, "And do you believe that? That 'a little love' can make a difference?"

Trip's mouth quirked into a tiny, calculated grin. He tipped his head slightly, checking himself out in one of the monitors as he deliberately adjusted his blazer over his T-shirt.

It took me about a split second to realize what he'd just done.

His alteration blocked out some of the lettering, leaving only:

visible between his lapels. He must have seen my shocked face, because he raised his lip into a half-smile before answering Perry's question. "Yes, Perry. I do believe love can make a difference. It can change the world, even. Heck, it worked for me." Then his small smile turned into a huge grin as he looked past the cameras and right at me.

I almost died. There was Trip, announcing that he loved me *to the entire goddamn world*.

Well, to the room, anyway. It's not as though a respectable news station like CNN would bother reporting on the person behind the initials branded across his chest.

A few eyes swung in my direction, and I hoped my face hadn't turned bright red. Perry had actually twisted in his chair at that, trying to get a better look at the woman who had stolen the infamous Trip Wiley's heart.

Then again, I couldn't very well steal what was rightfully mine.

* * *

Trip was saying goodbye, offering his thanks, and showing the last of his houseguests out the door. He threw the deadbolt, took his fingers off the handle, and turned to find me standing there with my hands on my hips.

"What?" he asked lightheartedly, knowing damn well what I was going to say.

"When did you have that shirt made?" I asked, pointing to the tee in question.

He took a few steps in my direction and wrapped his arms around my waist. He was wearing an evil grin, those perfect, white teeth smiling down at me. "Just last week. But I adopted the motto a year ago."

"You devil! You did that on purpose!"

"It was either 'Love Will Win' or 'I love bisexual women.' I thought you'd like the first one better. But on that note, is there any chance I can talk you into a threesome?"

I smacked his arm as he cracked up. He lowered his laughing mouth and kissed me, cutting off any snarky remark I was readying myself to offer.

He pulled back, just far enough to admit, "I figured after your public heartbreak, the least I could do was publicly *un*break it. Mission accomplished?"

The exasperating man in my arms was looking at me optimistically, those playful blue eyes waiting on my reaction. Just because he had very visibly announced his engagement to the underwear model didn't mean my *heartbreak* was public. No. That was a very private destruction which ate away at me from the inside.

But I appreciated what he was trying to do. His heart was in the right place.

It's not like anyone from CNN would bother making a fuss over what he'd done anyway. And thank goodness, because I was starting to learn how the Hollywood grapevine worked. If that interview had been with some corny entertainment show, my name would have been leaked to every gossip magazine in the country as soon as the cameras stopped rolling. And that would have been a shame, because Trip's foundation deserved to be the focus of that interview, not the woman he was sleeping with. It was a pretty risky stunt he'd pulled, but if *I* was able to figure out he could get away with it, *he* must have been dead certain. It didn't need to be a public outing. It was enough that he and I knew what he'd done.

"Mission accomplished," I confirmed, pulling his smiling face down for a kiss.

Chapter 17
CINDERELLA MAN

The next day, Trip had a "read-through" for *Slap Shot*, and he asked if I'd like to go with him. We took the Batmobile to the studio, and I can't say that I wasn't excited about it. Not only was I going to get a real insider taste of Hollywood, but I'd be seeing where Trip worked.

He stopped briefly at the gatehouse and gave a salute to the security guard, who did nothing more than salute back and say, "Good afternoon, Mr. Wiley," before raising the gate. Trip was well-known *everywhere*, but the familiarity vibe was definitely different on his home turf. He hadn't even turned into *him* yet. I guessed there was no need to amp up the Wiley just for the gatekeeper.

We drove past a few low office buildings, which Trip explained were for "the moneybags," and down a narrower street lined with trailers, for "the peons." He maneuvered around a million identical white structures that looked like airplane hangars, and I wondered how he knew just where to go. My eyes kept darting around between the buildings, hoping to see some action. I mean, this was a Hollywood studio lot! I'd never seen one in person and only had my impression of them from the movies. So, where were all the lions on leashes? The clowns walking around on stilts? The feathered showgirls and the zombies and the cowboys?

The only humans I saw walking around were a few harried-looking, but fairly normal people.

What a gyp.

We parked in the lot near a building with a big, black *B 124* painted on the side, and Trip let me out of the car. He held my hand and led me through the doors. It was bitter cold!

"Why is it so cold in here?"

Actually, it was only my top half that was freezing. Even though I was wearing a pair of shorts, the nerve endings in my legs had been deadened after four winters in my St. Norman's skirt. To this day, as long as my torso is bundled, I could brave the arctic tundra in a pair of bikini bottoms and be perfectly comfortable. True story.

He smiled and answered my question. "You'll see."

We walked through another set of doors—where it got even colder—and I saw the massive hockey rink that took over the space. "Oh my gosh! Is this the *Slap Shot* set?"

His smile turned into the full-force grin, proudly announcing, "Yep. All the interiors are going to be shot right here. Welcome to the home arena of the Charlestown Chiefs."

"Wow! Cool! So, you'll get to shoot it right here? No going on location?"

"Maybe just a few quick trips for the exteriors."

I snuggled against his side, trying to get warm. "*Quick* trips. Okay, I can handle that."

He rubbed his hand along my arm to warm me up. "It's not like you won't be coming with me, babe."

I caught the look in his eyes and was suddenly very warmed by his words. He said it like it was the most obvious thing in the world. It should have been.

He led us out of the freezer and across the lobby again, through another set of doors and down a hallway. The temperature was more bearable back there, and by the time we made it to a door marked "PROD," it was comfortable. It was a large, fairly nondescript room that reminded me of a gymnasium. There was a long table set up in the middle with about a dozen people sitting around it on folding chairs, getting ready to do the read-through.

An older, balding man spotted us first. "Ah! There he is now. Nice of you to join us, Mr. Wiley."

There was no malice in the man's voice, and Trip smiled as we made our way over. He gripped my hand a little tighter and whispered, "Brace yourself."

I didn't know what was in store for me, but I found out soon enough. As we neared the table, the Elmer Fudd guy said, "And it looks like you brought me a present," eyeing me appreciatively.

Trip snickered, "Not a chance, pal," before addressing the other people in the room. "Everyone, this is Layla Warren." He gave a warning look to Elmer and added, "And I brought her for *me*."

I smiled and said my hellos as the people around the table greeted me. I finally looked over at Elmer and stopped dead in my tracks. The balding old man in front of my eyes was none other than Patrick Van Keegan! I was practically weaned on his movies growing up. He was my father's favorite actor. A lot of other people's, too. He'd starred in some of the biggest films ever made. The guy was a legend, and positively the hottest thing to hit the screens post-James Dean, pre-Trip Wiley.

I was grateful when Trip directed me to sit over near the craft table so I wouldn't have to speak. I was completely star struck, and my hands had begun to shake. It was crazy. I was sleeping with the most famous actor on the planet, and I had firsthand knowledge that he was just a regular person underneath the fame. He just happened to have an irregular job that made him extraordinarily well-known. But there I was, getting all googly-eyed from being in the same room as Patrick Van Keegan. But hell. After all, Trip was presently the actor Patrick *used* to be. Who wouldn't get star-fuckery around that?

But my God he'd gotten old. It broke my heart a little bit. I almost wished I hadn't just met him.

The table Trip directed me toward was completely laden with snacks and drinks, and I grabbed a bottle of water out of the iced tub, but bypassed helping myself to any food. I took a seat on one of the folding chairs nearby and introduced myself to the other two girls who were there. Amber Lynn was fairly new to town. Chrystal Lynn was not. They didn't wait to inform me that they were both "dancers."

Chrystal Lynn gave me the once-over and promptly asked, "So, you're fucking Trip Wiley?"

She asked it so matter-of-factly. Like she was inquiring about my shoes.

Ummm... "He's my boyfriend."

I saw the two girls exchange a snarky look, and it was enough to make me want to go Jersey on their mini-skirted asses.

"Our friend Marcy was doing him a while back. He's really hot. You're so lucky."

Note to self: Remember to kill my boyfriend.

Amber Lynn piped in just then. "We're fucking Patrick."

I'm sure my mouth gaped open as I asked, "Both of you?"

Amber Lynn sounded as though she were trying to impart some newfound Hollywood wisdom when she taunted, "What, did you just come here from the farm?" They both shared a giggle at that before Amber continued, "It's a whole 'nother world out here, honey. You might want to wake up and realize it. Sex is money out here."

Chrystal Lynn high-fived her slutty friend and added, "And there's a helluva lotta rich people!"

The Bimbo Twins started cackling again, and it was enough to turn my stomach. They were both unbearably stupid, and they were both there with Patrick. What kind of world was this that Trip lived in? That *I* was living in?

I took a sip of my water when the old, ballbusting reporter in me decided to mess with them—I was just getting ready to ask their opinion on the situation in Darfur. However, I didn't get to open my mouth, because Patrick Van Keegan had opened his. Loudly.

His booming voice yelled at the director, "You think I don't know that? I was making movies while you were still in diapers, you little shit!"

His voice echoed around the large room, stunning everyone into silence. He stomped over to where we were sitting and grabbed at Amber's hand as he commanded, "Come on, girls. We're leaving!"

I caught Trip's attention and gave him the wide-eyes. He gave a casual shrug and went back to work. Thankfully, the meeting didn't take very long, and before I knew it, we were back in the Batmobile, wending our way through the lot once more.

"So, what happened at the table?" I asked. "Patrick Van Keegan lost his shit!"

Again, Trip only offered a shrug like it was no big deal. "He wanted to change some of his dialogue in a pivotal scene. Carlos refused to budge."

"You can do that? Isn't that the screenwriter's job?"

"Normally. But a script is written long before any actors are cast. The best directors will have a screenwriter tweak a scene to suit the actors after the fact. For the bigger names, anyhow."

"So… what? Carlos made Patrick feel like he wasn't big enough to warrant the change?"

"Nah. It was simply a bad suggestion. Carlos knew that and challenged him on it." He turned the car toward the gatehouse as he added, "Don't worry about it. He's just blowing off some steam. He'll come around. The Oscars are in a few more days. Makes everyone crazy."

I'd been witness to that phenomenon over the past week. Oscar season brought out the jitters in everyone in town. Not just the actors and directors, but the boutique-owners and the salespeople at the jewelry stores. Who was going to wear who? What megastar could best show off the diamonds? It was so weird to me that stuff like that was enough to throw an entire city into such a tailspin. It seemed so… *superficial.*

138

But I felt like Patrick's outburst was due to something bigger than a flipping awards ceremony, for godsakes. I was pretty sure he wasn't even nominated for anything. Was *that* it? Had his star gone so dim that he thought he'd simply fade away? It must be a bizarre transition, going from having the world at your feet to being shoved to the background, practically forgotten. It must have been even harder for Patrick to have the younger version of himself sitting right there next to him, knowing Trip's name would be above his in the credits, the hottest new thing since... well... him. At least it would explain The Bimbo Twins. It probably made Patrick feel like a big man to be nailing not one, but two cheap strippers purely for sport.

Hollywood was glamorous and exciting, but it was also the kind of place that could chew a person up and spit them out. The thought filled me with an unwarranted sense of dread:

When he had ultimately aged out of heartthrob status, when the cameras finally stopped flashing in his face, would Trip someday grow into the same, cynical, broken man as Patrick Van Keegan?

Chapter 18
LIPSTICK & DYNAMITE

We'd decided to treat our Academy Awards evening like a date and got ready in separate rooms. I spent most of my prep time in the guest bathroom—the beautiful, decorating-magazine bathroom—while Trip took over the master suite next door. I was anxiety-ridden, sitting at the dressing table, the stylist putting the finishing touches on my makeup, when I heard Trip through our adjoining wall, singing in the shower.

I had to strain to hear what the song was. The evening's selection was "You Got the Touch" from the *Boogie Nights* soundtrack, and Trip was belting it out with as much passion and pitchiness as Dirk Diggler. It was enough to make me forget my nerves for a minute, and I started laughing so hard that tears gathered at my eyes, enough so that Betty admonished me for threatening to ruin my eyeliner.

After she'd gone, I checked out her handiwork in the huge mirror over the sink. She did this crazy smoky thing with my eyes which looked really cool. I was sure that if I'd tried to recreate it on my own, I'd end up looking more like a heroin addict instead of a spicy vixen.

But that night, it was sexy.

She'd curled my hair so that it had these great, 1920s-type finger-waves going on, one side pulled up and held with a diamond and brown-topaz comb, on loan from Harry Winston.

That's right, kids. *Harry Effing Winston.* I was freaking out about the whole night, but just seeing those famous diamonds at my head pretty much sent me over the edge. I mean, I was going to the goddamn Academy Awards. Me. Layla Warren. On the arm of the biggest movie star on the planet.

Wearing *Harry. Winston. Diamonds.*

The same flower shapes from the comb were recreated along the delicate necklace in coordinating jewels. I had politely refused the earrings, though. I could totally have seen me losing the things and didn't want to worry about them all night. It would have been too much sparkle anyway, even for Oscar Night. I opted for my own, simple, diamond studs instead.

Oh. And don't tell anyone, but I was wearing Club Monaco Glaze on my lips. You know, that Monica Lewinsky shade that was all the rage twenty fashion cycles ago? But it was still the perfect color for my skintone, and if it ain't broke, don't fix it, you know what I'm saying?

I stripped off my robe and went out into the bedroom to slip into my dress.

Only it wasn't there.

Hanging in its spot instead was the cream gown I had picked out at Siobhan's.

It actually took my mind a few seconds to register what was happening. When it did, my only thought was, *He didn't!*

Sonofabitch, he did.

I stormed down the hallway to Trip's room and burst through the door. "Where's my dress?"

He was standing there in just a white towel, slung low on his perfect hips. If I wasn't so angry, I would have appreciated the view a bit more. He didn't even bother to look at me, and continued to debate the neckties in his hands as he answered, "Hanging in your room."

"That's not the dress I bought."

"No, but it's the one you liked."

"Trip! I know what you're trying to do, and it's very sweet, really. But it costs too much. It's why I didn't buy it in the first place! I just can't in good conscience allow you to spend that kind of money on such a thing."

He lowered the ties and turned toward me. And when he did, his jaw dropped to the floor and his eyes bugged out of his head like a Looney Toon.

Ayoooooogah!

I suddenly realized I'd been standing there in just my beige push-up strapless bra, a tiny pair of panties, lace-top thigh-high stockings... and garters. I figured it was a special occasion, so what the hell.

Trip's tongue rolled across the floor and back up into his mouth as he regained his composure.

He perched a hip against the dresser and crossed his arms over his naked chest. He looked so gorgeous standing there in just a towel, with his intentionally mussed hair and his calm, commanding stance.

A smirk decorated his face as he said, "Lay, I don't know if you've noticed, but I can afford stuff like this now."

"It's too much."

"Not by a longshot."

"Well, I'm just going to return it." I crossed my arms over *my* chest. See? I could be stubborn, too.

Trip dropped his arms and came over toward me. He put his hands on my shoulders and implored, "Look. Please don't deny me the pleasure of buying you things. Besides, you can't return it. It's already been altered."

"You could feed a small country for the price of that dress!"

"Babe. I give enough money away to feed some very *large* countries. Don't get all guilty on me. It's okay to spoil yourself every now and then. Just let me do this, okay?"

I pursed my lips and squinted at him, but didn't answer. He knew he was winning me over. Because honestly? I really freaking loved that dress.

"Besides, it's a big deal for Siobhan to see her stuff strutting down the red carpet. When you're asked who you're wearing, don't forget to add where you got it. Got it?"

Okay, I admit it. I was wrong. Fairytales *do* exist. I suddenly had a new appreciation for *Pretty Woman*, because all I could think at that moment was that I was Cinderfuckinrella. There he was like a kid on Christmas, so excited to unveil his surprise and I was yelling at him for it. What was I going to do for an encore? Kick him in the nards?

"Fine. Okay. Yes. Thank you, Trip. This is really an incredible thing to do. I'm blown away."

He was smiling as he bent his head to plant one on me, saying, "You can show me how grateful you are later."

Our lips met, and my fingers immediately went to the back of his still-damp hair. He slid his hands along my backside, pulled me tighter against his hips, and groaned against my mouth. I was feeling a little dizzy from his... *enthusiasm*, and wrapped my arms around his shoulders, raising up on my toes and pressing into him. Just as things started to get interesting, he tore his lips from mine with a grunt and said, "Shit, Lay-Lay. We'd better get dressed. The car will be here any minute."

* * *

Trip was sitting in an armchair in a corner of the foyer when I met up with him. He looked positively drool-worthy, lounging out casually in his formalwear, his fingers against his temple, *waiting for me*.

I stood in front of his knees, gave him a twirl and asked, "How do I look?"

143

He didn't break his pose, but appraised me with a scandalous perusal along my entire body. "I don't know, babe. It hurts to look right at you. Gorgeous, in any case."

Then he got up from his chair, wrapped an arm around my waist, and pulled me to him. "Stop smiling at me like that. It makes me want to blow off this whole night and just take you back to bed."

I almost let him.

I was a nervous wreck in the limo on the way to the Kodak Theater. Trip kept his hand on my knee, and he must have been nervous, too, because his fingers never slipped any higher. The limo had a bar alcove with a few decanters of liquor, and I wondered how many times he'd taken advantage of such perks in the old days.

We made it to our destination in decent time, but had to idle in a queue of similar cars, waiting for our turn to pull up to the main entrance. That was the hardest part of the whole evening, I think. Just having to sit there and sweat it out, the raucous cheers of the crowd pouring through the closed windows in an oppressive deluge of sound. Despite the waning sun, the strobe-like flashing of hundreds of cameras punctuated the sky. Up ahead, I could see the sentinel of monstrous Oscar statues, their heads glowing a fiery gold, lining the entrance to the red carpet.

Holy shit. I was really there. At the Academy Awards. Holy. Effing. Shit.

Are you there, God? It's me, Layla. It's been a while, and I'm really sorry about that, but I would be eternally grateful and all that jazz if you could help me make it down this carpet without stumbling, sweating, or otherwise embarrassing myself in any way, shape, or form. I'm guessing you've never given stilettos a shot, and let me tell you, you are one lucky dude. They are like spiky little torture devices designed solely to make your feet throb incessantly while mocking your lack of grace. And we both know grace has never been high on my list of positive attributes to begin with. So, yeah, any help you can give? Greatly appreciated. Oh. And please don't let me have a wardrobe malfunction and slip a nip. Muchas gracias. Amen.

My nerves were pretty well shot to begin with, but sitting there, crammed inside some claustrophobia-inducing limousine, waiting indefinitely for the night to get underway, was positively nail-biting. Plus, I was trying to forget that the last time I'd seen Trip emerge from a limo, my world fell apart.

But then I made myself remember that I had asked for this. I was the one who begged and pleaded with my boyfriend to bring me to this thing. And *he* was the one who actually had to get onstage and speak!

I took a few deep breaths, determined to lose my anxiety, and instead focused on making sure Trip was okay. "How you doing over there, pal?"

Trip looked cool as a cucumber. So handsome in his tux. He gave me a calm smile, which would convince anyone else that a night like this was a common occurrence for him.

Finally, it was our turn.

Our door was opened, and the dull roar that I could hear from inside the car became a deafening cacophony of screeching and whistles and screams outside of it. Trip held his hand out to me, a smirk on his face, and I was quite sure he was thinking about the last time I'd watched him escort someone out of a limousine. But he seemed much happier that this time, it was me. So was I. I made sure to exit the car while pressing my knees together, like Betty had warned me to do, and I utilized her tip so the cameras couldn't catch my hoo-hah in a Britney Spears shot.

It was still daylight outside, but that didn't stop my eyes from blinding from the flash of the million or so cameras aimed in our direction. All I wanted to do was get down the mile-long length of red carpet as quickly as possible, preferably without tripping and falling flat on my face. But every few steps, a photographer would call, "Trip! Over here!" and I'd feel Trip's hand at the small of my back, nudging me in the direction of a camera. We'd been there for almost ten minutes, and I don't think we made it further than ten feet down the carpet.

Trip had prepared me for that on the ride over. He'd explained that he always let the paparazzi take all the shots they wanted when he was at a work-related event like this. He did it in the hopes that they'd leave him alone when he was just out and about, living his life.

Not that they did.

But Trip was holding up *his* end of the bargain, turning toward each and every camera down that runway, smiling and waving to each and every person that called his name.

He leaned his head into my ear and said, "You're doing great. Only nine thousand more pictures to go."

I looked at him and he gave me a quick wink, which made me laugh and helped me to relax. There I was, a panicky mess, and my boyfriend was just eating it up. He flashed that megawatt grin, the full-force smile that always knocked me out. Me, and everyone else on the planet.

About midway down the carpet, I gave his hand a quick squeeze before releasing him out into the wild. At my insistence, we'd made the plan ahead of time for me to fade into the background for a few moments in order to let Trip be *him* for a while, soak up some of that spotlight on his own. After all, this was *his* world. I was simply along for the ride.

He was almost immediately intercepted by a certain up-and-coming starlet, and I recognized her from the tabloids as one of the many young women Trip had been linked with over the years. She was pencil-thin and beautiful, but had a big, poofy mop of hair that reminded me of Tina Yothers. The flirty way she talked with him confirmed that there was some history there. Thankfully, he kept the conversation to a minimum, and made his escape before she could tear off her Vera Wang and jump him right there on the red carpet.

He paused at the grandstand, listened to the screams from the women in the bleachers, and stopped for a few quick interviews with hosts from various entertainment shows.

At the end of the run, he reclaimed my hand again and we chatted with some of his industry friends who were gathered near the entrance. Introduction after introduction, I watched people's faces go from *Who's this chick crashing our party?* to *Awww, really? Your high school sweetheart?*

I got completely tongue-tied while being introduced to a particular silver-screen hottie who shall forever go nameless, in order to protect my cool. But I had the hugest crush on this actor growing up, and I kind of lost my shit to find myself standing there actually talking to him. Well, I guess *talking* is a relative term. I don't even know if I was speaking English to the poor guy as I babbled my hellos.

Finally, finally, we made our way inside the building, and I went to give Trip a look of relief. But his mouth was set in a firm line, a muscle twitching in his jaw, his eyes narrowed at me in a scathing glare.

"What?" I asked.

"*Clooney?* Really, Layla?"

His jealousy made me giggle as I answered, "Sorry. I used to crush on him pretty hard when he was on *Facts of Life*. Did you ever notice that he had the same mullet as Jo Polnachek?" Trip didn't find that amusing, so I leaned up to whisper, "But I'm kinda partial to *blonds* these days, anyway."

That thawed him out. "Good thing. Because *he* seems to be partial to anything with a *pulse* these days."

* * *

147

I sat there with sweaty palms all night. It's not like I was the one waiting there, listening for my name to be called. But that sadistic camera shot when they showed every nominee as the envelope was being opened... Christ. I didn't know how they could stand it. And then to have to sit there with a smile still plastered to their faces when their name *wasn't* called? Ouch.

Presenter after presenter, envelope after envelope. All night, I was a nervous wreck.

I was even worse when it was Trip's turn to get up there. Someone had come down to our seats to escort Trip backstage, and I found myself sitting next to some hot young tuxedoed stud. I wondered how someone went about obtaining a job as seat-filler and debated asking him about it. But before I knew it, Trip was being announced.

"Ladies and gentlemen... Three-time Academy Award nominee and Oscar winner for Best Actor in a Leading Role... Please welcome... Trip Wiley..."

And there he was, amidst the applause, strutting out onto the stage and taking his place at the microphone, preparing to address his peers. The thing of it was, though, is that *no one* was among his peers. Trip Wiley *had* no peers.

He was confident, polished, incredibly talented, undeniably hot. I was sure that the men in that room would give their left nut to live his life for even one day; the women would sacrifice anything to be in his bed for one night. He may have lived this part of his life *with* them, but he was most decidedly not *among* them.

He smiled as the cheering died down and his smooth voice proceeded to give a brief explanation of the category he was presenting before announcing the nominees... for cinematography.

There could be no more perfect category for that man to announce. He made sure to become familiar with the work of each and every nominee, subjecting me to an endless viewing of *The Proof Beyond*, where he paused practically every frame, pointing out "the brilliance" in every shot. It took about four hours to watch that movie, and I'd still really like to see it someday. My vote laid squarely with *Anya's Garden*, however, and it was a much-discussed debate between the two of us all week.

But sure as shit, he opened that envelope—and I swear his eyes flicked toward me for a split second—as he smirked and announced, "And the Oscar goes to... *The Proof Beyond*."

Oh, he was going to be impossible to live with after this.

A few minutes later, he was back in his seat, grinning smugly, but staring straight ahead at the stage. I flipped him the ten bucks I owed him, and he didn't even so much as glance my way as he wordlessly stuck the bill in his front breast pocket.

Jerk.

Just for that, I leaned my face in close to his ear and whispered, "*Congratulations. But there's something you need to know. I took my panties off before putting on this dress tonight.*"

That was a lie. I was totally still wearing my undies.

I sat back in my seat and waited for his reaction. I wasn't sure if he had heard me, because he was still staring straight ahead. But I noticed that his bottom lip had dropped just a fraction of an inch.

A whole five minutes went by before his mouth was at my ear, whispering, "*Did you leave the garters on?*"

I pursed my lips to keep from cracking up, then mouthed the word, "*Yep.*"

He was staring straight ahead again, but I watched a muscle working in his jaw and felt his hand tighten on mine as he shifted in his seat.

Ha! Sit on *that*, Fonzarelli!

Chapter 19
SEX, POLITICS & COCKTAILS

The after-party was at *Château Blanco*, and the vibe in the place was positively electric. For all the formality and nervousness before and during the show, it was replaced with relief and laid-back *after*. The men all loosened their ties and some even ditched their jackets. The women had changed into comfortable shoes, and I wished I'd known that that was a thing so I could have been more prepared. But seeing as it was Trip's first time at one of those things, he didn't know to give me the heads up.

We said hellos to a million people and were introduced to a million more before we found a booth along the wall that we could claim as our home base. Not that we sat for very long. There were elbows to rub, introductions to be made, asses to kiss. I'm not going to name-drop here, but let's just say I was blown away to be in the same room with most of those people. Faces you'd know; names you'd recognize. From rising stars and veteran actors to acclaimed directors and legendary producers. At one point, Trip pointed out Harvey Weinstein, and I thought I was going to bust a rib cracking up.

"You think he's forgiven you for dumping that pasta in his lap ten years ago?"

Trip raised an eyebrow as he shot back, "I *know* he hasn't."

We laughed at that as Trip excused himself to hit the bathroom. I kind of had to go, too, but there was no way I'd be able to get out of my dress on my own. Thank God I knew I'd have some help with that later, wink wink.

I saw that he'd gotten tied up talking to some people, so I went to the bar to grab him a club soda and lime. I couldn't find him after that, so I just decided to wait in the alcove near the restrooms.

"Well, hello, there!"

I turned and registered the lecherous man who had just greeted me. The look on his face and the way he was licking his lips made me feel like a triple-decker hot-fudge sundae. And not in a good way. I gave him a polite smile and said, "Hello."

"I don't think I've had the pleasure."

He extended his hand, so I took it, but before I got the chance to introduce myself, he added, "But I sure as hell look forward to it."

Ewww.

Again, I merely gave him the briefest of smiles, my expression and my body language clearly screaming *not on your life, pal.*

Only, he wouldn't release his death grip on my hand until I pulled it out of his grasp. It was all I could do not to dig out my bottle of Purell right there on the spot.

He gave a quick scan to our surrounding area before leaning in, still licking his lips like a lizard, so close I could smell the cognac on his breath as he sneered, "I'd almost say it would be worth *a million dollars* to find out." He raised his eyebrows suggestively, waiting for me to take the bait.

Now. I should mention that while this guy totally skeeved me out, I didn't know who he was. As obnoxious as his indecent proposal was—and dude. Seriously? We've all seen that movie—I didn't want to create any problems for Trip if this were some major player. I also didn't want to create a scene in the middle of the party. But even still, I didn't realize my free hand had been clenching into a fist at my side until Trip appeared.

Good thing he did. Apparently, I was gearing up to go full-on knuckle sandwich on this guy's ass.

"Robert. Good evening." Trip slipped his arm around my middle, never breaking eye contact with Robert the Lizard as I handed him his drink. It was enough to get the disgusting man to take a step back and resume life outside of my personal space.

151

Robert tried out a jovial tone. *Aren't we all just a bunch of silly friends, here.* "Mr. Wiley! I was just getting acquainted with your…"

"My girlfriend, Bert. My very serious, *very last* girlfriend. Get the picture?"

Every second I had to spend in that lecher's presence was worth it to hear those words come out of Trip's mouth.

"And she's not interested, so take a hike." Trip took a swig of his drink, staring off beyond Robert, already bored.

"Now, Trip. You don't think I'd have tried anything if I knew she was with you! I just saw this lovely creature standing here all by her lonesome and thought she might like some company. Isn't that right…"

I guessed that was the part where I was supposed to offer my name. But where did that smelly ballsack get off trying to get me to vouch for him? Who the hell did he think he was?

When I didn't fill in the blank, he staggered a bit as he added, "And it's not like I wasn't willing to *pay.*"

There he went, treating me like some streetwalker again! As infuriated as I was, I could tell that Trip was about to blow his top. His entire body tensed, his eyes turned to ice, and his jaw was clenched so tightly, I thought he must have been grinding his teeth into a fine, white powder inside his mouth. He started to lean in Robert's direction, but I constricted my hold on his hand as The Lizard finally wised up from the look in Trip's eyes. He put his hands up in defense and said, "Hey. Whoa, there. Okay, okay. I hear ya. No need to get all up about it."

Trip took that step anyway, inches from Robert's face, staring him down with barely leashed fury. "If you weren't such an old bastard, I'd pound your face into a pulp for the way you just spoke to her. Seeing as we may be working together soon, I'm going to refrain from kicking your ass."

Wait a minute. *This* was Bert Goldblatt? The director Trip had been meeting with?

Bert's eyes darted around the room, looking for someone to save him from a well-deserved ass-kicking.

Trip's voice didn't even sound like his own as he demanded, "Apologize."

"Trip. You're taking this all the wrong—"

"*Apologize. Now.*"

I wanted to step in and tell him it wasn't necessary. I wanted to just get the hell away from the guy. But Bert turned toward me, sticking his sagging chin out a bit smugly as he said, "I'm sorry."

He finally chose to take his leave, but tossed over his shoulder as he did, "I'm sorry I didn't get the chance to taste those tits."

Trip turned into the Hulk before my eyes. He slammed his glass down on a nearby table and lunged at Bert, but I was in the way. Bert jumped back and smiled, but there was fear in the weasely man's eyes. I put my hands on Trip's chest, trying to keep him from killing the guy. "Trip! Stop! Please don't do this. It's over, okay? Please!"

Trip looked from the man's retreating back to me a few times, still practically growling. I knew if he really wanted to go after him, I was no match to physically hold him in place. My words had already halted him, so I continued with that tactic. I put my hands to his face, and turned the focus of his eyes to mine. "Trip! Baby. Please don't. He's a pathetic excuse for a man. Please don't ruin tonight over him, okay?"

Trip's need to kill Bert was being overshadowed by his need to not destroy our evening. I could see the slight shift in his expression and used that line of logic to my advantage. "It will ruin our night, okay? Please don't let him."

He didn't say a word, but he didn't go after Bert, either. Instead, he grabbed me by my wrist and practically dragged me around the corner, slammed me against the wall and opened his mouth on mine.

Whoa.

I was caught off guard, but it didn't take me long to melt into his forceful kiss. Our tongues tangled as he groped at my breast, his other hand gripping my gown at my thigh, lifting and gathering it in his hand until he could slip his palm underneath and grab my ass. His hips jacked into mine, his hardening length grinding against the front of my dress, causing the body parts underneath said dress to clench from the heat he was creating between us.

I should have been more concerned with someone catching us, right there in a shallow alcove, where anyone could turn the corner and find us at any second. But Jesus, the kiss was freaking hot.

I grabbed his lapels in my hands, pressed myself against him, and I could feel how hard he was, that amazing fifth limb of his straining against the fabric of his pants. He let out with a growl and teased his fingers against the edge of my garters, pulling one of the straps away and letting it snap against my thigh.

"You're *mine.*"

My brain had shut off, stealing my ability to form actual words. "Mm hmm."

"You called me 'baby.' I like that."

"Mm hmm."

"You little liar. You're still wearing your panties. But not for long."

That one jogged me out of my trance as I giggled and answered, "Mmm hmm."

"Do you have any idea what I want to do to you right now? Feel this. Feel what you're doing to me." He took my hand and pressed it against the front of his pants. "It's torture, knowing what you've got on under this dress. You're leaving the garters *on.*"

Note to self: Always, *always* let Trip see what I'm wearing under my clothes at the *beginning* of the night.

I was coming unhinged, right there in a restroom alcove in the middle of Château Blanco. I mean, the guy wasn't just sexy. He was *sex*.

"Jesus," he hissed, exasperated. "We gotta get out of here. Unless..." He pointed to the restrooms nearby, and I took note of the signs on the door: Men's Room. Ladies' Room. Men's *and* Ladies' Room.

"Ewww. Is that one for what I think it is?"

"You didn't see that yet?"

"No! Do people really..."

"Well, they're not really *supposed* to, but it doesn't stop them."

"Grody! Let's just go back to your place."

"Good idea."

Walking back into the party, some boobified blonde intercepted us and wedged herself between Trip and me, her back in my face. "Trip Wiley," she purred, trailing a hand down his arm. "My, my, my. Where have you been hiding yourself, handsome?"

Ugh. Nice line, hosebag. Where did this chick get off? He was obviously there with me, yet she chose to completely ignore that small fact in her quest to make time with my boyfriend. *Again*, from the looks of it.

Smelly pirate hooker. Go back to your home on Whore Island.

Trip very politely excused himself from her clutches and led me over to our booth to grab our stuff. I'd been looking forward to diving into the SWAG bags as soon as humanly possible, but suddenly, I could care less about them. I was way too pissed to be curious about a sack of free tchotchkes.

Trip put a hand at my elbow, and the contact served to break my control. I spun on my heel and snapped, "Is there anyone in this city you *haven't* fucked?"

His shoulders sunk as he registered the broken look on my face, the barely restrained tears. "Layla, come on. That was before. You and I weren't together for a long time."

"Oh, but 'you never stopped loving me'. I was 'always with you'."

He slid his hand up and down my arm. "You were. You are. Babe. Don't do this. Don't be one of those crazy jealous girls. It's not who you are."

I didn't know where he got the impression that I wasn't a jealous person. I guessed we just hadn't ever been a couple long enough before to be able to find out.

The truth was, I was feeling pretty green right at that moment. Not just green-eyed in a monster-like capacity, but green about this entire world of fast and loose sex.

Green-skinned as I became sick to my stomach.

Trip was looking at me hopefully, unsure of just exactly what to say. He raised a hand to my face and brushed a thumb against my cheek. "I love you."

I let out a conceding breath at his words. "I know. I know you do. This is…" *just so much to handle.* "This is just not how I pictured the ending of our night. When I see hints of your life as *him*, it's kind of confusing for *me*. Understand?"

"Oh, Lay," he chuckled and wrapped his arms around me, holding me tightly against his chest. "It's not real. *We are.* I'm sorry if all this made you doubt that."

All this. The glitz and the glamour, the flashbulbs and the phoniness. I shouldn't have been doubting him. Just because he was playing Trip Wiley all evening didn't mean that's who he was to *me*. I'd have to do a better job of reminding myself I was in The Land of Make Believe. To be honest, it felt as though I were playing some sort of part, too. The jealousy thing *was* a tad out of character.

He tipped my chin to his face, bent down and gave me a sweet kiss along my lips.

A very real, very sincere kiss. A Trip Wilmington kiss.

The gesture thawed me out and allayed my concerns. And thankfully, by the time we got back to his house, we'd both decided to table the incident.

It was easy to overlook almost anything when Trip was intent on making me forget.

He made leisurely love to me for hours, and after that, I couldn't even remember my *name*.

Chapter 20
COME AWAY HOME

We had a couple free weeks to take it easy, considering *Slap Shot* wasn't due to start filming until the end of March. We went out into the world sometimes, but mostly, we just enjoyed staying in. It was easier to relax when we were able to take up residence in our own, private cocoon.

Because going out was always a spectacle.

In spite of the baseball cap, Trip was stopped everywhere we went; people asking for autographs, tourists snapping pictures. He took it all in stride, but it was a little overwhelming for *me*. I was astounded at the attention he attracted. I mean, I knew he was famous and all, but knowing something and living it were two totally different things. I watched his interactions with awe, seeing "Trip Wiley" the way the world saw him, the pieces of this public figure they thought they were entitled to. Who was this sexy, urbane man that had emerged from the clunky (but okay, yeah, still sexy) teenager I once knew? When Trip was being *him*, he carried himself with an inflated confidence which managed to come off as almost... *graceful*.

I spent some of our time in seclusion getting some writing done, and thank God, because I had barely thought about work since the moment Trip walked back into my life. Aside from that notable distraction, it was just simply too hard to get back into the grind out there. California was so laid-back. Content. Peaceful.

At first when I'd taken over Trip's office, I spent more time staring out at the sunshine than doing any work. I daydreamed. I called Dad. I called Lisa.

My best friend was such an enabler during that time. She'd call every few hours with questions about the Academy Awards. Who was hotter in person; how tall was so-and-so *really*? I told her a few stories, but kept most of the slimy stuff to myself for the time being. I didn't want to tarnish her impression of the glamorous Hollywood façade that she'd come to know; the shiny, star-studded lifestyle of her imaginings. Besides. Lisa was never one to let me get more than a few words in edgewise. I was saving the details for when I got home.

I was also, apparently, saving my productivity for another time. I did everything *but* work during those first days.

I watched every one of Trip's movies that I hadn't yet seen, then I watched the ones I already had. I collected all the entertainment magazines that had covered the Oscars and clipped any pictures I found of Trip and me together.

I swam. I cooked. I organized my notes.

I was totally stalling.

Finally, out of nowhere, inspiration struck and I spent three solid days banging away at my keyboard, barely coming up for air. Trip was busy preparing for his movie, so I was able to get some words down without feeling too neglectful. But even so, when an idea for a book finally sets off a creative spurt, I have no choice but to run with it.

My big epiphany had come from that read-through the other day. After meeting Patrick Van Keegan, I'd come up with a story about a washed-up Hollywood actor in the days leading up to his suicide. I'd hardly call Patrick Van Keegan a has-been, but seeing him that day gave me the idea. You just never know when a muse will present itself. I'd already titled it "The Last Act," and the ideas for it just wouldn't stop flooding my brain.

I'd called Diana with the pitch, and she just went nuts for it. That added motivation was what had me tapping away on my laptop the past few days, practically nonstop. Which was a good thing, because between the fiction novel for Diana and the memoir for Trip, I had a lot of writing to do.

I was starting to burn out.

But I had to keep going. Not only was I on a self-imposed deadline, but I truly loved it. I knew, though, that I had to find my balance between loving it and loving Trip at the same time. It was too easy to get lost in him, and I didn't want that to happen.

Trip seemed to be stressing a bit as well. I had walked in on another heated phone conversation that morning and quickly realized it was Bert coercing Trip into doing his film. It wasn't the first call like that, and I knew Trip was tired of the incessant pressure and schmoozing. My impression of Bert at the Oscar after-party still lingered, and I felt it was pretty insane that either of them would even consider working together after almost trading fists.

But this was Hollywood. Things were a little different out there.

Bert was a complete ass, but a talented director, and Trip thought that the script was amazing. The whole situation was absolutely crazypants to me. Where else on Earth can a potential employee threaten to beat the shit out of a potential employer and still be pursued for the job? I thought the man was a skeeze and I hoped Trip would flat-out turn him down. But it wasn't my decision to make. Trip wasn't even surprised to find that the guy still wanted to work with him, which was more than a little disconcerting. He'd become almost used to the way things were done in that city. I didn't think I ever would.

His moody outbursts had become more frequent over the past few weeks, but I made a point to remind myself that it wasn't personal. The old Layla would have assumed she had done something wrong; the new Layla trusted that he would come to me if I were the source of his frustrations. Striving for better communication wasn't always easy, but our recent efforts had been an improvement between us, and that certainly counted for something.

Between his dealings with Bert and his preparations for his upcoming movie, Trip was burning out, too. He must've finally decided to take a break from studying his script as he made his way into the office and slumped down in a leather chair across from the desk. I looked up just long enough to acknowledge him as he shot me a contented smile. He didn't interrupt my frenetic pace and just sat there watching me for a while. It was nice having him there, his silent presence a cozy encouragement.

I was in my zone and had barely registered that he was even still in the room when he asked, "Hey. You in the mood to catch a concert? The Chili Peppers are playing at the Bowl. I can get us tickets."

I had a pencil between my teeth and didn't even look up from the keyboard. "Can't. Writing."

"How 'bout some dinner? You want to go out or stay in?"

"Hmm. Sounds good, hon." I registered that I wasn't really paying attention to whatever it was that he was asking, but whatevs. We'd talk about it later. *Tapatapataptap.*

"You want to move in with me?"

I was still pounding away at the keys, and wasn't even sure what he'd just said. It took an extra minute for his words to finally sink in, and when they did, I stopped dead in my tracks. My hands went motionless and I looked up to meet his eyes. The pencil dropped out of my mouth as I asked, "What?"

"Well, *that* got your attention!" he said, cracking himself up.

Did he seriously just ask me if I wanted to move in with him? "Wait. Did you… what?"

He came around to my side of the desk, knelt down on the floor, and swiveled my chair to face him. He rubbed his hands against my knees and said, "I know you're heading back next week, and I kind of figured you'd be coming back, but I wanted to *officially* ask you to do so." He pulled a mini Rubik's Cube keychain out of his pocket and dangled a silver key in front of his face. "I had this made for you."

161

"Trip!" I shouldn't have been so stunned. I mean, how did we plan on being together if I lived on the opposite side of the country? But just hearing him actually say the words, seeing the sweet, shy look on his face... my body's response to his gesture just caught me by surprise. My heart started pounding and my eyes actually welled up as I took the keychain from his outstretched hand.

And then I kissed him.

Right there on the floor of *our* office.

* * *

Trip's birthday was on March 15th.

He had yet another meeting with the *Slap Shot* crew, as they readied to start shooting in a few more weeks. I was amazed at how much time and work went into filming a movie even before the cameras started rolling. Trip informed me that it was nothing compared to the time and work that goes into a movie *after*. But at least his bodily presence wouldn't be required too often during that phase until it was time to start promoting it.

His meeting was first thing in the morning, so I barely had a chance to wish him a happy birthday before he was out the door. I felt bad that the guy had to go in to the studio on his special day, but he assured me it wouldn't take very long. It ended up working out great, though, because it gave me a few hours to throw an impromptu "party" together. The guests would only consist of his immediate family, but I figured they were the people he'd most like to spend his day with anyway.

What was interesting to me was that he had numerous acquaintances out there, but not too many close friends. He was tight with his agent, David, and he'd bonded instantaneously with Carlos, his director from *Slap Shot*. I saw the way he interacted with all those industry people at the Oscars, laughing and chatting and having a great time. But he wasn't really *friends* with any of them. I guessed since he spent most of his time trying to avoid the limelight—and the drinking that went with it—he was kind of insulated from the social aspects of that world.

He'd been talking to Pickford pretty regularly since the wake, though, and I was glad that between his old buddy and his new pals, he at least had a small handful of people to make up his inner circle, a reliable group of friends that would make sure not to lead him astray.

I was just putting the finishing touches on the dining room table setup when Sandy arrived to help me decorate the house. She put the baby down in her bedroom, the pink-and-white space that her uncle had painted himself in anticipation of her arrival months before.

Sandy and I got to work decorating, and we really pulled out all the cheese to do so. She actually picked up some crepe streamers and balloons on her way over to the house. Sandy started in with hanging the streamers, and I took over balloon duty. But since we didn't have a helium tank, I just blew them up and piled them all along the bar.

It was ironic that Trip had a fully-stocked bar in his home, so huge it took over an entire wall of his living room. I mean, not only was he a recovering alcoholic, but he didn't do much entertaining. I couldn't quite grasp why it was even under his roof, much less in the most lived-in space in the house.

I had just finished with the balloons and recovered from my lightheadedness when I decided to join Sandy with the rest of the decorating. Out of nowhere, she took a deep breath and blurted out, "I owe you an apology."

"For what?" I asked absently, balancing on a step ladder.

Sandy rolled the leftover streamers around the spool as she slumped down onto a side chair. "For not...you know... For not trying to step in and straighten you two out all those years ago."

I was startled by her words and came down off the ladder. "Sandy... Why would you owe me an apology for that? *We* screwed that up, not you. It wasn't *your* fault."

"It was just difficult, you know? It's so hard working for family sometimes. I never know when to draw the line between being an employee and being a sister-in-law to him. I really try to separate the two, and normally, I do a good job of it. But that thing in New York... I just want you to know that I know I chose the wrong role."

I sat down on the chair next to hers. I was touched that she was taking my life so personally, but I really didn't want her to keep beating herself up about it. "You were only doing what Trip asked you to do. I wasn't happy about it, but I never blamed you."

"But I should have told him to get his head out of his ass. I should have told him to at least speak to you." She played with the roll of streamers in her hands before adding, "You should know that I came right over here as soon as he got back and tried to talk some sense into him. But he said if I ever even so much as mentioned your name to him again, he'd not only fire me, but cut Claudia off as well."

That sounded a bit extreme to me, but I was sure he was only lashing out at the world because I'd hurt him so deeply. It didn't make it right, but I understood the feeling. All too well.

She put the streamers on the table and met my eyes. "I knew he didn't really mean it, assumed he was simply too raw to discuss it at the time, and just figured I'd give him a few days to cool down about it. But then I made the mistake of trying to talk to him one day when he had a few in him. He shot me a look—God. I'd never seen that look on his face before or since—it just froze me to the bone. I didn't want to take the chance of riling him up if it meant he was going to make good on his threat. We'd just bought the house in Santa Monica, we were looking into adopting the baby… we knew we needed his help with those things. I've always been ashamed that I didn't bring it up again."

"Oh, Sandy. I'm so sorry you got mixed up in all that! You didn't do anything wrong. In fact, you did exactly what he asked you to do. I'm so sorry I turned him into such a monster."

"He really was," Sandy snickered out. "It took me some time before I was able to figure out he was only taking out his hurt on us. I should have known that sooner and stepped in. I should have stepped in anyway."

She looked so guilty sitting there, but I truly didn't want her to hold herself responsible for Trip's and my stupidity. "No. Please don't question yourself about it another minute. Please stop being so hard on yourself! Really. Everything is working out exactly as it was supposed to. I just feel bad that you've been so stressed out about it all this time. If anything, *we* owe *you* the apology. Did he ever…?"

"He did. A while back. Took me out for dinner and apologized for being an evil ogre. Still didn't want to talk about you, but he was in a better place by then, at least."

We were in the midst of sharing a teary-eyed hug when Claudia came in with Mrs. Wilmington. She'd flown in for the occasion, and the two of them had spent the whole day house hunting. I guessed now that her husband was gone, Mrs. W. could make that long-anticipated move out west.

Sandy sobbed, "I'm just… I'm just so glad you're here right now. We all are. Trip's never been happier."

I hugged her even tighter. Her words carried more weight than she could ever realize. "Thank you for that."

Claudia stood in the living room, watching as Sandy and I swiped our eyes. She knew full well what we'd been discussing, because she put her hands to her hips and busted, "Sandy. What the heck did you do to the poor girl *now*?"

That made us laugh. Claudia threw an arm around my shoulders and said, "She really couldn't get over it for the longest time. I didn't really understand until I saw you two together, but I gotta agree; it's good to have you around, kid."

The approval of Claudia Wilmington. Jesus. Now I *knew* Trip and I were doing something right.

Mrs. W. came into the room then, bouncing Skylar in her arms and sing-songing, "Look who's up from her nap!"

Claudia released her arm from my shoulders and said, "Yeah right, Ma. Like we don't know you just went in there and woke her up." She rolled her eyes and announced she was going to the kitchen to heat up a bottle.

It was really pretty awesome to have the Wilmington women in my life. I'd always been surrounded by men. And actually, after growing up with so many male relatives, it was a breath of fresh air to have some female family members around, even if they weren't my own.

Chapter 21
BACK IN THE DAY

By the time I pulled the meatloaf out of the oven, Trip had come home. He walked into the kitchen to find all his women standing there, ready to celebrate his thirty-second birthday.

Jesus. Thirty-two. Remember how old you used to think that was when you were a kid? I remember as a little girl, doing the calculations until the millennium. I figured on New Year's Eve of 2000, I'd be twenty-six, married, and with four kids by then.

We all know how that turned out instead.

Trip had a shy smile on his face as he entered the room. He was only partially surprised to see his mother there and went over to give her a hug, before kissing Claudia, Sandy, and Skylar hello. Then he came up behind me and wrapped his arms around my waist as I stirred the creamed spinach at the stove. You'd think with his money, his tastes would have gotten more extensive. But when I asked him what he wanted for his birthday dinner, he immediately requested meatloaf, mashed potatoes, and the aforementioned spinach. After the diet and exercise binge I'd gone on leading up to the Oscars, I was more than happy to indulge in a little soul food. At least for one night. I still had an entire city of beautiful women to keep up with.

He nuzzled his face against my neck and said, "Mmm. Smells great." I didn't know if he was talking about me or the food until he asked, "Did you make everything yourself?"

"I did. Used your mom's recipe for the meatloaf, though."

"Perfect. Can't wait to dive in." At that, he bit my earlobe, and I *knew* he was talking about me that time.

"Okay, kids, that's quite enough," Claudia snarked as we laughed. "All this cute is making me a little sick to my stomach, and I haven't even eaten Layla's cooking yet.

After dinner, we retired to the living room for dessert. Sandy had made a phenomenal brownie cheesecake, and I was only slightly annoyed that she had picked something even more fattening than Trip's dinner selection. *Et tu, Brute?* Again, I tried to ignore the calories. It was my boyfriend's birthday, and I justified the sliver of cheesecake.

I wasn't much looking forward to the extra-intensive workout in the morning, however.

Trip and I took over the couch with the baby, and I was bouncing her on my lap, watching her beautiful, chubby face splinter with drooly smiles as she chewed on her hand. She had a great laugh, and I was pulling out every trick in my repertoire just to hear it as often as possible.

"You're a natural," Trip's mom directed at me.

I chuckled and responded, "No. I'm *practiced*. My best friend had twins a few years ago." A pang gripped my heart as I mentioned Caleb and Julia. God, I missed those little fuckers. "Baby number three is due this summer. And. I. Can't. Wait," I added, bouncing Skylar's feet against my knees on every word. She started squealing in response. Jackpot.

"Oh! Look at her face!" Mrs. W. exclaimed. "Oh, she reminds me so much of your father when she laughs like that."

Trip spat, "Skylar's adopted, Ma."

"Even still. She's a Wilmington." Mrs. W. leaned over from her chair toward her granddaughter. "And you know it too, don't you, baby girl," she added, grabbing at Skylar's pudgy toes.

"She's a Wilmington-*Carron*. And stop comparing her to that asshole."

We all went silent at that, the room turning quiet enough that I could actually hear the hall clock ticking away the seconds. I kept my focus trained on the baby on my lap, miming happy faces in her direction, trying to downplay the awkwardness that had suddenly crept into the evening. I was well aware that it wasn't the first confrontation Trip's family ever had regarding Terrence C. Wilmington II. Despite the fact that their mother was their saving grace in that house, neither Claudia nor Trip had ever understood her loyalty to the man. I didn't feel it was my place to join the conversation, so I simply placed my hand at Trip's leg and gave an inconspicuous, reassuring squeeze.

Finally, Mrs. W. broke the silence with her calm but firm voice. "Your father was a good man, Terrence. I won't have you speak of him that way in my presence."

"He was a *drunk*, Ma."

Trip's mother sank back into her chair, her tone conciliatory. "Can't you try and remember the good times? Yes, he fought his battles with the bottle, but then, so did you. What if I had given up on *you*?" Trip stayed silent at that. "Terrence, you never forgive. Look at you right now. You've got your arm around Layla, and yet you still haven't *forgiven* her. I love you, but you can be stubborn as a mule sometimes." She shook her head and looked at him earnestly before leaning forward on her chair and placing a consoling hand against his knee. "Sometimes, you just have to learn when to let go. *Let it go,* honey."

There was a heavy pause before Claudia let out with a long whistle. "Well. On that lovely note, I'd say it's time to get this kid to bed." Trip's sister reclaimed her daughter from my arms as Sandy gathered up all of the baby's things.

Mrs. Wilmington stood up to leave as well, brushed a hand over Trip's hair, and kissed him on his forehead. "Goodnight, my sweet boy. Happy birthday. I love you."

Trip was still stewing from his mother's reprimand, but he answered, "Yeah, love you, too, Ma. Thanks for coming out for my birthday."

"Lunch tomorrow?" she asked hopefully, her attempt at a truce.

Her invitation allowed a small smile to escape his lips as he answered in a resigned voice, "Yeah. Yes. I'll call you in the morning."

After they'd gone, I finished cleaning up the kitchen and then collapsed onto the couch next to Trip. He was busy checking out his new gifts: a Tag watch from his mother, and a mini digital palmcorder from his sister and Sandy.

I watched him in silence for a few minutes before asking, "You okay?"

"Why? Because of that thing with my mother?"

"Well, yeah."

He shrugged his shoulders and said matter-of-factly, "It's not the first time we've disagreed about the guy. I just wish Claudia would back me up a little more sometimes. She had her problems with him, too, you know. But it's like she and my mom are content to just forget all about it now that he's gone."

"But you can't? Or *won't*?"

He gave another shrug, indifferent to the conversation I was trying to start. I already knew how Trip felt about his old man, but he'd never allowed himself to *deal* with those feelings. Denial had been his coping mechanism for way too long. Forgiveness isn't really something you can force on a person, but I thought if I could just get him to talk about it, maybe we could sort it out together.

I tried the indirect route. "Hey. What did your mom mean when she said you haven't forgiven me? I thought we were past that."

Trip didn't look up from the pamphlet he was inspecting. "We are. Now. But I spent so many years angry at you that I guess she figures old habits are hard to break."

"Kind of like you and your dad when you think about it, huh?"

That got his attention as he looked up and met my eyes, a blank expression in his. "You're you. He's him. It's not the same at all."

I thought he was being intentionally evasive, but I realized the

170

guy probably didn't want to get the third degree on his birthday. Maybe my timing wasn't so great. "Do you even want to talk about this?"

"Not really," he said as he went back to his gifts.

"But you're okay, right? I feel like your birthday party has this big cloud hanging over it now."

He stopped futzing with the palmcorder to meet my eyes, a lethal smirk decorating his face. He put a hand under my chin and tipped my face toward him. "It's not the first time my mother and I have had that discussion. It won't be the last. You're making too much of it. Nothing could ruin tonight. Thank you." At that, he brushed his lips against my forehead in a sweet, pacifying kiss.

Even if I felt my psychoanalysis had been a big bust, I at least knew that Trip was at peace about the evening's events. I figured we'd be tackling his father situation with baby steps, and that maybe we'd taken enough of those for one night. I could try again another time. A time when it wasn't his birthday. So, instead of hitting him with the Spanish Inquisition, I pulled a gift bag out from behind the couch and plunked it on his lap.

A huge smile spread across his face.

"You seem surprised," I noted.

"I just thought the party was my present."

"Oh my God, Chester. You're so cute. And stupid. You're kinda stupid, too. Don't hurt yourself there, big guy. You just sit there and look pretty, okay?"

He shoved a forearm into me, then tore into his gift.

The first thing he pulled out was a manila envelope. Inside, there was an 8 x 10 photo of us from Oscar night, a really great shot where he was whispering in my ear and I was laughing. I'd contacted *US* Magazine when I saw it, and asked to buy a print. "Wow, great shot," Trip said, admiring the picture. "We should frame this one." He shot me a wink, and it made me smile, but I was anxious for him to see the something-even-better in that envelope.

Trip peeked inside and started chuckling when he saw the folded piece of notebook paper. "Oh, man. You're not going to make me read this, are you? I'm already cringing."

I nudged into him and explained, "It's not *your* Mind Ramble. It's mine."

His eyebrows raised in anticipation, plunging his hand into the envelope and pulling it out.

Here's what I wrote:

Hey Dummy.

After spending too long in the Hallmark store, I realized that no pre-printed card was going to cut it. I thought it would be best if I wished you a happy 32nd birthday in my own words.

My own words? Okay, here they are:
I'm crazy, sick, head-over-heels in love with you.

These past weeks have been the most amazing of my life. Not just because I'm in an exciting new place and taking part in your exciting life.

It's because of you.
The person you are. The incredibly generous, and fun, and hardworking, and incredibly beautiful person that you are.

Do you even know how beautiful you are?

I wanted this gift to take us back to the beginning, to where it all started.
The start of US.

Here's to looking back... But more importantly... Here's to what's yet to come.

Happy birthday, Chester.
I love you.

Lay-Lay

Trip sat there staring at the sheet of paper in his hands for way longer than necessary, and I knew he must have read my letter at least twice during that time. When he finally raised his head, his eyes met mine in gratitude. "God. Is this what you felt like when you read mine?"

I smiled and asked, "I don't know. What do you feel like right now?"

He gave a shake to his skull, slid a palm over my hair and answered, "Like I'm the luckiest bastard who ever lived."

"Well, then, yes. Same for me. Except, you know, for that whole bastard thing," I confirmed.

He laughed at that, gave me a lingering kiss on the corner of my mouth.

Just to thwart any further corniness, I pulled back and joked, "If that's the reaction I get for your card, I can't wait to see what I'll get for your present!"

He snickered, then turned his focus back toward the gift bag. Inside, there were three wrapped packages of varying sizes. In true Trip fashion, he unwrapped the biggest one first. When he did, his lips pursed into a smile and his shoulders slumped as he viewed the Dukes of Hazzard lunchbox in his hands. "You kept it."

"Of course I kept it. Hidden in a wad of beach towels and shoved to the back of my closet... But I kept it."

He ran a palm over the front as I said, "Well, open it, dummy! There's more inside."

He broke out of his daze to flip the latch, cracking up as he did so. "Holy shit. It's us!"

His hands dove into the treasure trove, pulling out the bag of Skittles, the package of Twinkies. The pack of Juicy Fruit, the snack-sized bag of Cool Ranch Doritos, the scattered pieces of saltwater taffy.

Underneath all the junk food, he unearthed his nametag from Totally Videos that I'd saved as if it were a voodoo talisman. "Oh my God! I can't believe you have this, you stalker!"

I laughed and admitted, "I slept with it under my pillow that whole winter."

"Loser."

The last item was a broken piece of cork. He held it up and asked, "Our wine from the tent?"

"Yep," I smiled back.

He shook his head in disbelief. "You are just the best, you know that?" he asked, before his lips came down sweetly on mine.

It was hard to tear away, but I was too excited to concentrate on kissing him when there were still unopened presents. "There's still more! Keep opening."

He grabbed the small, square package out of the bag and ripped off the paper. He was smiling like a loon at the Guns N' Roses Greatest Hits CD in his hands as I explained, "You don't know this, but 'Paradise City' is our song."

He didn't even miss a beat as he asked, "Why? Because it's the first one we listened to together?"

My mouth gaped open. "Tell me you don't actually remember that."

"We were in my truck—God, I miss that Bronco—and I was driving us back to your house after school. Of course I remember. I was the one who put it on."

"But... But..."

"All I wanted to do was pull over and see what you had on under that skirt. I had an uncontrollable hard-on the whole ride home."

"Shut up! You did not!"

"The song still drives me insane whenever I hear it."

"Where's your CD player!?"

He laughed at that, but noted, "Cool your jets there, horndog. I still have another present to unwrap."

He took the last, small package out and tore off the paper. He was holding a disc in a clear jewel case. He looked it over, asking, "R and J? Who's that?"

I must have confused him with the G N' R. I bit my lip and hinted, "I had it burned from video to DVD."

Understanding dawned across his face. "Get out. Our movie? I can't believe you did this!"

He immediately hopped off the couch to throw it in the DVD player when I stopped him. "No! Popcorn first. I haven't watched this in fifteen years either. Let's do this right."

So, it was a few minutes later when we were situated on his couch, wrapped up in a fuzzy tan blanket, the coffee table strewn with a junk food buffet. I settled into his side with a Twinkie in one hand and a Coke in the other, delaying my worries, yet again, about the calories until a more convenient time. Trip had one hand around the bowl of popcorn and the other on the remote control.

"You ready?" he asked, his smile infectious.

"Just promise me something."

Trip paused in the act of pressing play, a wrinkle appearing between his brows. "What?"

"Please don't analyze it. Just watch. Okay?"

That cracked him up.

We watched as the scene faded in on my father's den—Friar Laurence's room—the two of us frantically pacing about, Trip wearing a black leather motorcycle jacket and me in a pair of scrubs (We'd decided to make Romeo into a very *Eddie and the Cruisers*-type hoodlum and put a literal spin on "the nurse"), and I kept whining about how his main squeeze "Julie" had been moping around the castle.

"Look at you," Trip laughed out. "God, you were so in love with me. But look at that skinny little fuck. How could you not be?"

"Oh my God, you're right!" It was so mortifying, watching the teenaged me looking at him all googly-eyed and hero-worshippy. "Oh, this is so embarrassing! No wonder everyone thought we were a couple. I wasn't even playing Juliet! Yikes. It looks like the nurse wanted to get it on with the Montague boy."

"She still does, I hope."

I smiled at that as we directed our attentions back to the television.

By the time "Robbie" finally accepted the mood ring that Julie had asked the nurse to bring to him, we were cracking up, and the movie was over almost as soon as it had begun. I always thought it was like an hour long. Seriously, it was probably no longer than seven minutes.

The screen went blue, and all I could do was sit there and groan in humiliation. "How on God's green Earth did you not realize I was crazy about you? How could you have possibly been so blind?"

"I knew. Well, I hoped, anyway. You thought you were so slick."

"I did! Oh, God. Kill me now."

That made him laugh. "Just shut up and kiss me or I'll have you bani-shed from this couch."

I was still giggling as his mouth met mine, but it didn't take long for me to stop laughing and melt into those soft, inviting lips. He wrapped his arm around my middle and slid my body underneath his as my hands ran over the muscles in his arms. I was practically obsessed with Trip's new body, tracing my fingers over his new bulges every chance I got. I loved his involuntary response to my touch, the muscles in his back, or his chest, or his abs jumping under my palms.

He groaned as his hips jacked into mine, his tongue teasing against the seam of my lips, coaxing them to open, but he didn't meet much resistance from me. I opened my mouth and moaned into his as our tongues tangled against one another.

Things had heated up quickly, but I was jogged out of the spell when Trip tore his lips from mine. "Hold on," he said gruffly, before bounding off the couch.

He threw his new Guns CD in the stereo and skipped to "Paradise City." He turned from the sound system, looking at me with a wicked smirk, slowly stalking back toward the sofa like a predator and scooping his new palmcorder off the table. "I think we need to make a *new* movie...."

...And that's how only a handful of people (okay, just he and I) know that Trip's greatest film was actually a riveting two-person performance opening to unanimously positive reviews in the winter of 2005 during a private after-party on his couch in Hollywood, California.

Chapter 22
THE UPSIDE OF ANGER

I was in the pool early the next day, trying to work off the feast from the night before. Trip's plan was to run some errands all morning, then take his mother out for lunch that afternoon.

I thought he'd left hours before, so I was surprised when he came outside, holding a sheaf of papers in his hand.

"What is this?" he asked derisively. I didn't know what he was holding, but I *did* know that I didn't like the tone of his voice. I stepped out of the pool and wrapped a towel around me, coming closer to take a better look.

I was just coming to the realization that the papers he was holding were mine when he spat out, "Are these the notes from your book? *My biography*? You're *publishing* this? How could you do that to me, Layla?"

Hey, whoa. Hold on there, sparky. One minute, I was swimming around the pool. The next thing I know, I'm getting a tongue-lashing. And not the good kind.

I couldn't even address his anger yet. I had my own anger to deal with. "I didn't do anything! And why are you reading my stuff?"

"You left it scattered around my office. I couldn't *avoid* reading it."

His office.

But crud. He was right. I did. "It was supposed to be a surprise. And I wrote this for *us*, not to sell. If I wanted to sell it, I could have done so years ago."

"Bullshit. You *did* sell it! You sold *me* out!"

I was really shocked at how he'd just blown off my explanation and at the way he was ranting at me. I'd only been the target of his rage once before, years ago when he exploded on me at that diner.

Only, he was drunk that night. This time, there was no excuse. I wondered what the hell was going on.

I tried to counter his yelling by keeping my voice calm. "I did no such thing. Trip, I swear. Those are my *personal notes* from years ago, and I didn't even use them for that first book. I only pulled them back out to write our story for *you*. It's the one that they wanted, but I didn't do it. Just read the book. You'll see I'm not lying."

He ignored my rationalization, his ire too far gone to listen to reason. "And this! What the hell is this? A washed-up actor? Is that where you see me headed?"

He had my memoir notes and my "Last Act" notes all jumbled together, thinking I was writing a tell-all about his past and making dim predictions about his future.

I ignored my anxiety at seeing how he'd messed up my "filing system." There had been order to my chaos, and Trip had just lumped all my pages into one, discombobulated stack. "That is for a *fictional* novel that has nothing to do with you!"

Something changed in his expression and I knew my words were finally getting through. His shoulders deflated as he swiped a hand through his hair, staring off across the patio. He wanted to believe me; I could tell that he did. I wasn't a liar. Trip knew that. He knew I wasn't like them. He couldn't help but get his defenses up about something like this. He was surrounded by users and sellouts.

But goddammit, I wasn't one of them.

Maybe I should have told him about being asked to write that first book, but since I never actually did it, I didn't think it was important enough to mention. It's not like I was specifically trying to keep that information a secret from him.

Besides, I got the impression that something else was going on. Trip was being moody and accusatory, both of which were definitely not features of his normal personality. He was all stressed out, and I knew it wasn't just because of my manuscript.

So, why the temper tantrum?

"What's going on here, Trip? This is about more than just some diary passages."

He met my eyes for a quick second, opened his mouth to speak, but then must have thought better of it. Instead, he stormed into the house and I followed him. The conversation wasn't over.

I was getting ready to ask him about his abandoned explanation when he growled and slammed the papers onto a side chair of the living room. "Goddammit! I need a drink."

I watched him head for the bar and brace his hands along the edge, eyeing up the rainbow of bottles along the mirrored wall.

Oh no. No, no, no.

As riled as I was feeling, I still knew I had to stop this. Our fight took a backseat to the more immediate situation that had just presented itself.

I wanted to beg him not to do it. I wanted to sit him in a chair and talk him down from the ledge. But he'd started pacing around the room like a caged animal, hands clenched in fists at his hips, in his hair, against the bar. Talking wasn't going to do it right then.

I intercepted him mid-pacing, halting him in his tracks with my hands at his shoulders, jogging him out of his stupor. He'd been in such a state that his eyes met mine in confusion, his expression glazed over momentarily. It was like I was awakening a sleepwalker as I dropped my towel, grasped his hands, and placed them on my breasts, trying to jog him out of his trance.

It worked.

His eyes suddenly turned dark and his lip curled into a leer.

I clashed my lips to his, kissing him hard, fisting his shirt in my hands, pulling him toward me and ramming my tongue in his mouth. Trip took the bait and grabbed me around the waist, pulling me to him fiercely, sliding a hand down to grip my ass, pressing my body into intimate contact with his, bending me backwards from the force of his kiss. Feeding off me. Taking.

My heart was beating a crazy rhythm, my body melting from his eagerness. I suddenly forgot about trying to create a diversion and just got caught up in the electric jolts that were invading my entire length, making me dizzy, the room spinning. His impatient lips tasted sweet, as always, his sugary warmth consuming me. The heat of us sharing the same gasping breaths, the power of his hunger overtaking mine. There was no tenderness there; there was no reason for it. There was only want. There was only need. There was only now.

Oooh. Angry sex.

He abruptly spun me around and pushed me away, forcing my body to bend over the back of the couch, holding me fixed there with a hand at my spine. I snuck a look at him over my shoulder as I hooked my thumbs into my bikini bottoms, ripping them down my legs quickly, hearing Trip groan.

The preliminaries were over as he released his hand from my back, tearing at his fly, the both of us standing there with our clothes around our ankles. He grabbed a fistful of wet hair at my nape, knotted his fingers in the mass and tugged, forcing my head back. His other hand was at my backside, positioning a certain body part against me. He leaned over my back and hissed into my ear, "You want this? *You want me to fuck you hard?*"

Well, Jesus. Hell yeah, I wanted it. How freaking hot was he? I could only nod my head in answer.

He let go of my hair and grabbed my hips, driving full-length into me as we both screamed. He slammed into me hard and fast, grunting on every thrust; once, twice, maybe only a dozen times before he lost it, growling and cursing as he came, pouring himself out in me, forcing every last ounce to spill inside, before slumping across my back, shuddering and exhausted, breathless and spent.

We were both ravaged animals, panting heavily, coming down. Trip gave a quick rub to the back of my head, soothing the spot where he'd practically ripped out my hair.

"You okay?"

"I'm great!" I said, elated and overcome. Who knew a quickie could be so satisfying?

He put his forehead against my shoulder blade, and I could feel his heaving breath against my bare skin. "I wasn't going to do it, you know. I wasn't going to take a drink. It's important that you know that. I've been here before. I would have talked myself down."

"Coulda told me that before slamming me over the sofa. Ow. My ribs hurt."

Trip pulled his pants back up and I managed to wrap a towel around me before sliding onto the couch, where he joined me, curling up against my side. We were both invertebrates, melting into one another as I played my fingers through his hair. I thought about the fight we'd just had and wondered what was going on. We definitely had to straighten some stuff out.

But it was hard to concentrate on anything more than getting my breathing back to normal while I reveled in the delicious afterglow, his limbs tangled up with mine.

That is, until the question that had been bothering me for weeks made its way out of my mouth. "Why do you even keep it in the house?"

He didn't even wait a beat before answering resolutely, "To test myself. Like Sam Malone. Remember *Cheers*? Reformed alcoholic relief-pitcher-turned-bar-owner? That's me. If I know I can fight it in the privacy of my own home, when it's right there for the taking at any time, I know I can fight it anywhere."

We lay there for a moment, settling into one another as I mulled over his logic. Trip's heartbeat was still pounding rapidly, the sound a nostalgic melody against my ear.

Out of nowhere, he sighed, "I'm sorry."

"Huh?"

"I'm sorry for raising my voice, for accusing you like that."

I was grateful for the apology. But it still didn't explain his outburst. "Thank you. I appreciate that. But Trip, why would you just come out like gangbusters and blast me like that? Even when I explained myself, you refused to believe me."

"I know. I guess I just got caught up in my own head about it."

I was all too familiar with that scenario. I think I've proven beyond all reasonable doubt that I am Queen of the Mind-Splooge. "I'm really sorry if it looked as though I were writing some tell-all about your life. I hope you know that I'd never do that. Even the 'biography' I was working on for you was more of just a sweet story about how we'd met; a memoir from my point of view. It's not a retelling of every sordid detail about your life."

"I only scanned the pages long enough to see that it was about me."

"I kind of figured that out on my own."

He sighed and repositioned himself more comfortably on the couch, my body wedged in tightly along his side. I ran a hand up his bare chest as he tangled a strand of my hair around his fingers, the both of us lost in thought.

Finally, he asked, "Is it any good?"

His question made me chuckle. "Well, it's not finished yet, but I'd like to think so, yes."

It suddenly occurred to me that Trip had no idea whether or not I could actually write. Yes, he'd read the article I'd written about him, but that was hardly a valid example of my work. I'd written entire novels since then.

I was mulling that over when his next words caught me completely off guard. "Then you should publish it if you want. Just have your agent send over the release forms."

What the? I was stunned by what he was asking. I twisted myself to look him in the eyes as I asked, "Seriously? You want me to essentially sell a piece of your life story, here."

He swiped a hand down my jaw, his fingers playing under the hair at my neck. "Babe. I trust you. And anyway, it's *our* life story. You and me, remember?"

Of course I remembered.

How could I ever forget?

When it came to Trip, I remembered everything.

Chapter 23
FRAGILE

The next day, it was my turn to come barging through the door in a huff. Trip was in the den, listening to his Guns N' Roses CD and reading... shit. My book. I was flattered by that, but I was too riled up to acknowledge it right at that moment.

However, I was not going to come at him guns blazing the way he had with me the day before. I was simply going to present an opportunity to engage in a conversation about what was bothering me. This would be good. A big, mature step in our communication.

I took a deep breath and slapped a copy of *The Backlot* down on the coffee table (a little harder than I'd intended), causing him to look up from his reading. He peeked over the book and saw what I had placed at his feet. "What's that piece of crap doing in my house?"

"Did you see the picture on the cover?"

He lifted the book in front of his face again as he answered, "I'm really not interested in seeing a picture of myself on that birdcage liner."

"It's not just a picture of you," I swiped the magazine off the table and held it up toward him. "It's a picture of you *with Jenna*."

He ignored me, so I flipped in a couple pages and read from the article. "*Trip Wiley and Jenna Barnes together again! The estranged pair were recently seen leaving the St. James hotel, where a source confirmed the tumultuous twosome are plotting to work on a new movie together. Does this mean a possible reunion is in the works for the star-crossed couple?*"

I was fuming about the whole situation, but that last line *really* twisted the knife in my side. *They* were not the star-crossed couple. I'd been through way more with Trip than that witch.

"You know not to believe anything in those rags. Why start now?"

"Is it true? Is this why you've been growling around this house like a bear, crabby and stressed out?"

He finally put the book down and swiped the magazine from my hands. "Did you really look at the picture, Lay? Yes, it's the two of us out front of the hotel, but it's two *separate* photos. They just doctored it up to make it look like we were there *together*, when in fact, we just happened to be in the same place at different times."

I'd been so disgusted at the sight of them together that I hadn't looked at the photo for more than two seconds. But okay, yeah, on closer inspection, he was right. The photo was totally 'shopped.

"Fine. But is it true?" I asked again.

He ran a hand through his hair and lurched to his feet. "She wasn't even there! I made sure she wouldn't be there when I went to meet with Bert."

"You *knew*? You knew she was going to be hired for this movie *before* that meeting?" I was astonished at his admission. He may as well have kicked me in the spleen. Oh, this "conversation" was gearing up to turn into an all-out brawl.

"I knew it was a *possibility*, yes."

"And you didn't bother to tell me about it?"

"Kind of like how you never told me that your first book was supposed to be about me?"

He was grasping at straws and he knew it. "*Really*, Trip?"

His posture deflated as he conceded, "I didn't think it was worth upsetting you when it wasn't set in stone. I'm still hoping she won't be cast."

I couldn't even respond to that. I had my arms crossed over my chest, unspeaking, waiting for him to explain himself.

He put his hands over his face and growled into them before throwing his arms out to the side. "Look. It's just a job! I'm not the boss here, okay? I didn't pick her for the part. There are producers and who-you-know and anyone she's ever promised a blowjob to, including the director who's had a hard-on for her for years and he'd be a full-time pervert if it weren't for the fact that he's a filmmaking genius!"

I was aware of the man's pervy side. I'd experienced it for myself on Oscar night. But why did he have to perv over *Jenna Barnes*? Of all the people!

I was positively stewing about the blonde whore from hell.

Amongst others.

All those women from his past. I couldn't take it. My prior resolve to handle things maturely got thrown out the window. "Who's *Marcy*?"

Trip stopped pacing, caught off guard by my change of subject. "Who?"

"Oh, you don't even remember her name?"

"Who's name?"

"Marcy... *Something*! According to The Bimbo Twins at the read-through, you used to fuck her."

He braced his hands on the back of the wing chair and stared me down. "I used to fuck a lot of women, Lay. A *lot* of them. Is that what you want to hear? How I spent years going to bed with every hot blonde in the city? Do you really need to hear this? Do you really want to go down this road?"

No. No, I most certainly did not. But the fact was, *he* was the one that took a road trip down the Whorey Highway, not me. If he hadn't, there'd be nothing *to* discuss.

"That was then. *This*?" he motioned his fingers in the gaping space between the two of us, "This is now. And right now, *this* is all that matters to me."

"Right now."

"If you want the truth, it was all that mattered to me then, too. But I couldn't... You weren't..."

"So, you just decided to have sex with *everybody*?"

He sighed, looking at me intently, trying to find the right words. The air left the room as he lost the heated tone and brought his voice down to a calculated calm. "Maybe that was wrong of me, and I apologize for it. I can only imagine what you must think of me right now. But I was only with them because I couldn't be with *you*. I've always loved you, Lay. It's always been you."

Ouch. My heart cracked at that admission, because I knew it was the truth. He'd always been it for me, too. He'd always been the love of my life.

And, yeah, okay, to be honest, it's not as though I had joined a nunnery while we were separated. My numbers weren't anywhere near his, but could I really blame him for living his life, doing whatever he did, *before* we were together? It's not like either one of us could pull a Superman and spin the world back in time to change things.

"Patience" was playing on the stereo, and it was enough to make me want to cry. I looked over at Trip, who'd sat down in the wing chair, elbows on his knees. His hands clamped into two white-knuckled fists and his head dropped to his chest, staring at his feet as he said, "Please don't leave me over this. Please don't break me again."

He thought I was going to leave him over it? I just wanted to be a regular girl for a minute and bitch about it. I wasn't planning on *leaving* him.

"Oh God, Trip... no. I'm not..." I sank down to the floor at his feet, put a hand to his knee. "I love you. I'm not going anywhere." He looked positively wrecked, which was never my intention. I guess I could have explained things better. "I'm sorry, too. It's just strange for me. We can't seem to go anywhere without running into one of your ex-girlfriends. All these California blondes with their big fake tits. Can you even imagine what that would be like for you if every time you turned your head, some guy I slept with was standing there? Some guy who still wants to sleep with me.

Gives you dirty looks like you don't measure up. How would that feel for you?"

He raised broken eyes to mine. "Babe. Think about it. Yeah, they're all blondes. I couldn't bear to be with a brunette ever again after you."

What? I thought on his words for a moment and holy crap, realized it was the truth. Damn that man and his selective adorableness.

I tried to contain my smile at his revelation as I teased, "Maybe I should dye my hair."

He grabbed a handful at the back of my head and pulled, tipping my face up to his. "Don't even think about it."

The old Trip was back as his mouth crashed down on mine and kissed me roughly, his teeth clenched, the sound of his growl vibrating against my lips. He wasn't going to distract me this time. We still needed to sort some stuff out. But his admission and his kiss had at least served to change the tone of our confrontation.

My voice was almost playful as I said, "Okay, okay. But *Jenna*? C'mon, Trip. You have to understand why I'm so upset. Not only is she your ex-fiancée, but she's super-skinny, with humongous boobs, and she..." I trailed off.

"What?" Trip asked, finally cracking a smile. "And she what?"

"She went to Yale! *YALE*, Trip!"

"Why do I get the impression that you're more jealous of that than of her tits?"

"I *have* tits. What I don't have is a diploma from YALE."

"Neither does she."

Wait. What?

He could see the confusion on my face, and clarified his statement. "She didn't go to Yale. That was just part of her packaging."

"Packaging? I thought they only did that in like the fifties."

189

"You'd be surprised. I could give you a list of people in arranged marriages that would make your head spin."

"Arranged?"

"For a few guys who are a little light in the loafers. Ruins their box office as romantic leading men if people can't buy them as straight."

I let that sink in. Hollywood was the weirdest place, I swear. "So, no Yale?"

He was laughing as he put his arms around me, hauled me up to sit on his lap. "No. Actually, she wasn't too bright. I couldn't understand how someone who went to Yale could constantly use the word 'supposably.' Made me cringe every time."

"How did she even get away with saying she went there? Someone could easily find out the truth. I mean, there are records for that sort of thing."

"Only if someone cares enough to dig for them."

It seemed Jenna escaped a bit of the Hollywood grapevine simply because she wasn't famous *enough*. Huh. Maybe I could slip by it as well.

I snuggled in against his chest, played with the edge of his T-shirt at his neck. "I can't believe you were engaged to her."

"In my defense, she didn't start out as such a vapid tart. I was impressed with the Yale thing, too. And believe it or not, in the beginning, she was nice."

That made me just a smidge jealous. But she was his *ex* for a reason, right?

"So, you just expect me to suck it up and deal with this?"

"I'd appreciate it." He put a palm against my cheek, holding my head against his chest. "Have a little faith, sweetheart."

Faith wasn't an easy thing to come by, and not a concept with which I was too familiar. It was too scary. Too... unpredictable. I wasn't used to throwing caution to the wind, just leaving my fate in the hands of another person.

Then again, the person in question was Trip.

I was still kind of seething about it, but what could I do? It was just work, like he said. After the numerous stories he'd told me about the technicality behind all those steamy love scenes in his movies, I knew all that chemistry was just make-believe.

But shit. *Jenna?*

I suddenly understood why he'd been so edgy the past days. He was all stressed at the thought that I'd actually leave him just because her name was being thrown around as a possible choice for a possible project. I supposed he could've had a bit more faith in *me* than that.

But if he thought it was going to freak me out so badly, why was he even considering it?

I knew I needed to just chill the hell out. I trusted Trip to do the right thing, make the right decision in regards to his career. Sure, I was hoping he wouldn't even take the part, but if he *did...* well, if he did, I knew it would be for the right reasons. He was right when he said I wasn't normally a jealous girl. I realized I was just lashing out due to fear. Fear of knowing how easily we'd been torn apart in the past.

We weren't those same stupid kids anymore. We'd gone through a lot to get to this point, and *this* wasn't going to just slip away like it had the last time. Or the time before that.

When it came to our relationship, *this* was all that mattered now.

I hoped I wasn't being naïve when I chose to believe him.

Chapter 24
SUNSET STORY

I'd felt bad about all the ridiculous fighting we'd been engaging in. It wasn't really our style.

Well, it didn't *used* to be.

I blamed it on the smoggy air out there. It messed with a person's brain.

Not that I'm making excuses for our behavior.

But even if we still had some major communication skills to hone, at least we were making it a point to actually talk about stuff. In the old days, we'd just bottle everything away and assume the worst. Fighting was an improvement over silence, right?

I knew Trip had only lashed out at me because he was under stress. Plus, he'd gotten too used to the idea of being sold out. That didn't make it okay, and his outbursts were something we'd have to work on. I didn't sign on to be his punching bag.

He didn't sign on to be mine, either.

I went into that Jenna conversation determined to be calm. Zen. Rational. Instead, I'd freaked out at him because... well, because I obviously didn't like the idea of Trip's name being thrown around with hers again. Or any of those other women.

I'd dealt with that enough while we were separated.

In the weeks after The Lunchbox, I kind of went a little nutty. I holed up in my old bedroom and watched *E!* religiously, torturing myself with every report about Trip's new movie, every mention of his engagement. The only times I left the house were to buy up all the movie magazines and rag mags that had his picture on the cover. There were a lot of them.

As usual, Lisa was my saving grace.

She came over every day, made me shower, put on clean clothes. She brought over mindless romantic comedies and snacks to pig out on while we watched them. She took me shopping. She bought me that membership to the gym so I could use the pool. Eventually, she dragged me to her Lamaze classes. She tried to keep me focused on *life*.

She even tried to get me to swear off the tabloids, but those things were addictive. It took quite a while before I could wean myself out of their grasp. But even though I stopped buying them, I couldn't ignore the covers. So, it was hard to avoid Trip altogether. With so many entertainment magazines, his face was everywhere, all the time. Normally, not alone.

During those years after rehab, he went back to his playboy ways. I couldn't go more than a week without seeing him on some magazine, some new girl on his arm, living it up with some random woman or another.

A few months back, he was even named as *People*'s Sexiest Man Alive.

For the second year in a row.

So, in my defense, you need to understand that I was acting out because of more than just plain old jealousy. Any reminder of that period of his life inevitably reminded me of mine, and that wasn't really the greatest time for either of us.

He'd spent our years apart with a fake smile plastered to his face, concentrating on nothing more than his career and turning fully into *him*.

The newfound stardom forced Trip's alter ego to appear more often than usual, and he hid behind that persona for so long that there were times I was sure he didn't even realize he was slipping into it.

Like the night we went to *The Viper Room*.

Trip decided that I couldn't come all the way out to Los Angeles without experiencing at least a taste of the famed Sunset Strip. He chose that place not only because he was friendly with the owners, but because it was practically pitch black inside. I could barely see

193

my hand in front of my face, much less would gawking fans be able to recognize him in order to swarm him all night.

He kept ordering Tanqueray and tonics for me, and after about three of them, I suddenly decided I felt like dancing. There was a great band playing, and we abandoned our private booth in order to make our way closer to the stage. It wasn't the smartest move on either of our parts, because the lighting was a bit brighter near that part of the club.

People noticed.

A group of girls that were dancing nearby started nudging each other and looking our way before I realized our mistake. They were young—in their early twenties—and I immediately felt like The Old Lady at the Bar. I'd already come to the conclusion that the Sunset Strip was a younger person's game, and I'd most likely missed my window for optimal clubbing a few years before. I was hoping that maybe since I was there with a celebrity that it shaved a couple years off my tally.

One of the girls finally mustered up enough bravery to walk right up to Trip and ask, "You're Trip Wiley, right?"

I could see the hint of white powder along the edge of her nose. God. Coke was so eighties. Wasn't ecstasy or meth all the rage nowadays? I didn't even know. That's how uncool I was when it came to the club scene.

Him made his appearance as he smiled and answered, "That I am."

Fangirl shot over her shoulder, "Told ya!" as her girlfriends started giggling and closed in around him. I was unceremoniously shoved out of the way as they asked for his autograph and tried to buy him a drink. Trip just ate it up. He shot me an apologetic look as he signed their scraps of paper, gave hugs, posed for pictures. I wanted to just get the hell off the dance floor before more people recognized him.

At one point, Fangirl gave me the once-over and said to Trip, "Why are you here with *her*?"

Ummm, excuse me, Cokey McWhoreslut?

She should've used daddy's credit card to invest in some etiquette lessons instead of blowing it up her nose. I put my hands at my hips and got right up in her face to respond, "Maybe because I have more *class* than to say something like that?"

She stood there, speechless. She might have had youth over me, but she sure as hell didn't have my years of *cultivated wit*. Or my boyfriend. Fuck her.

Trip grabbed my hand and led us back to our booth. He looked pretty pissed. I was, too. I mean, who the hell did that coked-out bitch think she was, right?

But when we got back to the booth, Trip said, "Layla. You can't say stuff like that!"

"What? You're kidding, right? I'm pretty sure she had it coming."

"Those are my *fans*, Lay. They're the ones who'll actually buy a ticket to my next movie. You can't ream every one of them out every time one of them says something stupid."

I looked at him in astonishment. "Well, maybe if you had put her in her place first, I wouldn't have had to. But you didn't say anything!"

His eyebrow quirked at that. "I would have. You jumped in before I could."

Crap. He was right.

I started laughing. "Well, okay, Mr. Cool. How would *you* have handled it?"

He slid along the pleather bench seat, close enough to rub a hand along my bare thigh. "I would have asked her kindly to treat my girlfriend with a little more respect. That's all it would have taken. She's young and catty; she was showing off for her friends. A simple reminder that she was acting out of line would have done the trick. But now...."

"Now what?"

He raised my chin to face him and smirked out, "Well, now she has a story to sell. You're the one that gets all bent out of shape about the tabloids, and now you know how these stories happen, Lay-Lay. She could call up any of those damned magazines and those bloodsuckers would be able to pull an entire article out of a two-minute incident."

"I highly doubt she even knows how to read."

That made him laugh. "You're right. I'm sure it won't turn into anything. But please just let me handle this stuff from now on, okay?"

I snuggled in a little closer against his side. "Fine. You're the boss, Chester."

He just chuckled and shook his head.

Then his hand rose a little higher as his mouth came down on mine.

"*Oh my God*! I'm kissing *Trip Wiley*!" I busted, as I ran my hands through his hair and opened my lips, right there in our darkened booth. The music was pumping through my body; Trip's tongue was invading my mouth.

We were totally making out.

I slid my hand down his chest, my fingers traveling south on their way to his jeans, pressing my palm insistently against his—

"I'm sorry to interrupt, but you didn't sign my paper."

My hand stilled as I broke away from Trip's mouth. I looked up to find one of our new friends from the dance floor standing there expectantly, holding a pen and a piece of paper.

"*What?*" Trip asked her gruffly, his thoughts clearly on my abandoned handy.

Dance Floor Girl said, "You signed all my friends' stuff. You walked away before you could sign mine." She stepped closer and shoved the paper in his direction. "Do you mind?"

My first thought was to answer her with *Do you?* but I kept my mouth shut. Trip smiled politely, signed her stupid napkin, and sent her on her way.

He shot an apologetic look my way and I just rolled my eyes.

And then we went back to making out.

My thoughts were more on the evening we'd had rather than the evening still ahead of us. I mean, the first night we went out in weeks, and we had to spend it dealing with strangers. That night, I felt like he belonged to the world more than he belonged to me. Maybe he always would.

Trip went to the bathroom, so I hit the dance floor. It's not like I was the one who needed to live my life in hiding, right? No one would give a darn about me.

But just in case, I stood off to the edge of the floor where it was a little darker. I was feeling the effects of those gin and tonics, and figured I'd look like a drunken idiot if I busted a move anyway. So, I was just kind of swaying along and bobbing my head to the music when a voice behind me asked, "Good band, huh?"

I turned and found a really cute guy standing there. Young. Probably early to mid-twenties. Fantastic eyebrows. "Yeah. They're great. I'm enjoying the hell out of them!"

"You know what I'm enjoying?" Eyebrows asked. He leaned in closer and said, "Watching you dance." I just gave him a courteous smile and a *yeah right* smirk as he added, "Can I buy you a drink?"

I was feeling like an old lady in that club filled with twenty-somethings, so it was flattering that some young stud was laying on the charm. He was sweet, but I politely thanked him and explained I was there with someone.

Suddenly, that someone swooped out of nowhere, grabbed my hand and hauled me out of the club. Once we got outside, I gave a rub to my shoulder where Trip had practically pulled my arm out of the socket. "Whoa, there, pal. What's with the—"

SLAM! My back was suddenly plastered against the black walls of The Viper Room, Trip's mouth descending on mine. I was a little buzzed from the drinks, but I was positively drunk from Trip's drugging kiss. I melted under his assault, his body pressed along the length of mine, his breath against my lips as he pulled back and said, "You tease. Wiggling around in this little skirt. You thought you'd go unnoticed? I leave you alone for five minutes and you've already got some guy hitting on you."

I bit my lip to keep from smiling. Jealous Trip was just too hot for words. I decided to stoke the fire. "You were only gone for three."

He growled, smacked me on the ass and gave me a sham dirty look out of the corner of his eyes. "You're asking for it, Warren. Just wait until I get you home."

Trip gave his ticket to the valet just as the flashing started. A group of photographers came practically out of nowhere and immediately surrounded Trip and me as we waited for the car. It was positively blinding and more than a little scary. I had my hands over my face, trying to shield my eyes from the onslaught of their flashbulbs. One of the photographers nudged my shoulder, shouting at me, "Layla! Layla, let me see that face. Come on, honey. Smile!"

Smile? It was all I could do not to break down in tears. Who was this man and why were his hands on me? I didn't know him; we weren't friends. Why was he calling me by name as if we were?

Trip tightened his grip around my shoulders, saying through a chuckle, "Come on, guys. Back off a little, huh? We're just headed home. Nothing newsworthy." His voice was lighthearted and joking, which goes to show what an incredible actor he truly was. Here were these six or so men invading our personal space, hell bent on blinding us one way or another and Trip managed to sound like it was all in good fun.

Trust me, it wasn't.

The valet finally brought the Batmobile around and Trip basically shoved me into the passenger seat. The paps were still taking their stupid pictures, but I was able to see past them to the line of awaiting club-goers gawking at the scene we'd just made. Shit. Forgot about them. A few Blackberries made their appearance, and I wondered how long *they'd* been snapping away.

Trip started the drive home as we both put the madness behind us. I was still a bit flustered, but I was trying very hard not to let it ruin our night.

So was Trip.

His hand slid up between my legs, under my skirt, teasing a look at my panties.

"Eyes on the road, cowboy. Let's remember where we are."

He snarled, "There's only one place I want to be right now and it's right here. Maybe here. Or *here.*"

The last of my concerns vanished as I found myself practically melting into the seat. It was going to be a long ride home.

Like a total gin-head, I unzipped him and slid my hand inside his jeans as he wound the car up Mulholland Drive. He was already hard, and he groaned as my hand worked him over. I was a bit worried that he'd drive us over the edge of the cliff.

Maybe I shouldn't have had my hand down his pants.

Rationality returned as I shook my head, trying to get my brain straight. "I'm thinking this can wait a few minutes," I said as I reclaimed my hand.

Trip let out with a frustrated breath. "I'm only agreeing because we're almost home. Christ. You're such a tease. I'm dying here."

I giggled as I watched him zip up and readjust himself.

We finally made it home—in one piece—and Trip hit the button to open the gate, but didn't drive through. "Huh," he said. "That's weird."

He got out of the car and checked his mailbox, which was gaping wide open. Slightly odd.

He pulled an envelope out and ripped it open right there at the end of the driveway, read the card inside, then promptly folded it up and shoved it in his pocket before coming back to the car.

"What was it?" I asked.

"Nothing."

"Let me see it."

"It's nothing. Don't worry about it."

"Well, if it's nothing, then you won't mind me looking at it."

He reluctantly pulled the card out of his pocket and handed it over. I took note of the googly, bubbly lettering, hearts over the "i"s and everything.

Trip-

I am in love with you and want to show you how much.
I heard you were going to The House of Blues tonight. I'll be there, too.
I can do things to you that you've only dreamed of.

Xoxo♥ Sarah

P.S. I will be wearing a purple dress. But don't worry, I'll find YOU.

I folded the card back up and put it in the envelope. "This is a little weird, don't you think?"

"It's just some stupid teenager or something. I wouldn't worry over it."

The fact was, we almost went to the House of Blues. It was on our short list of possible places to hit that night. What if we had gone there and Psycho-Stalker thought it was for *her*? What if she had some burly maniac there with her, waiting for the opportunity to slip something into Trip's drink before throwing him in the trunk of her car or something? What if they came to the *house* to carry out their plan? "Well, this 'stupid teenager' knows where you live! She was here. That doesn't disturb you?"

"It's not like she hopped the gate and snuck into my bed. Really, don't worry about it."

"How can you not worry about it? Trip, maybe we should call the police."

He let out with a heavy breath. "Babe. They'd laugh at me for something like this. It's not the first time some crazy girl stuck some letter in my mailbox. It probably won't be the last. I have the best security system money can buy. No one's getting in here. You're making too much of it."

Not the first time? This had happened before? And my God, he was okay with it happening again? How could he just be so calm about something like that? I was trying to keep my cool about it for Trip's sake and my sanity, but the truth was, I was pretty flipped out. The snotty fans were just a nuisance. The photographers were a pain in the ass. But that little gift in his mailbox pretty much sent me over the edge.

For all the foreplay and teasing leading up to his house, I suddenly wasn't in the mood. That card had freaked me out enough that we decided it was better to just go to bed.

I didn't fall asleep until dawn.

* * *

I awoke to a certain body part prodding me from behind.

I'd barely slept the night before, which only added to the half-asleep, dreamlike quality of Trip's body nudging against mine.

Wordlessly, he slipped his hand under the sheet and around to my front, grasping at my breasts as he continued to shove his hips against my backside.

Mmm. Good morning.

I was only half-conscious as I reached up and back, pulled his face in tighter against my neck, his hot breath against my skin, his hand sliding down inside my panties. He ripped them down my legs and I kicked them off my feet, his fingers exploring again, making delicious circular motions against my pinkest part. Kissing that spot behind my ear where the skin meets the hairline. Is there a name for that spot? I decided to name it a *fleeb*.

His face was at my ear, his panting, snarling breaths against my neck, the most thrilling shivers traveling along my spine. I let out with a moan, and Trip pulled my tank top off, groping at my skin. I felt him stripping down behind me, then he pushed the sheet down and lifted my leg up, back, and over his hip, exposing my naked body to the breeze.

Heart beating, breath catching, he speared himself into me.

I rocked with him, half in a daze, the cadence of his thrusts driving me over the edge. His body slamming against my backside, his growling against my ear, his hands at my breasts, sliding down my stomach, his body moving inside mine, his fingers pressing in just the right spot, *oh my GOD, I'm going to come.*

"*Yes.* Come for me. I want to make you come," Trip whispered, and until then, I hadn't realized I'd said that last part aloud.

202

The electric charges ran along my entire length, the feel of his huge cock smashing into me, filling me, his noises at my ear, the biting of his teeth against my shoulder.

I reached back and grabbed his ass, pulled him tighter to me, deeper, *oh God, oh God please, oh yes*, and Trip's fingers were still making those circular motions against my front, his hips still rotating at my back, driving into me as deep as I could take, his voice rough with madness and want, begging me, *"Oh babe. I can't do this much longer. I..."*

And I screamed as I came and Trip thrust deeper, faster into me, groaning and swearing and pumping himself into me, so violently as he rolled me to my stomach and flattened me to the mattress, holding my hands fixed to the bed above my head, my face buried in a pillow, muffling my screaming as he jacked into me once more, twice, shuddering and growling as he came, collapsing on top of my back, the weight of him pinning me underneath him, possessing me, owning me.

Breathless. Spent. Euphoric.

Eyes wide open now. Awake.

His.

Chapter 25
NAKED FAME

The day before I was scheduled to head home, I went shopping down in Venice Beach for some souvenirs. If I had spent my time in Los Angeles fruitlessly searching for the clichéd Hollywood scene, Venice Beach is where I found it.

The promenade had a stretch of shops and restaurants along the sand. It is there where I saw bikini-girls rollerblading, meatheads working out at Muscle Beach, a group of guys playing a pickup game of basketball like a scene straight out of *White Men Can't Jump*.

There was a Rastafarian on roller skates playing electric guitar. There were random people on soapboxes, speaking to the gathering crowds. And there were lots and lots of tourists like me.

I took advantage of the fabulous shopping, however, and found two different wind chimes for Sylvia and Lisa's parents, and a hand-carved pipe for my father, all of which were purchased from an aging hippie wearing a Che Guevara T-shirt and love beads. I picked up an awesome black leather saddlebag for Bruce's motorcycle, then stopped at a children's boutique to get T-shirts for Caleb, Julia, and the new baby, scoring an adorable little bikini for Skylar while I was at it. I was finishing up my shopping with a watercolor from a streetside artist that I knew would look perfect in Lisa and Pickford's sunroom when I headed next door to the newsstand for some gum.

That's when I saw the naked pictures of me on the cover of *The Backlot*.

Oh my God!

I immediately scanned my eyes around the store, hoping my ass wasn't recognizable to the oblivious patrons milling about the magazine display. I could've just died right there by the racks of cellophaned doughnuts.

I'd promised Trip I wouldn't bring home any more of those awful tabloids, and it was kind of hard to avoid buying up every copy of the one with the picture of *my naked body* on the front cover. But, with great restraint, I kept my promise and didn't get a single one.

I stood there staring at the headline: "Trip Wiley and Mystery Vixen Heat Up Poolside".

The picture was of me sprawled out naked on his chaise lounge in the backyard, Trip still wearing his shorts, but between my knees. It was the day I'd gone dress shopping and came home to surprise him with my newly waxed nether regions. The photo was obviously taken from far away, probably from a freaking helicopter or something based on the angle of the shot. It was fuzzy—thank *GOD*—but clear enough that they still had to black-bar out some private parts.

And that was the thing. That was the *private* part of our life. That moment was never intended to be broadcast to the world. I couldn't even think about the collection of pictures they *didn't* publish, probably stashed away in some pervert's literal spank file.

What the ever-loving fuckity fuck fuck???

It was unsettling and weird, to say the least. I mean, *I* didn't sign up to be famous. Yes, I was a slightly well-known author, but even a public career like that was fairly detached. Faceless. Anonymous. Private.

There was nothing private about my naked body sprawled out across the cover of a nationally-distributed periodical.

Oh dear God. Please, please don't let my father see this.

I may have promised not to bring any more tabloids into Trip's house, but he hadn't said anything about me reading them *when I wasn't there*. And there was absolutely no way in hell I was not reading this. I mean, those were my hooters on full-out display. My

205

all-natural hooters that up until that moment I had always found to be one of my best attributes, even in The Land of Unnaturally Perky Fun Bags.

So that's how I found myself standing in the middle of a run-down magazine stand on my last day in California reading a brazen article reveling in my sexual escapades.

Prior to this story, any time I'd seen a photo of myself in a movie magazine, I was normally referred to as: "and date," which was just fine by me. However, *The Backlot* had taken things a step further that day. The pictures were bad enough, but I cringed when I saw that they actually *printed my name*!

In a bombshell Backlot *exclusive, we revealed that author Layla Warren is the mystery woman who Trip Wiley escorted to the Oscars last month. But* Backlot *has just received insider information that the bookish beauty has since taken up residence at the playboy's compound.* The Backlot *exclusively revealed photos last week of the wily actor leaving the St. James Hotel with his ex-fiancée, model Jenna Barnes, and one can only wonder at Miss Warren's reaction to the Academy Award-winning actor's secret trysts with the leggy lingerie looker. Well, wonder no more.* The Backlot *nabbed the insider scoop that the fiction-writing femme fatale is fuming about the fornicating film star stepping out with his ex-fiancée. "She's going bonkers over those photos, but come on. Everyone knows Trip Wiley is no saint," said a source. "Everyone knows he can't stay faithful." The source went on to reveal that Warren is not only Wiley's current girlfriend, but that the twosome has known each other—and dated on and off— for years. "Oh, yeah. He was cheating on Jenna with her the whole time they were engaged. Guess it's Jenna's chance for payback."*

Enough was enough with this frigging magazine. I flipped to the inside front cover and checked out the stats; *know thy enemy* and all that garbage.

Only, it turned out that I *actually knew* my enemy.

Right there in the editorial credits, a very familiar name popped out at me.

Thine enemy's name was Devin Fields.

Okay, God. Now I know you're just fucking with me.

* * *

I had a ton of packing to tackle and I sure as heck wanted to be able to spend my last hours with Trip before having to get on a plane the following day. But I had one last stop to make before I could go back to the house. I knew Trip had lawyers, but this was a situation I wanted to handle personally. It was too important to simply let slide. I wanted to make things right before I left.

I pulled the Jeep into the lot of *Starz Publications*, a large, glass structure located in the heart of Century City.

I made my way into the lobby and waved cheerily to the security guard at the desk. "Good afternoon," I said as passively as possible. It wouldn't help my case any if I came storming into the building like the furious wrath-monster I actually was.

I cruised into the elevator as if I knew exactly where I was headed, as if I belonged there, so as not to provoke suspicion. It didn't take a brain surgeon to press the button for the top floor. Devin wouldn't be stationed anywhere else.

I channeled my old reporter skills and made my way to the receptionist's desk. "Good afternoon! I do *not* have an appointment," I said jovially, shaking my head at my oversight. "But I'd like to see Mr. Fields. Is he in?"

The receptionist picked up the phone and called his office. I didn't even know if she really dialed an extension, but I was positive that if she *was* speaking with someone, it wasn't Devin. "A young lady is here to see Mr. Fields? Okay, thank you. I'll tell her."

The receptionist hung up the phone and gave me the standard runaround. "Mr. Fields will be tied up with meetings all day. I can make an appointment for you to see him next week, if you'd like."

No, bitch! I need to wring his neck now, and I'm not going to wait a week to do it!

I smiled pleasantly and asked her to call again. "And this time, please have his secretary ask him *personally*. Just let him know Layla Warren is here. He'll see me."

The receptionist didn't look pleased, but she could tell I wasn't going anywhere until she carried out my request. This time, she hung up after the call and looked at me in curiosity. "You can go right in. Through the glass doors, all the way down the hall."

I thanked her, then headed down the hallway, trying to steady my breathing and get my rage under control.

Devin's secretary buzzed me into his office, a huge, windowed expanse with an enormous oriental carpet along the floor and rich, mahogany paneling along the walls. And there was Devin, standing in front of his massive desk, two black leather club chairs framing his commanding pose.

Some things never change.

"Hello, Devin."

"Warren! I was wondering when you'd come to pay me a visit. Welcome to the West Coast!"

He spread his arms out in a sweeping gesture, and I didn't know if it was to exaggerate his statement or to invite me in for a hug.

Aside from the extra gray around his temples, he looked almost exactly the same as the last time I'd seen him. The day he fired me.

I stopped a few feet in front of him—arms at my side—and tried to keep my voice calm. Even though I was fuming internally, I did my best to keep the conversation professional. "This is hardly a social call, Fields."

"Oh, I'm guessing you've seen my new magazine! No need to be angry. Hasn't anyone ever told you that you shouldn't pay attention to anything you read in the tabloids?" He started to chuckle, like the fact that my naked body was currently splashed all over the country was an amusing little aside.

"It's not funny, Devin. Why are you doing this to me? Why are you trying to destroy Trip?"

He didn't even miss a beat to answer, "Oh, you mean aside from the fact that you left me for him?"

Wrong. "Let's just get one thing straight. I left you for *me.*"

He wandered over to the built-in bar, grinning smugly as he said, "Now that hurts, Layla. I always thought we made a great team." He poured some Perrier into a glass, held it out to me and asked, "Care for a drink? Or maybe Wiley's gotten you used to something a little stronger these days. I have some whiskey, if you'd rather."

That's it. I snapped.

"Okay, that's enough! You'd better pray I don't sue your ass. You have *no right* to print those pictures of me and those lies about Trip. And you know it!"

"I'm well within my rights. And I have quite the legal team at my disposal if you need confirmation." His answer was collected, but I knew him well enough to recognize that my threat had put a bit of fear in his voice. The thing was, I didn't even know if I had a case. So, I guess I was bluffing, too.

"I don't know what kind of game you're playing here, but I don't like it. I don't deserve this."

"You reap what you sow."

"What's that supposed to mean? You can't stand here and tell me that you're still hurting from our breakup."

"Hardly. I'm actually getting married in a few months."

Huh. *That* was certainly interesting. I wondered who the poor girl could possibly be. "Well, congratulations," I said flatly.

Devin smiled a genuine grin at my well-wishes, but he looked even more pleased with himself when he said, "What I meant was that this is the life you signed on for, this is the life you chose. You want to date a guy like Wiley, you have to be prepared for this kind of attention."

"I didn't *choose* to have my naked body gracing the cover of your magazine. Trip didn't *choose* to have you trash him every chance you get."

He shrugged, dismissing my complaints. "Better get used to it."

I couldn't tell if he was being snarky or genuinely offering advice. I didn't care to figure it out. "When did you become this vindictive person?" I shook my head in disbelief, taken aback by the new Devin in front of me. "How can you print that stuff about him? Do you have any idea what he needed to go through in order to get his life back?"

"It's not personal. It's *The Backlot*, for godsakes. It's what we do here." He gave a chuckle at that, and that one, little, trivializing guffaw managed to make me feel like I was in way over my head. As if this was just the way things were done in that city, and *I* was the oddball for not adhering to their rules. What was wrong with these people?

Devin didn't notice my epiphany and just continued with his self-inflating commentary. "I turned this magazine around. We went from relative obscurity to the third-highest-selling tabloid in the entire country. I turned this place into an empire, and you're looking at the king, baby."

"You're sitting on a throne made of porcelain. It's a kingdom of crap."

He stammered a bit at that, caught off guard by my dig. "It pays the bills."

"Destroying people? I can't imagine any amount of money is worth that."

He snickered, but I knew my words had gotten to him. "Always with your high ideals, Layla. You may want to join the real world sometime."

If that was the real world, I didn't need to be a part of it. I was much happier living in my delusional bubble, thank you very much. "You've changed, Devin. I mean, you were always ambitious, but I never knew you to be *cruel* before."

I saw his face fall, but he quickly regained his composure as he shrugged and defended, "It's just business, baby."

"It always was with you."

I paced a few steps around the room, ran a hand over my hair. "Okay, look. I didn't come here to argue with you. I came here to offer you a deal."

I stood there with my arms crossed, eyeing up the man I had almost married. I was pretty disappointed in myself at that moment for ever considering it and grateful that I'd finally woken up in time before I did. Granted, he wasn't always this much of a jerk, but the signs had always been there.

Moving out to a sink-or-swim place like Hollywood didn't help matters any. That city was like a drug in the way it amplified a person's character. Like that Bill Cosby bit. During one of his standups, he made a joke about talking to some guy, asking what was so great about being on drugs. The guy said, "It intensifies your personality." Cosby responded, "Yes. But what if you're an asshole?"

Ladies and gentlemen, please observe Devin Fields overdosing on Hollywood.

His ambition had been enlarged to epic proportions and he was letting it dominate everything, destroying reputations just for a little extra cash in his pocket.

Trip, on the other hand, had used that Hollywood drug to become a mega-star. A generous philanthropist.

And I... well... I found out my insecurities were alive and well, bigger than they ever were.

Devin was staring me down, trying to hide his intrigue. He mirrored my pose, crossing his arms over his chest and leaning back against his desk again, an incredulous look on his face, a lip snarling above his teeth.

"What kind of deal?"

Chapter 26
TWIST OF FAITH

"You're letting your ex-fiancé publish my biography?! What the hell are you thinking?!"

Trip was feeling uneasy enough as it was that I'd gone to see Devin without telling him first. I'd told him the whole story, explained why I was there. But by the time I told him about the book, he just about blew his top.

"It's a *memoir*, not a biography, and I was thinking I was arranging for our life together to be a little more private. I was thinking that you'd be grateful to have him off your back. I thought I was protecting you, protecting *us*."

"I already told you that the crap in those rags doesn't bother me."

"Well, it bothers *me*! I'm sure it's real easy for you to wash your hands of it when it wasn't *your* ass on the cover of that thing!"

Trip opened his mouth to respond, but must have thought better of it. He knew there was no way to excuse such an intrusion into our lives.

"Are you even going to do anything about it? Can't we call your lawyers or something?" I asked.

"There's no case, Layla. They covered up most of your body and they weren't on my property when they took the picture."

"How can that be legal? How can *you* be okay with it?"

"I'm not okay with it, but what do you expect me to do? I'm also not okay with your *ex-fiancé* getting a book deal out of the situation."

Was that... *jealousy* I was hearing? "Are you serious? He means absolutely nothing to me. To *us*. He can hit the lottery or get hit by a bus. It doesn't matter. He's on my pay-no-mind list. So, it shouldn't really matter if he's the one to turn this book into a

213

raging success. If it does well, that will only mean that *we* benefit from it. Understand?"

"I could give two shits about the money he'll make off it."

"Then what's the problem?"

Trip raked a hand through his hair and looked at me, a line drawn between his brows, a muscle twitching in his jaw. I gave him a moment to gather his thoughts, but when he did nothing more than let out a breath through clenched teeth, I filled in the blank space.

"Look, Trip. Don't you see how this makes everything work out? Diana still gets the fiction novel to auction off to the highest bidder *and* she gets to option the built-in deal for the memoir. Devin calls off the dogs because he won't want any bad press leading up to the release. *The Backlot* is the only magazine writing all that negative stuff, and now they won't do that anymore. You go back to being Golden Boy in the tabloids. I sell lots of books. Everyone wins."

Trip finally found his voice. "Especially Fields!"

"What?"

"Oh, I'm *so sure* he'll hate every moment of working so closely with his ex-fiancée."

That wasn't the case at all. And wow, yeah, I guessed Trip actually *was* jealous. It was kind of strange to see him getting so angry just from the mere mention of Devin's name. I didn't do anything that would warrant suspicion on Trip's part. And where did he get off being such a hypocrite? "He's not my agent. He's not my editor. He won't be working with his *ex-fiancée* at all!" I should have just shut up after that. I should have just let the comment stand on its own. But in true brain-vomit fashion, I had to go and add, "Unlike *some* people."

"Oh, Jesus. Don't start in with this again."

"Are you going to do this movie with her?"

"Stop changing the subject."

"Are you?"

"I haven't decided yet."

"What's to think about?"

He paced a few steps, ran a hand over his face. "Why don't you trust me? I'm not that same guy anymore, Lay."

Knowing that didn't make the situation any less outrageous. And besides, he was getting all bent out of shape because of a *meeting* with Devin. I wasn't the one that would be rolling around naked with my ex in front of dozens of people for some movie that the whole world would see. I thought I was content to let Trip make his own decision about it, but obviously, I was fooling myself. So was he. "I *do* trust you, but why would you even want to do it? You hate Bert; you want nothing to do with Jenna. It just feels like you're trying to punish me somehow by even considering this role. I've already apologized for the mixup five years ago; the fact of the matter is that I'm here with you *now*. Doesn't that mean anything to you?"

Aaand get ready for some more inappropriate brain-vomit in three... two... one...

"Your mother was right. You don't know how to forgive. Maybe I deserve a little of that, but this is going too far. I'm not your father."

The look Trip shot me froze me in my tracks. "Now you're bringing my *father* into this? Way to go for the trifecta, there, Lay."

I knew I was opening a whole new can of worms at what was most likely not the most opportune moment. But screw it. I didn't want to waste a good argument. We weren't normally fighters. It wasn't every day that we had a big blowout to hash out all our crap. Well, prior to the past few days, anyway.

May as well lay *everything* out on the table.

"You say you can't forgive your father even though you know what it must have been like for him. You know what it's like to have that weakness. But I think that wake was a really good first step. You made sure that it was beautiful."

"I did that for my mother."

"You did that for *you*. To say goodbye properly. And there's nothing wrong with that. It's cathartic."

He stopped pacing around the room and looked at me like I'd just shat in his Corn Flakes. "You know what? Don't go standing there psycho-analyzing me, Lay. That's a shitty thing to do. I could toss out a ton of jargon to describe your fucked-upness, but I'm not doing that to you. I don't try talking you into forgiving your mother; why is it so important to you that I forgive my father? Why can't you just let it be what it is? Why can't you just let it go?"

"Why can't *you*? Stop shutting me out. Stop treating me like I'm constantly *betraying* you. Stop *punishing* me!"

"Stop. *Pushing*. Me!" He turned and stomped a few steps away, tearing at his hair with his fists. He flung his hands out to his sides and threw his head toward the ceiling as he let out with a screaming, frustrated, "*Fuuuuuck!*"

He bent in half, braced his hands against his knees and took a cleansing breath, coming down, refocusing. It was enough of a tantrum to wipe him out, and I watched his torso slump in fatigue. He was trying to keep his rage in check as he turned back to me and said in a measured voice, "Just think about it. We can't change the stuff we have no control over, remember?"

"What do you mean?"

"It means that I can't change the fact that my father was an asshole. You can't change the fact that your mother left. I can't control what the tabloids say about me—or *you*—and it shouldn't matter what they say anyway. I can't control who gets cast in a movie and I can't change the list of women that I've slept with. I can't stop the fans from asking for autographs. I can't stop a photographer from taking a picture. We can't control other people's behavior. We can only control our own."

I couldn't believe he was content to just throw me to the wolves. I wasn't used to being tabloid fodder, he knew that. Because we couldn't change what happened meant that we should just do nothing about it? That was *his* ideology, not mine. "That's a bit of a cop-out, don't you think?"

His newly-found calm cracked at that as his voice rose a notch higher. "A cop-out? I've been living my life by those words for three years now. You're going to stand there and tell me the theory I base my life around is nothing but a cop-out?"

"No. I didn't mean it like that. What I was trying to say is that it's a little too convenient to write everything off to a simple catch phrase. Sometimes, you have to get down in the mud and get your hands dirty. Sometimes, you have to actually figure some stuff out for yourself. And sometimes, you need to ask for help."

"I don't need anyone's help. I've been doing just fine on my own."

"How can you say that? Your mother and Claudia have been there for you every minute of your life. I'm really sorry *I* wasn't, but you need to stop holding that against me. I want to be here for you now. I love you, Trip. I want to help you through this." Would he always resent his father? He'd acted like I'd gone for his jugular just by bringing it up. Would he ever let me break down that wall? Was I even supposed to try?

I let the dad thing go for the time being, in order to drive my point home. "But what I meant was that *I* need *your* help."

A line formed between his brows. "With what?"

With what? Couldn't he see how hard it was for me out there? How I was struggling? This was the life he chose; this was the world he lived in. I felt out of control within it, but how could he just be *used* to this madness by now? The entire universe expected pieces of him—from his fans to the women to the people he worked with. The only piece of him I wanted was the *real* him, but there were so many other things standing in the way.

217

"I don't know how to deal with this life. I feel like I've been thrown into this ocean without a life vest, and I'm afraid of sinking, Trip. You've had ten years to become a part of the way things work out here. I've had four weeks. I just don't—"

"You think I'm like *them*? That I'm part of this whole stupid, shallow—"

"No, of course not. You're—"

"Because I'm not just some fucking *sellout,* okay? I might play the game, but it doesn't mean I like it. It doesn't mean I'm *used* to it."

"I wasn't saying that! I—"

"Let me tell you something, Lay. You *never* get used to it. Never. All you can do is navigate through it."

"Okay, fine. I'm just trying to figure out *how*. I don't know how to be *you* through something like this!"

He stood there staring at me for a long minute, and I couldn't read the look on his face. We were both breathing heavily, caught in a stand-off, each of us waiting for the other one to flinch first. My heart was beating in a crazy rhythm, watching him looking at me like a lion ready to pounce. Every muscle in his body was poised, tensed; his eyes were icy, blue slits aimed in my direction. The moment was wrought with unease, the air between us charged with crackling electricity, edgy and heated. I got the impression he was battling with himself over whether to wring my neck or slam me up against the wall and kiss the last of our fight away.

It hadn't occurred to me that he'd been considering a third alternative entirely.

"Well, from the sound of it, you've already got it all figured out perfectly."

At that, he walked out of the room.

I stood there, shocked and speechless, having no idea what to do. I didn't want to run after him, even though we still had a ton of stuff to work out. Because "working it out" had only led to huge fights between us thus far. Talking about our problems shouldn't trigger even bigger ones.

We needed to find some better ways to get our points across, because fighting about everything was definitely not cutting it.

Ignoring our stupid crap hadn't ever cut it, either, and at least we'd gotten in the habit of *addressing* our problems, even if we had no clue how to deal with them.

It was a small consolation, however, while I was feeling so despondent.

We didn't speak the rest of the night and spent those last, uncomfortable, waking hours avoiding one another's company. Finally, I just went up to bed.

Trip never did.

* * *

Late the next morning, I gathered up the last of my things and got ready to leave. I still had a little time before my flight, however, and figured we'd have the chance to make everything right before I stepped on that plane.

Trip was sitting outside with the paper when I found him. He didn't look up from his reading as he said, "I called a car for you."

I was stunned by those words, the sense of finality that they held. "You're not taking me?"

He still couldn't find it in him to tear his eyes from the newspaper in his hands. "I didn't do it to be a jerk. I have to have a final sit-down with Carlos before we start filming next week."

No matter what he said, his tense pose and standoffish lack of eye contact confirmed that he was still annoyed about our fight. So was I.

There was no way I could get on that plane with things so up in the air between us. At the very least, I needed to know that we were going to be okay, that I wasn't leaving his house for the last time. All the stupid things between us could be resolved later, but there was one thing I really needed to clear up right then. "Why do you love me?"

That got his attention. He finally looked up and met my eyes. "What?"

"I mean, why do you love me? Why have you loved me all these years?"

He was clearly confused, judging by the crinkle drawn between his brows. "How am I supposed to answer that? I just do."

"I'm getting on that plane in a few hours, and I need to know that I'll be coming back here for the right reasons. Because I know I love you for you, but I need to know you love me for *me*, not just because I'm the only girl who's ever seen beyond the movie star. I'm not that teenage girl anymore, Trip. I'm a grown woman who's going to want to talk stuff out when there's a problem, and I'd like to think you'll try to understand where I'm coming from when I do. It's not always going to be all rainbows and unicorns, you know? It's hard for me out here. And just because I'm having a hard time with your fame doesn't mean I only think of you as a famous person. You know that. But is that all I ever was to you? What if I'm just your Rosebud?"

He knew exactly what I was asking. And he didn't say anything to ease my mind.

Instead, he did the complete opposite.

"Maybe a little distance wouldn't be such a bad thing right now, Lay."

Chapter 27
RETURN TO THE LAND OF WONDERS

This isn't a breakup.

That's what I kept telling myself on the entire plane ride home.

We were not broken up, we were simply… disagreeing. Couples do that all the time, right? He was just doing his clamming-up, uncommunicative thing.

Right?

I'd had some niggling concerns about the success of our relationship since the beginning, but that was the first time I'd had actual *doubts*. The paparazzi, the women, the cage he lived in. The issues we both had with our parents, the piss-poor fighting skills with each other. It was all so much to deal with.

What kind of life was this? We never had any privacy. Outside of his fortress, anyway. And as evidenced by those intrusive pictures of us in his backyard, sometimes not even then.

I didn't sign on for that.

I didn't sign on for the photographers in my face, the interruptions from his fans. I didn't sign on for the constant worries about our security, our safety. The tabloids. Other women. An ex-fiancée-slash-costar.

That was *his* world. I didn't know if I could handle it. I wanted him, just not the world he lived in. Was there a way to separate the two? Wouldn't Trip's fame always be a huge part of who he was?

Hollywood was no place for an idealist. A dreamer, sure. But not an idealist.

I got home pretty late and tiptoed into the house so as not to wake my father. I went right to bed, but I hardly slept at all that night.

That's three nights in a row for those of you keeping score at home.

I must have fallen asleep at some point, because the morning light seeping through my windows caught me by surprise. Of course, the first thought that invaded my brain was my fight with Trip.

I needed to talk about it.

At such an early hour, Lisa was probably in the middle of her morning craziness, getting her kids off to preschool. Dad had already left for work. Bruce had most likely been at his construction job since dawn.

My go-to support system was officially MIA at the moment.

But would any of them understand anyway? This wasn't just your average, run-of-the-mill relationship stuff I was dealing with. I didn't have too many people in my life who knew what it was like to deal with dating a celebrity.

Although... I knew my cousin Jack had dealt with a touch of super-stardom back in the day. It's not like he was as famous as Trip, but back in the mid-nineties, his band was pretty well-known. That was around the same time he'd met his wife, Livia.

I decided to give her a call, and thank God, she was home.

We chatted for a few minutes, making small talk about my trip out to Cali. I knew Livi was pretty unaffected about the fact that my boyfriend was a movie star, and I was grateful that I'd picked the right person to call with my concerns.

"How do you deal with it?" I finally asked. She knew I was talking about the madness of being in love with a famous person.

Livia laughed and answered, "I don't know. I don't really think about it. I mean, it's not *him*, you know?"

Of course I knew. But just because I viewed Trip as a normal person didn't mean the rest of the world did. It was the other people on the planet that I had the problem with. "No, I know that. I just meant, you know, the whole *being famous* thing. The invasion of privacy thing."

"Oh," she said. *"That."* She chuckled again and added, "Well, I can't say that your cousin was ever in the same league as your boyfriend in that department. But yeah, I guess the women grated on my nerves a bit. They were just always *there*, always hanging around."

I certainly knew what that was like. "But like, did you ever feel... violated? Like how the press and the women are all odds stacked against you? Like you never have a private moment, that you can't go anywhere without being recognized, worrying about stalkers, hounded by people asking questions, asking for autographs, taking pictures, like anything you do is made public the second you do it, like the problems you *should* be working on are lost in the background because of it...?"

I realized I was rambling and that of course Livia had no real experience with those things. Few people did.

"I'm sorry," I finally said. "I guess this past month has been a little overwhelming."

"Look, Layla. I can only imagine that all that stuff must be pretty hard to deal with." She gave a sigh at that and said, "The bottom line is, if you love him, then you learn to deal with it, right? Some people get annoying in-laws; we get the fame. Every relationship has their burdens to bear. What matters is how you deal with those burdens *together*. The little bit of fame we went through was no picnic, though, so I know I wouldn't go back to that life for anything. Jack starts missing the whole rock star thing every now and then, but I just send him out to get a new tattoo and that normally calms him down."

"What about Lutz Hamburg?"

"The producer guy? What about him?"

"The Super Bowl last month. Trip said he ran into Jack and him there. He's going to do that soundtrack, right?"

Livia was silent for a beat too long, and I thought there was a chance I'd spoken out of turn. *Shit. Did she not know about that?* I hoped I didn't just inadvertently get my cousin sent to the doghouse. But she allayed my concerns when she said, "Oh. Yeah, that. He hasn't really decided yet."

She wrapped up the conversation quickly after that, and I sat there for a few extra minutes, trying to figure out what to do about Trip.

Yes, I was pissed and unsure about just exactly what was happening between us, but I wasn't even allowing myself to consider the possibility that we were over. I decided to concentrate on the memoir. It would be a special gift for him, a way to show him how much I loved him by getting every detail down perfectly.

An assignment like that was an obsessive-compulsive's dream.

I had to drive into the city to do the proper research, get the right vibe for the New York chapters of our story, maybe take some pictures. I knew there was plenty of time to send Livia back in to take some more professional shots for the actual book, but for right then, I just wanted to give her an idea of the visuals I'd be going for.

I hit the *TRU Times Square*, and prayed that Concierge Cat would be behind the front desk. The girl had a serious ass-whooping coming her way, but she wasn't there. I assumed she'd probably been fired a long time ago. I snapped some shots of the lobby, then headed back outside. Down the street was the movie theater where we'd caught a showing of *Swayed*, and the diner around the corner where we'd pigged out afterward.

Then I zoomed down to the Village to my old apartment building, but wasn't able to finagle my way up to the roof, much less my old apartment. I took some exterior shots of the building instead.

The last stop was Beth Israel Hospital, where Trip was treated after he'd broken his arm.

I'd just made my way to the front desk when I turned and collided into a woman coming around the corner. We were both holding folders, the contents of which had gone flying through the air upon impact.

That's when I realized I had literally just bumped into Kate.

Kate Warren.

My mother.

Chapter 28
A HOLE IN MY HEART

I was frozen with shock. I knew it was her just as sure as I knew my own name. My name that she'd lifted from a Clapton song over thirty-one years before. It was a killer song, but still. That's a pretty lame-ass thing to do to a kid.

She hadn't really looked at me yet, and she *definitely* didn't recognize me as she started apologizing profusely, bending down to pick up our collective papers, separating them on the receptionist's counter into two piles, hers and mine. I stood there glued in my place, jaw slightly agape, watching the woman who'd given me life giggle casually as she cleaned up her mess.

I didn't know what I should do. Talk to her? Introduce myself? Run? I sure as hell was eyeing up Option Three right at that moment.

Before I could make a decision, she stood and met my eyes.

Her smile abruptly disappeared.

We stood there like that for a long while, my heart beating out of my chest, my words caught in the back of my throat, my mind racing. I hadn't seen her since I was twelve, but she looked almost exactly as I remembered her. I stood there and assessed her, compared my memory with the woman standing right there in front of me.

Same honey-colored hair—although, I was sure that by then it was coming from a bottle—shoulder-length and wavy and hanging over her forehead.

Those same brown eyes—*my* eyes—sporting a few new crinkles, as well as some long, faint creases around her mouth.

Laugh lines. How dare she.

I only came back to Earth when I heard her voice—that oddly familiar, melodic voice—ask, "*Layla?*"

226

I couldn't speak. I wanted to deny it. I wanted to run away. But instead, my head shook up and down on its own, as my shaking, traitorous voice answered, "Yes."

There was an awkward second where it almost looked as though she were going to hug me. I tensed visibly and she must have thought better of it.

"I can't believe how much you've grown!"

Yeah, Kate. That's what kids do. They grow up. Most parents stick around to witness it.

I didn't know if she was expecting an answer, but I wasn't giving her one anyway.

"You look just like Kenny. My God. It's uncanny. You always did, but…"

"What are you doing here?"

She shifted on her feet for a moment, ran a hand over her hair, tried out a smile. She tipped out her bottom lip and gave a quick breath to the wayward curl across her forehead. I'd forgotten how she used to do that. "Well, I work here. What are *you* doing here?"

For some reason, that casual question made me angrier than had she slapped me right across the face. But I suppose anything she said would have been met with the same venom.

"I'm researching my *book*," I answered with added vengeance. *See that, Kate? Look how well I'm doing without you.* "What do you mean you work here?"

"I mean I work here." She held her hands at her sides, palms facing me. Trying to make me notice that she was wearing scrubs.

"You're a *nurse*? You take *care* of people?"

"Yes. For about ten years now."

"That's rich."

My words were laced with a bite I didn't even recognize. Who was this person trying to have a pleasant conversation with me? Where did she get off talking to me like we were a couple of long-lost friends just catching up?

Her face dropped at that, her attempt to remain smiling abandoned at my answer. Her shoulders deflated, her gaze focused on the two piles of papers she'd scooped off the floor. I watched, flabbergasted, as she nudged each of the two piles into perfect stacks, setting them at exact right angles along the countertop.

"Guess that's *one* thing you gave me," I said, nodding my head in the direction of her busywork. "Thanks." No way she could've missed the sarcasm.

She stopped fiddling with the papers, laying a flat palm on top of each stack, her eyes closed as she said, "You're angry."

That made me snap loudly, "Ya think?"

She tried to give me a *shush*, even though there was no one else around. Well, save for the two other nurses at the far end of the desk. But fuck her. Let her coworkers see what kind of person they were working with. The kind of selfish bitch who abandoned her family for her latest boy toy.

"How's Ke—How's your father?"

"Still around. How's *Rick*?" I asked her, my eyes like slits, my mouth barely able to form the word.

She actually looked wistful when she answered, "Oh, he and I haven't been together for a long time now."

What the...?

"Oh, really? He was so fucking important to you that you *left us* for him, but you're not even *together*? What kind of succubus are you?"

She actually looked like she was trying to contain a smile. Was she for real?

"Layla I—" She bit her bottom lip, trying to find the right words. "I know what you must think. But I didn't leave you for him. I left... I left you for *you*."

"What's *that* supposed to mean?"

"I wasn't happy, Loo. Not for a long time."

Who cared if she was happy? Who really gave one flying fuck about her happiness? The woman made everyone around her miserable for years after she left. She didn't deserve to be happy.

"Don't call me that," I spat.

"I'm sorry."

"You should be." Only, she and I both knew she owed me an apology for things way bigger than using my family nickname.

"I was young, Layla. Your father and I... we were so young when we had you. I didn't know who I was."

"Is this the part where you tell me you needed to *find yourself*? If that's the case, you can just save it."

"You need to understand—"

"I don't need to do anything."

She took a steadying breath. "You're right. I have no right to ask anything of you." She bit her lip and continued, "Just please know that... Well, sometimes your life doesn't turn out the way you plan. Sometimes, you make choices and—"

"The motherly advice is really warming my heart, here, Kate. But you know what? We've been fine without you. We've done just fine. We didn't need you. So spare me your sanctimonious explanations. At least be honest." I ran my hand through my hair and tried to find my equilibrium. There was only one thing I needed from this woman in front of me. Only one question I'd always wanted to ask. "Just answer me this. Just... *How could you do it*? How could you walk out that door? Leave your husband and your kids and never look back? What kind of person can do a thing like that?"

She gave a defeated sigh, then turned broken eyes to me. The pang in my heart was only out of an instinctual sympathy. I didn't feel badly for *her*. I didn't feel *anything* for her.

"I'm trying to tell you. I was young. One minute, I was a teenager. The next, I was a wife. And a mother. It was just... *too much*. I never... I never knew how to handle things back then. I was insecure and there were younger men who paid attention to me. Who made *me* feel young and carefree, too. Like them. And then Rick came along…"

"Okay, eww. Got it."

"He offered me a way out. I didn't realize I'd been looking for one. But I never… I never thought it would be forever. After only a couple weeks, I missed you and your brother terribly. I called your father. He told me to meet him at his office so we could talk things out. I never showed, Layla. I never went to meet him."

The weight of that statement and the forlorn way she delivered it almost made me feel badly for her. Almost.

"Why not?" I asked, more gently than I intended.

"Because Rick made me choose. Made me choose him or your father. I knew I wasn't happy before, why would I expect to be happy a second time? So, I chose Rick. Mistakenly believed my happiness depended on something outside of myself. But he didn't make me happy either. We broke it off after only a few months. I went to the house that day. It was fall. I parked my car at the end of the street and watched you two playing in the leaves with your dad. And you looked… *joyous*. It's the only way I can describe it. You had on that rainbow hat? You remember, the one with the tassels that hung down to here? And you were smiling, and Bruce was laughing and… I knew you were better off without me."

"How *noble* of you," I said, trying to regain the proper snottiness to my voice. It wouldn't come.

"I wasn't well in those days, Layla."

I tossed her a bone on that one. "I know. It took me a while to figure that out."

"But I straightened out. Truly. I had *lots* of therapy." At that admission, she actually let out with a tiny giggle. The sound was so completely unexpected, so achingly nostalgic, that I hadn't realized I'd let my guard down.

I took in her trim physique, obvious even in the scrubs, and found myself hoping I had inherited those genes. I peered at her lips—lips that were tipped ever so slightly into a smile as she giggled. I knew that if she'd smile just a bit wider, I would see the crooked tooth, the one my skull had shifted one afternoon when she was tickling me. She had refused to get it fixed, insisting that it would forever remind her of me. Before I could wonder if that too had been erased, she grinned uncomfortably at me, and I could just make out the slight turn of that incisor. My eyes snapped up to her face, and I took a step back, bumping into the desk.

I was having a conversation with my mother. Almost more dumbfounding than that, I found that I was actually hearing her. Hearing what she had to say. And even if I didn't agree with her choices, agree with the way she had left us so easily… I allowed myself to let her be human.

She must have sensed this shift in me, because her voice had changed from tense and beseeching to simply… *pained.* I bit my lip until I tasted blood, trying to hold back the looming tears.

She gave another burst of air toward her forehead and continued. "I was so impressed with everyone at the hospital that I went back to school and got my nursing degree. It was a huge turning point in my life. I continued with my therapy, realized the gravity of my selfish mistakes." She put a hand to her heart and said, "I was filled with such *regret*, Layla. If you listen to only one thing I've said today, please hear that. Please know that it's the truth."

I believed her. I couldn't forgive her, but I believed her.

She was caught up in her retelling, shaking her head at the memories before she continued. "By then, *years* had gone by. I couldn't quite believe it. I wanted nothing more than to try and make things right. But after so much time, I knew it was too late. I never thought you, or your brother, or your father… I knew that you had built your own life together. I knew I wasn't a part of that. By then, there was nothing left of *me* in you kids. You were all his, and he deserved you. He earned it from you. You, especially. You and your father were always so much alike." Her eyes were glistening with genuine tears as she added, "But I did love you—so much—and I *am* sorry. Truly, Layla."

Okay, fine, yes, I was crying. I admit it.

I wasn't feeling badly for her, exactly. After all that time, there was no way I was going to feel sympathy for her after what she'd put us all through. And even in that moment, I knew it was pretty damned unlikely that we'd be able to salvage any kind of relationship after something like that. And trust me, I wasn't looking for one. This was a chance encounter. It's not like she tracked me down to tell me these things. I was only willing to give her so much credit.

I was simply crying from the sheer *waste* of it all. The utter helplessness, the lost time, the alternate life. I was crying because I understood her regret, her indecision, her insecurities. I was crying because that was *my mother* standing there in front of me, for the first time in almost twenty years, practically begging for some sign that I might someday forgive her. Absolve her guilt. Maybe even lose just a smidge of my long-held hatred for her.

Sometimes, you just have to learn when to let go.

I made the decision that I could toss her just the slightest morsel here. I couldn't grant her my absolute forgiveness—I'd spent too many years cultivating my anger to give that up so easily—but I could at least give her *something*. I could at least leave her with just the smallest bit of peace.

"Thank you for that." I swiped my eyes and met hers as I added, "You're wrong about something, though, you know. I look a lot like Dad, that's true." My hand reached out on its own as I laid it against her arm. "But he always said I was more like *you*."

Chapter 29
EVERYTHING IS ILLUMINATED

I really wanted to call Trip, hear his voice, tell him about my day. But not like that. Not by using the encounter with my mother as an excuse to talk to him. I could tell him everything once things between us got squared away.

If they got squared away.

Right then, what I needed was a dose of my best friend.

The twins would be in school for a couple more hours and Pickford was at work, so I probably couldn't have planned a better time to have a breakdown. I went right to Lisa's house and came in through the sunroom door at the back. She turned from her seated position in the middle of her family room, and I could see that I'd interrupted her in the middle of packing up her winter clothes.

I was familiar with this ritual, as I'd seen her perform this task twice a year, every year, since the day we met. She had towers of clear, plastic bins stacked around the room, labels informing her as to the contents of each box. And not just boring categories like "shorts" or "sweaters." No. Lisa's bins sported terminology like "Kate Spade Summer Bags" and "Ass-tastic 7 Jeans."

She was excited to see me after so many weeks and lunged across the room to give me a laughing hug hello. I hugged her back, happy to see her, but gutted from the day's events.

That's when she saw my face.

She knew I was there for something big, even before I said the words. "I just saw my mother."

Her eyes went buggy, but then she promptly put her hand in the air, halting further speech. "Hold that thought."

If I weren't feeling so miserable, I'd have laughed at the torn label she was holding in her hands: "Marc Jacobs Fuck-me Heels."

I guessed it was time to re-categorize now that the twins were learning how to read.

She led me to the kitchen and poured me a big ol' glass of wine, then we settled in on a couple stools at her island. Lisa ignored the clothes explosion in the adjoining room to give me her undivided attention. She propped her elbows on the granite surface in front of her, rested her chin in her hands, and said, "Okay. Spill it."

So spill it I did.

I told her everything that had happened at Beth Israel, every single word of the bizarre conversation, every thought that had run through my mind during the whole encounter. Lisa offered wide eyes or questions or words of comfort throughout my tale, helping me to sort out the myriad of emotions racing through my brain.

As I neared the end of my story, I actually felt a hundred times better than I had only moments before.

Thank God for best friends.

"Wow," I said on an exhale. "I feel like a weight has been lifted off my shoulders. I never understood that saying before, but I feel... lighter."

"Screw you. I'm feeling heavier than ever."

Lisa's belly had bumped out considerably in the weeks since I'd been gone. She still had four more months to go, and I could only imagine she'd be bigger than a manatee by then.

"So, Miss Red Carpet," she said, changing the subject. "I feel like I haven't talked to you for more than a few minutes since The Key. How's Trip? When are you heading back out there?"

I didn't know if it was the mention of Trip's name, the emotional trauma from having just seen my mother, or the half bottle of wine I'd polished off, but Lisa's question immediately sent me into a fit of tears.

"What? Oh no! Trouble in paradise? I thought things were going so great!"

"They *were*," I bawled out, not even trying to pull myself together. "But Lis, so much bad stuff happened between us this past week. I don't know what the hell is going on."

"What do you mean? What happened?"

Lisa and I hadn't spoken as much over the past few days as we usually did. She didn't know about the fights between Trip and me, didn't know about the downward spiral we'd been on all week. Trip's lifestyle in Hollywood was so isolating and I guess I got sucked into the vortex. But there I was, back home, sitting on my favorite stool in my best friend's kitchen, finally able to talk some stuff out, tell her everything face to face.

"He puts ketchup on his steak and I'm his goddamned *sled!*" I sobbed. I literally, actually sobbed.

"Uh, Layla, honey, I think you've had too much wine."

I sniveled out, "He doesn't love *me*. He loves the fact that I'm the only woman who doesn't think of him as a movie star. He even told me as much! I'm his Rosebud. *Citizen Kane*, remember? The one thing that brought him happiness before the fame, before the money. Rosebud was his special thing *before* all that."

"Yeah, um, that sounds like a pretty good thing to be thought of as."

Lisa is pretty smart, but I guessed she wasn't able to understand what the problem was. Truth be told, I didn't really understand it myself. "I thought so too, at first. But don't you get it? He was always so paranoid about women wanting him just because he was Trip Wiley: Big Bad Movie Star. But now I'm the one who's freaking out because he only wants Layla Warren: The Teenager Who Loved Him Before All That."

"I still don't see the problem."

"The problem is that I'm not *her* anymore! I'm *me*! Get it? I don't know if he's really fallen in love with *me*." I took a shaky breath and another swig of wine. "The sick thing is, that's not even our biggest issue."

I didn't even wait for Lisa to ask before I proceeded to spew everything out in a rush, just completely brain-vomiting all over my best friend.

Sorry. That sounded a lot grosser than I meant it to.

I told her about Robert the Lizard Perv and the possible movie with Jenna. I told her about my nudie pics and Devin and the memoir and the fights leading up to it and the huge one after. I told her about Trip's father and my mother and trying to force him to forgive. I told her about the *real* Patrick Van Keegan and the Bimbo Twins and all those blonde sluts and the autograph hounds and the paparazzi and that weird card in Trip's mailbox at the fortress.

I talked and I talked until I was exhausted, my throat actually sore and raw, my breath catching on choppy inhales.

When I finally came up for air, I saw my best friend practically laying over the counter limp, her arms bent over her head, her mouth gaped open in pure shock.

I swiped the tears from my cheeks and commanded, "Well? Say something!"

She sat up slowly, letting out with a huge breath. "I don't even… Layla, I'm speechless here. I got nothing."

Holy shit. Lisa was speechless? Things must've been worse than I thought.

She got up from the table and returned with a bottle of cherry vodka and a shot glass. "I've got booze, though. Here. You wanna do a shot? You're drinking for two now, don't forget."

I almost laughed at her comment. Just purging the entire story from my brain was enough to make me feel a little better. "No. I'm already buzzed enough from the wine."

"C'mon. Drink it. You need it."

"No, I'm alright."

"What are you, chicken?"

That one *did* make me chuckle. "Peer pressure! Peer pressure! I need a grown-up!"

We were able to laugh for a minute, until Lisa got serious and said, "Hey Layla? We *are* the grown-ups, now."

"Well, that certainly sucks."

She snorted at that, but added, "I'm really sorry things got so crazy out there. But this is big girl stuff right now. You two aren't those same teenagers anymore. This is what it's like to be in a real, adult relationship. You think there're days I don't want to kill Pick? Because I do. But we find a way to make it work. I know your problems are different, but it's all just the same, stupid relationship garbage. We've all got our crap to sort out. If you guys are meant to be, you'll just have to figure a way to sort yours."

If.

I was getting pretty sick of *if* when it came to Trip.

* * *

Part Three of my disastrous day commenced once my father got home from work.

I had to tell him about my little run-in with his ex-wife.

He gave me a gargantuan hug the second he came through the door as if it had been years since we'd seen each other instead of only a month. I asked about Sylvia, he asked about my flight. Before he could inquire about my time out west, I diverted him with questions about his work.

That always distracted him.

237

We chatted about his day, talked about his new clients. He finally settled himself down at the kitchen table, where I joined him, eyeing him warily.

Dad eyed me back. He knew something was up. "Okay, Loo. Out with it."

I took a deep breath and said, "I wanted to talk to you about Kate."

He looked at me questioningly, but didn't say anything. Finally, I just spilled the news. "I saw her today, you know. She's a nurse at Beth Israel Hospital."

I expected my big revelation to shock him. But instead, he simply responded, "Yeah, I'd heard that's where she might be."

It turned out *I* was the one who was shocked. "You knew?"

"Not at first, no." He paused at that, trying to find the words. The ones he came up with weren't the ones I was expecting. "I want to apologize, Loo. I always felt like I should have tried harder to find her, should have been able to figure out what she needed from me in order to keep her here. Bruce was too young to even remember much about her, but you were the one that put her on such a pedestal. Do you even remember any of the bad times?"

Bad times? *Before* she left?

"What do you mean?"

"The Episodes, as your Aunt Eleanor and I used to refer to them. The singing out on the front lawn in the middle of the night when she was happy. The days she'd spend in bed, reading the encyclopedia when she was depressed. The baking jags. The shopping trips. The way she couldn't go to sleep until she double-checked that everything in the pantry was alphabetized." He gave a shake to his head and let out a sad chuckle at the memories.

"I remember the baking and the singing," I said. "But I guess I must've been oblivious to the rest."

"I never felt like I did a very good job of being both father and mother to you kids."

I looked at him in astonishment. "Are you kidding? Dad, you've been amazing. Kate couldn't have done any better."

"It was hard on you, growing up without her."

That was a bit of an understatement. But the fact was, it was hard on all of us. Yet somehow, we all survived. "It was. You're right. But Dad, when I think about how close you and I always were, I wouldn't trade that for anything. You loved us enough for a million mothers. Bruce and I know that."

He cracked a small smile and gave me a light fist bump before rapping his knuckles on the table, ending the conversation. I guessed Dad heard everything he needed to hear and didn't really want a rehash of my entire conversation with his ex-wife. I hadn't even mentioned that she'd given me her phone number. I didn't think any of us would ever need it, but I'd stuck it in my pocket anyway. You never know.

It was cleansing, in a way, to see that the encounter didn't mean too much to him. I was happy that he'd come to the same conclusion as I had after so many years: There was no reason for hate, or remorse, or nostalgia. It was what it was. She was simply a part of our past.

"So," he started in, smiling, "I haven't gotten the post-mortem on the rest of your California trip yet. How was it?"

I hadn't spoken to Dad for more than a few check-ins since the Oscars. Lisa and Pick had invited him, Sylvia, and her parents over to watch the show. They made a ton of food and sat around the TV, trying to catch every glimpse of Trip and me. Lisa said I was giving dirty looks to Joan Rivers.

"Post-mortem. Interesting choice of words," I answered back, practically scowling at the sudden shift in subject matter. "Everything feels like it's dying between us."

"Oh, come on. Surely, you don't mean that."

"I do. And don't call me Shirley."

He chuckled at that. "You compared every relationship you ever had to Trip. I'm sure that whatever happened between you two can be fixed."

"Maybe."

I was lost in that thought until Dad startled me out of it. "He came to see me, you know. I think he was really looking for you."

"What? When?"

"Oh, a few years back. He was visiting his mother up there in that big house of hers on the hill, and stopped by to say hello. His arm was all bandaged up from when he broke it, remember? When he was filming that movie in the city and you interviewed him? We sat out back and shot the breeze for a while."

Remember? Was he kidding?

I was knocked out. "You never told me that!"

"He said you wouldn't give him the time of day, wouldn't go out with him while he was in town. I guess you'd just gotten engaged to that Fields guy—stop looking at me like that. Of course I knew—and you were trying to do the right thing by staying away from him. We both had a chuckle over that one. That you didn't trust yourself to be anywhere near him."

"You *knew* that? *Trip* knew?"

"You were always nuts about that kid. Heck, I always liked him too. He was a good kid. And now he's a good *man*. But you need to decide whether you're going to keep trying to find someone else who measures up, or settle down with the real thing. No relationship is perfect, Loo. You have to decide to accept the imperfections and realize that what matters is that you're perfect *together*. All the other stuff is just the small stuff. It doesn't matter."

"It's actually kind of big stuff, Dad," I said, picking at the linen placemat in front of me.

My father leaned back in his chair, folding his hands across his belly. "Did he beat you? Cheat on you? Start drinking again?"

"No, of course not. Nothing like that."

"Then it's not 'big stuff.' It's just stuff you haven't figured a way through, yet." He got up from the table and gave me a kiss on the top of my head. "You two'll figure it out. Have a little faith, sweetheart."

Chapter 30
FINDING HOME

I needed air.

I decided to go for a walk to try and sort some stuff out.

The ground had thawed while I was gone, and the rainy season was about to begin. I watched as little rivulets formed along the curb and dribbled down the street. Spring was well on its way, and I hoped its return would make *everything* new again. Maybe the coming season would be a good time for rebirth. Renewal.

Repair.

What the hell was wrong with me? Here I had everything I'd ever wanted. No. Wait. Not just wanted, but prayed for, begged for, spent countless years hoping for. How dare I even question it? It took us forever to get there. It took us forever to just *be in love*, to give ourselves over to it. There it was. Right there in my hands.

And we were threatening to ruin everything.

Every person I had ever loved was still a part of my life. Except one. Trip had lost a parent of his own. Why were we punishing *each other* for abandonments we had nothing to do with? We spent more time condemning each other for stuff we didn't do, accusing each other of being people we never were.

If I wasn't so focused on my fear, I could have seen that he'd done *everything* to show me that he loved me. Hell, he repeatedly said it flat-out, which, for him, let's face it, is a fricking miracle. What had I done to convince him that *I* did? I should have spent my time out there reveling in every joyous moment of having him back in my life. Instead, I pushed him about other women, I pushed him about his ex-fiancée, I pushed him about his father.

I pushed him away.

When he had never threatened to leave.

I swiped a tear from my eye and breathed in the mild, late-winter air. It was time to let go. Let go of my insecurity, my anger, my fears. It was time to let my life happen.

Everything that had gone wrong between us was due to outside forces and the stupid ways we went about dealing with them. It shouldn't have to be like that. It should only be about us. Our *us* had nothing to do with our *them*.

By the time I'd made the trek back to my block, I started formulating a plan to come back to him in some big way. I hadn't really settled on anything, because all my ideas seemed half-baked and insignificant. I needed something *huge*.

Out of pure habit, I jumped up to grab a leaf off my tree and sat down at the curb, turning it over in my hands.

And when I did… I noticed that something was *written* on it:

I love you

I ran back to the tree and noticed even more marked leaves, so I climbed up as quickly as possible (skillfully as ever, I might add), and sat my butt in my old favorite spot. Every single leaf along the lower branches—*every single one*—had writing on them, and they all said the same thing:

I love you

My stomach just about burst into smithereens. I sat there, trying to catch my breath as I looked at the pieces of Trip's heart scattered around me. There I was, thinking of hiring a skywriter, and Trip had hired someone to do *this*.

I pulled my Nokia out of my back pocket and called him. I was actually hoping he wouldn't answer. If he didn't pick up the phone, it would mean he wasn't there. And if he wasn't there, then maybe he was…

"Hello?"

No such luck.

I had barely said hello back when he launched in breathlessly, "Where are you?"

I pictured him sitting out by his pool, enjoying the warm weather, the California sun shining on his beautiful face. "Oh, you know. Just sitting in a tree."

He didn't say anything at that, and I knew it was major confession time. I had my reservations, but I owed him this. "I'm sorry, Trip. I should have just said I was sorry. I shouldn't have pushed you about your dad; I should have tried to be more understanding about your life out there."

I heard his release of breath, the breath he'd probably been holding for the past twenty-four hours. "*I'm* sorry I let you leave. I let you walk out that door thinking that I wanted you to go."

"I was a jealous lunatic about those other women."

"I wasn't exactly rational about seeing the way other men looked at you, either."

"I was a total bitch about your ex."

"So was I."

That made me laugh. I gripped the phone in my hand, wishing I could turn into vapor and slide right through the receiver to be with him.

"Look," I said. "We're not doing this anymore. If this is going to work, I don't think either of us should leave the room anymore if there are unanswered questions. I don't know if you've noticed, but we didn't used to be the best communicators. I thought we were making some pretty good strides in that department, when we could calm down and just talk about stuff. Even the fighting was better than just clamming up and wondering. I'm not going back to that. I'm not wasting any more time. If there's something that needs saying... *we're going to say it*. We've wasted too much time by not telling each other what we really mean. Got it?"

"Brain-vomit at every turn. Got it."

"And I swear I'll try to be more understanding about the fame thing. I'll lay off the tabloids. I'll be polite to your fans and your ex-sluts. They don't matter to me. They have nothing to do with us. And I won't push you anymore about stuff you're not ready to face. I'll help you along, but I'll let you work on it at your own pace." I snickered and added, "Maybe we need a safe word or something."

"My *ex-sluts*—and my sanity—thank you." I heard him chuckle as he added, "And yeah. You're right. There were times when we did pretty great with all that relationship stuff. I don't want to go backwards either. *I'll* try to stop exploding and start talking from now on."

Oh, *God*, was I in love with that man. Every part of him. I realized right then in that second that that love even included his past indiscretions, his present stubbornness about his father, his future fame. It was okay to just let that stuff be what it was. We were so much more than the sum of our parts.

"But even more important, it's time to let go, Trip. We need to let go of our bad habits from the past. Let go of the hurt. The hurt we caused one another, the hurt other people caused us. Can we do that? Do you think that we can try?"

Suddenly, a black truck screeched to a stop in front of the house, and Trip's voice was coming from two different directions. "Damn. The birds have gotten huge since I left town."

I watched his beautiful form walking toward me as my jaw dropped. I flipped my phone shut in a daze, my heart practically bursting out of my chest. "You're here! What are you doing here?"

"What do you think?"

"I think you're here to check out my vandalized tree. Wait. You got a cell phone?! And you learned how to have your calls forwarded?!"

He crammed a fist into the front pocket of his jeans as he laughed. "Well, who do you think did all this?"

"I thought you hired somebody. When did you do this?"

He rubbed a hand along the back of his neck. "Middle of the night. You have no idea how much self-control it took not to throw pebbles at your window."

I smiled, reminiscing at the sweet memory. "You really did this? You're such a jerk!"

"Call me crazy, but I was expecting a different reaction."

That made me laugh. "No, I meant I was just sitting here trying to think of something awesome to do for *you*, and you go and beat me to it."

"Guess I'm just more awesome than you. Why? What was *your* plan?"

I bit my lip. "It *may* have involved an electric guitar-playing clown singing 'Paradise City'."

"Damn. I would've liked to have seen that. Can we pretend I didn't do this leaf thing?"

"Like I could ever forget this." I jumped down from the tree and stood in front of him, feeling almost shy as I did so. "You're here."

"I'm here."

Holy balls! He really was! It felt like way longer than just twenty-four hours since I'd seen him. I'd already gone into withdrawals. So much had happened in that time. So much still needed to happen before we could be okay. But I knew we would make things right. We'd get through it eventually; it just didn't have to be right then. Because right then, he was actually standing there in front of me.

All I ever needed from him was him.

We stood there, staring into each other's eyes as he spoke. "Look. I should've noticed that you were having a hard time out there. I should have put all those girls in their place for trying to make you feel second-rate. I should have stood up for you about that magazine cover; should have gone and kicked Fields' ass instead of letting you think you needed to do it on your own. And I get why you made that deal. I get it now. I'm sorry you—"

"Shut up. Just shut up. You had me at 'Damn the birds have gotten huge'."

He looked at me in barely contained hysteria, his lips pursed together, stifling a laugh at my *Jerry Maguire*.

Oh, now I just *needed* to break him.

I exaggerated a shaky voice to repeat, "You had me at 'Damn the birds have gotten huge'."

At that, he cracked the hell up, and I joined him before wrapping my arms around his neck and planting a big, sloppy smooch on his laughing mouth.

Trip pulled back, his hands smoothing up and down my arms. "You're right about how that outside stuff doesn't mean anything. The only thing that matters is *us*. Screw everything else." He brushed a hand through his hair, his eyes meeting mine in a sheepish grin to add, "We also need to stop relying on singing telegrams and Skittles and leaves on a tree to show what we should be telling each other instead. I guess I've always been afraid to put myself out there like that. I can jump off an exploding building, but telling you how I feel has always been even more terrifying. So I relied on *things* to tell you instead. If I had told you that day in your apartment... If I had just come right out and said that I loved you, you wouldn't have had any doubts. But instead, I sent that stupid lunchbox to tell you for me."

"If *I* hadn't been so dense and insecure, I would have heard you."

He smiled at that; a sad, happy, lopsided grin for all the things that had gone wrong between us, for all the things that had gone right. "You were right about another thing, though, Lay. You *are* my Rosebud. But not in the way you think. I'm not using you to try and get back to the last time my life was innocent and wonderful. Because you were a part of that, no doubt—a huge part of it—but only because I loved you then. And I love you now. *You*, not the slice of life you represent. I knew it that first day I saw you sitting in that desk in Mrs. Mason's, trying not to look at me while I introduced myself to the class, and I never stopped. It's always been you and me, Lay, and I think you know that; or you would, if you'd get your head out of your ass long enough to realize it. You know it's true. I'm trying to get back to *you*. Hell, I just flew clear across the country just to tell you this in person. I'd like to think I'm gonna get *some* credit for it."

I stood there staring into the pleading eyes of that incredible man, the tears streaming down my face. Aside from that whole 'head in my ass' thing, it was the most beautiful thing he'd ever said to me.

That was, until the *next* thing he said to me.

He slipped a hand around the back of my neck, holding my teary eyes fixed to his. "You were my first love, babe. I want you to be my last."

I threw my arms around his shoulders, just bawling like a big sap into his neck. "I *know* you love me, Chester. I love you, too. More than anything." I kissed him then, my heart positively overflowing for the awe-inspiring man within my grasp. His arms wrapped around my waist, lifting me to him, crushing me against his length. I pulled back, looked right into those gorgeous blue eyes and saw the truth I'd always known:

"I'm not me without you."

JULY 2006

Chapter 31
THE WEDDING DATE

I was standing there, in my blush-colored gown, staring at the sliver of glass in the door of my church, checking out my reflection. My makeup… was perfect. My hair… was cooperating for once. Over the past year, I'd learned that that's all it took to look good: Lots of money to hire professionals.

The wedding ceremony was about to start, so I took my place at the back of the aisle. I looked to the front of the church and saw Bruce, so handsome in his tux, and shifted my gaze over to my father… standing at the altar. I peeked over my shoulder to find Sylvia just beaming gorgeously and looking as beautiful and happy as ever. Dad and she were finally making this thing official.

The music started, and I counted ten Mississippis before starting down the aisle. It wasn't difficult to keep a smile plastered on my face during my walk, but once I spotted Trip in the pews, I'm sure I looked like a complete doofus with my uncontrollable grin. Then again, he was smiling at me like I was the only person in the room.

Sitting next to him were Lisa, Pickford, and all three kids. The twins were getting ready to start Kindergarten in the fall, and I made Lisa promise me she'd always send them to public school. Where does the time go? I felt like it was only yesterday when *we* were in school, and now my childhood best friend was getting ready for *her kids* to start. Before we know it, those two will be in high school, living it up as hard as we did back in the day.

Lisa grabbed the baby's chubby fist and waved it at me as I walked past. Allison was just as beautiful as her big sister.

And her mother.

I said a quick prayer that all her children would be lucky enough in their lives to find a best friend as amazing as mine.

* * *

The reception was at the country club one town over. We were blessed with a perfect day—sunny and breezy—affording us the opportunity to take advantage of the outdoor party area.

By the time we made our way inside to the ballroom, we were stuffed from the endless fare of the cocktail hour, and still had a whole sit-down dinner to look forward to.

I grabbed Trip out of his chair and pulled him onto the dance floor, figuring we could work off some of that food before Round Two of the feeding frenzy.

Plus, I just wanted to dance with him.

The floor was packed with the people I loved most in my life. Dad and Sylvia were dancing nearby, and next to them were Mr. and Mrs. DeSanto. Bruce and his new girlfriend were swaying to beat the band, Pickford was twirling Julia around in his arms, and Lisa had partnered with Caleb. Aunt Eleanor and Uncle Conrad decided to join in, and my cousins were there, too, along with a bunch of other family and friends that we didn't get to see too often.

Aunt Eleanor and I had a pretty big talk one day about my encounter with her sister. Well, I guess I did most of the talking. Aunt El spent most of our conversation with a sad smile glued to her face, tears brimming in her eyes as she squeezed my fingers off. I almost got the impression that she was more relieved to hear about *my* closure on the situation, rather than revel in the peace I'd hoped to bring *her*. Between Bruce's shoulder shrug, my father's non-reaction, and Aunt Eleanor's happy tears, I realized I was the only one out of the four of us who hadn't already let my mother go years before.

The wedding wasn't the first time my cousins had been back in the same room as Trip. A few months after The Tree, I'd brought him to my dad and Sylvia's engagement party. I'd given Stephen the heads up, but I was still worried about how the meeting was going to go down. My cousin had practically arrested Trip a few years back, and had expressed some initial concerns when he heard we were back together. We all had a long talk before dinner, and Trip and he had since found a way to make nice. I wanted any lingering awkwardness from that incident to be settled long before the wedding, and mercifully, it had been.

Because there I was, dancing with him once again.

He was spinning me around, crooning along to "Chances Are" as he did so.

He stopped singing to smirk out, "Hey babe? This place is no rooftop, but I guess we can cut one hell of a rug anywhere, huh."

He pulled my waist in tightly against his side and dipped me backwards over his arm, planting a smiling kiss against my breastbone. I smacked his arm until he straightened us back up and then playfully chastised him. "You smoothy. Still working the moves on me? Don't you realize you already *got* me?"

"Oh, I realize. I guess I just still can't believe it." He spun me out and back in again as I giggled, watching one of his eyebrows raise comically. "Should I have kept my distance that night instead?"

Every moment had led us here. Every second of our lives. Every beat of our hearts. The answer was a big, fat *no*.

I pursed my lips to keep from smiling. "Hey Trip?"

"Yeah?"

"I wouldn't have changed a thing."

He grinned wickedly at that, pulled me in close, and buried his face in my hair. I heard him take a huge inhale before he said, "God, Lay. What *is* that? Do you have any idea how many random shampoo bottles I've sniffed over the years, trying to find this scent? 'Cause I *know* what kind of shampoo you use, and that's not it. I'm beginning to think it's just *you*."

My shoulders started shaking, cracking up at his admission. I'd spent the same years sniffing bars of soap. Even during that first trip out to his California house, I'd come to the same realization that he had: It was just him.

It was always him.

The wedding guests spent their time gawking at Trip all evening, despite the warning we put out to the family not to treat him like a sideshow freak. Thank God for my cousins. They took shifts running interference for all the curious rubberneckers intent on bugging him all night.

Not that I couldn't deal with it or anything. I'm kind of used to it by now. After all, that part of him is just make-believe. The part that's all mine is what's real.

After all that we'd been through—all the laughs and the heartache and the mistakes—the reality was that we were who we were. Not perfect. Just perfect together. More importantly, while the future wasn't mapped out, we at least had the knowledge that we'd always be together through it. The words spoken at our high school graduation came back to me: *We know what we are, but know not what we may be.*

Whatever it was, I knew it was going to be great.

NOVEMBER 2006

EPILOGUE

Trip bought my old apartment building in the village.

The plan is to rent out the other eight units, but keep the entire top floor for ourselves. I'd originally wanted to knock down *all* the walls on the fourth floor, but Trip wouldn't hear of it. He's making me leave my old apartment exactly as it was when I lived in it. So, I have to content myself with remodeling the other three units on that floor into a penthouse suite instead. I'm not complaining. The plans my father and Jack have drawn up are beautiful. Trip and I spend most of our time in Jersey anyway, but it'll be nice to have a space in the city to hide out when we're not at the *TRU*, or when Lisa and Pick or any of our other friends want a place to crash for the night. As with our California home, we plan on doing a lot of entertaining there.

My downstairs neighbor Angelo passed away, and his son found three letters addressed to me from way back in ninety-four. Trip had written the wrong apartment number on the envelopes and they'd been sent to Angelo, who never bothered to give them to me. One day during the demolition, Anthony showed up and just handed them over, apologizing and explaining what had happened. Trip put down the sledgehammer and the two of us sat right there on the floor amidst the rubble to read them. I won't bore you with the details contained within those letters—most of what he'd written had been about his daily life out in Los Angeles; auditioning, playing hockey, etc.—but there's a part of that first one I think that's worth sharing:

It started off as all the others, telling me about the latest dramas taking place in his seedy apartment building

but hey, it's near the beach

talking about his latest audition

257

I don't know. I don't think I got the part. Tawny Everett was there doing the readings, though. Right there in the room! She called me "cute". It was so freaking awesome!

and mentioning how he was dropping out of school

It's not why I'm here anyway. How's the new apartment?

But then, a few paragraphs down:

It's hard out here. It's lonely. It's fake. I'm thinking of packing it in and coming home.

Will you be there if I do? You've only got this last year of school and I thought maybe we could make some plans. I miss you like crazy and I just want to come home to you.

You're my home, Lay-Lay.

And yeah. He was right. If I had read that back when I was twenty-one, I would've been scared half to death.

But I would have taken him up on his offer. I would have welcomed him back into my life with open arms.

And then where would we be? Would we have torn each other apart, so young and so clueless, or would we have built each other up? Would I be writing? Would Trip really have given up acting? Would he have grown to resent me because he did?

I could ask myself those questions until my head hurt.

Thankfully, I'm not tasked with having to find out the answers. Somewhere in a parallel universe, Trip and I are miserable together. Just not in this one.

Along with the apartment building, Trip bought his old house in Norman from his mother, and she bought a new one out in Malibu to replace it. I never thought in a million years when I was standing in that foyer back in '91 that someday it would be my house. The demons of that first night have been exorcised, triumph over my first memory of the place. It's a beautiful home, and we shared our first kiss right out there in the driveway, confessed our love properly for the first time right there in his old bedroom. It's the good memories my mind keeps alive.

I suppose it helps that we christened every room within the first two weeks, however.

A few days after we'd moved in, Trip replaced the destroyed portrait of his father, hanging it in the same spot in the hallway where it once was. I still work on him from time to time—*unobtrusively,* nowadays—trying to help him heal his conflicted feelings about his old man. We're making progress. But for now, the little things let me see that he's learning to forgive. He doesn't need to say the words.

I set up my office on the third floor, in a room whose window can see the hiking trails out in the woods. Hidden from the trees, underneath the boughs, is our clearing. The place where we'd spent one amazing night in a shabby, turquoise tent; the place where I found out Trip was in love with me. Tucked in a drawer of my desk is a stack of letters and cards he and I had written each other over the years, reunited at last, and tied up with a bow, as if they were a gift. They are. Framed on the wall—in spite of my too-cool boyfriend's protests—is the first letter Trip ever wrote me, his Mind Ramble. He has some reservations about his sappiness being put on display, but I had a promise to keep to myself.

My fiction novel, "The Last Act" is coming out this winter, but my Trip memoir was released a few months ago. It's doing well. Trip was finally able to get on board with Fields as the publisher, once he realized that aside from the random call relayed through my agent, I didn't need to have much contact with the guy. Devin's book-publishing branch had pretty much cornered the market on celebrity tell-alls and was the most logical house to ensure it would be marketed with the proper enthusiasm. His *magazine*, however, is still spewing out the same old celebrity gossip, and reporting on the latest "news" with their usual brand of cheese. Their cover story last month was about Ella Perez having a love child with Sasquatch or something. I don't know. I don't really pay much attention to those things these days.

Case in point: Don't believe everything you read in the tabloids.

I'm working on my next novel. It's a story about a twenty-six-year-old writer in New York City who's trying to break into a journalism career when her ex-boyfriend suddenly pops back into her life.

I just *wonder* where all these book ideas could possibly come from.

I've written under some different pen names, but most of the time, I write as L.P. Warren. The P stands for Prudence, which, God help me, is my middle name. Aside from Clapton and Springsteen, my mom was a pretty big Beatle fan, too. I make a modest living from being a writer, and that, amongst other things, keeps me happy.

I may not be at the top of the New York Times Bestsellers List—*yet*—but I love what I do, and I'm pretty sure that's more important. No matter what stories I write, however, I kind of hold a special place in my heart for that memoir. I hear some other people do, too.

Actually, you may have heard of it. It's called "Remember When."

* * *

We're at the Meadowbrook Ballroom in New York City's Times Square for our reunion. Our last shindig was originally scheduled for early fall of 2001, but in the weeks after 9/11, a high school get-together didn't seem so important. So, in true St. Norman's fashion, we bucked conventionality and decided to have a fifteenth in order to compensate for that canceled tenth.

Everyone has turned out in full force for the thing, and it's pretty incredible to have the whole gang back together under one roof again.

I see Penny and her husband all the time, being that she still lives in Jersey and is related to Pickford and all. But that hasn't stopped us from hanging out most of the night, boogying with Becca and her husband. He's a really nice guy, but I can't help but be startled by his appearance. He looks an awful lot like Cooper.

Coop had come up for a visit over the summer, but this is the first time I've been in the same room with his wife Suzy since their wedding last year. She's a gorgeous redhead with a pixie cut that I'd never be able to pull off. She's also a very patient woman. Not only did she tough it out waiting on that ring for so many years, but she's smiling through this entire evening, getting along really well with her husband's old crowd.

We're not the easiest bunch to take.

Rymer's already tied one on, and I keep waiting for his inevitable queries to poor Suzy, wondering aloud whether the carpet matches the drapes or something. He's always had a thing for redheads. Then again, he may be a little distracted, as he's been spending the whole night hitting on Margie Caputo. He always said she gave him the best head he's ever had, and I guess he's looking to recreate history.

At least she's got that going for her, because hot damn, that chick's ass has gotten fat.

Oh hey! I just realized Lisa owes me ten bucks!

My best friend will probably kill me for this, but...

Speaking of fat... Lisa finally dropped all the baby weight and looks terrific. She says that "High School Reunion" is the best diet she's ever gone on. She thinks we should have one every year.

She also thinks she should play matchmaker to get Heather Ferrante and Mike Sargento back together. Sarge got divorced a few years back and Heather came here alone. She looks fantastic, and I'm pretty sure he's already noticed. Those two haven't left the dance floor all night. I think Lisa's meddling may be thwarted once again, because it looks as though those two are reuniting just fine on their own.

Even still, Lisa has Pick making arrangements for us all to go to a Knicks game this winter as his guests. It should be a blast.

It's good to have old friends.

Speaking of old friends... Trip is currently in cahoots with Miramax to direct his next movie. With all that obsessive attention to detail, I don't foresee any issue with a transition from working in front of the camera to being *behind* it. I don't think he'll ever give up acting, but for now, this is the avenue he's choosing to pursue. He's really excited about it.

The Jenna/Bert movie got shelved once Trip turned down the role. At first, I thought he was trying to appease me, and I found myself in the unfathomable position of trying to convince him to take the part. If the script was as great as he claimed, I didn't want him to miss out. That show of trust earned me an appreciative grin, his astounded gratitude, and a sound tongue-lashing (the good kind this time). Ultimately, though, the decision to bail on the project was made on his own. He finally realized that the idea of working with his ex-fiancée and The Lizard Perv simply turned his stomach, and didn't want to deal with their pain-in-the-ass personalities over the many months of filming. No script was worth putting up with that.

Slap Shot came out late last fall. It gave good box office, but it wasn't the kind of film to get nominated for a ton of awards. But that's okay. Trip was never in it for the accolades.

Speaking of accolades... I'd finally met Paul Newman at the premiere. When Trip introduced us, Paul kissed my knuckles, gave Trip a wink, and told him, "This one's a keeper."

I almost died. It seriously has gone down in the history books as one of the (many) highlights of my life.

Almost any time Trip and I find ourselves getting into a pointless argument, one of us will remember to defuse the situation with our adopted truce phrase, "What would Paul do?"

It may sound stupid, but it works for us.

Trip's foundation had been doing really well already, but the buzz has really picked up since that CNN interview. When Hurricane Katrina hit, Trip was one of the first celebrities to speak out about how poorly the residents had been treated, and his organization soon partnered with the American Red Cross to aid in the disaster recovery. Not long after, my cousin and my brother got on board, and arranged for ERF to team with Habitat for Humanity to start the rebuild. With Jack and Bruce leading the project, Trip's foundation has been responsible for over twenty new houses in the New Orleans area this past year alone.

The collaborations with such like-minded organizations have been ongoing.

Trip took me with him on a couple visits to Africa. He'd been all over the continent as a teenager during his globetrotting phase, and never forgot the conditions in some of the countries there. We're currently in talks with UNICEF, putting the funds together to build a school in Uganda. I joked and suggested we name it *St. Norman's.*

Speaking of our alma mater... Our former classmates have been going a little gaga over him all night. People he'd never spoken a word to back in school are suddenly bringing their spouses over to be introduced to their "old friend Trip." As always, he's been able to handle all the attention with his usual charm.

I took a break from dancing to come and check out all the pictures on the wall. Carolee Simcox chaired the reunion committee, and I guess she and her fellow rah-rahs thought it would be a great idea to blow up a bunch of shots from our yearbook and plaster them all over the reception room. It really was a great idea.

Not.

I'd forgotten how huge our hair really was in the eighties and early nineties. I guess that was the general idea behind hanging all these pictures. It's important to remember history so that we're not doomed to repeat it.

There's one shot in particular that caught my attention, however, and I've been standing here staring at it for a solid five minutes, now. It's a huge poster-sized picture of Trip from *Guys and Dolls*. He's leaning against a brick wall with his arms crossed against his chest, a fedora dipped precariously over one of his smiling, blue eyes.

God. I didn't just imagine it. He really was Golden Boy.

Trip sidles up behind me, slips an arm around my waist, and asks against my fleeb, "Having fun yet?"

I can't help the grin that spreads across my face at that, as I feel the length of his body pressed right up against mine from my shoulder to my calves. Yeah. I'd say I was having fun.

Still.

I lean back against him, cross my arms over his. "*You're* here, aren't you?"

I twist my head and catch him smiling at me. That devastating grin, that melt-me-down-to-my-core-smirk, splitting the beautiful face of this beautiful man.

He's so handsome, and it's still so disarming, even after all these years. And yet, he's always been even *more* gorgeous on the *inside*. His heart has always been his most attractive quality.

Either that or his sweet, sweet ass.

I can't wait to get out of here, drag him into our penthouse suite at the *TRU*, and have him all to myself again.

And again.

There's an electric current running down my length as I turn in his embrace and ask, "Actually, you think there's somewhere around here we can 'go talk'?"

My meaning is not lost on him, and he surprises me with a kiss, right there on the edge of the dance floor, in front of all our old classmates.

Surprises are good.

I kiss him back, thinking of how far we've come, how many years it took us to get here. I've loved him as both a girl and as a woman. I have both a history and a future with this man. This man I will love forever.

Thank you, God. Thank you for giving him to me. I owe you one.

Trip pulls back, a mischievous look on his gorgeous mug. "Yeah. We can head out soon. But there's something I need to take care of first."

I can't help but smile, because I've been waiting for this all night.

Even though he's been trying to keep it a secret, he knows that I know he's got a diamond ring in his front pocket, occupying a space right under his heart.

But what he *doesn't* know about yet is the baby occupying the space under *mine*.

THE END

Acknowledgements:

I just… I don't even know what to say, here.

There are way too many people to thank, and too many things to be thankful for.

I'd like to start with you, the readers:

You have made this journey one of the most incredible adventures of my life. You've written to tell me how much you've enjoyed this story. You've written to offer praise or encouragement or anger or impatience. You've fallen in love with Trip and Layla right along with me, and I'm as sad as you are right now about having to tell them goodbye. But I know we've left them in a good place. After two books of angst, I hope you've enjoyed finally seeing their LOVE STORY, and I know you join me in wishing them well. While this is the "end" of *their* story, we'll be able to keep tabs on them in the background of future books starring some new, just-as-lovable characters. ;) For all your comments, your excitement, your loyalty… I can only offer my heartfelt thanks.

Next up, I would like to thank Crystal Light Lemon Iced Tea for the caffeine and Tylenol Extra Strength for the inevitable caffeine headache. I would like to thank Sandwiches for keeping me alive during my creative spurts, and Eon Smoke for the nicotine that kept me sane. Special mention goes out to TUMS, and I'd be remiss in my expression of gratitude if I didn't give a super special shout-out to two very dear friends who work so well together, Svedka and Diet Fresca.

But seriously, folks.

I'm a bit hesitant to name the bloggers this time around. Not because they don't deserve the accolades, but because I don't want to forget anyone! Please don't egg my house if I leave your name off this list. I assure you… I am aware of you, and I am grateful to you.

First and foremost, yet again, I gotta give props to my girls at Totally Booked. Jenny and Gitte are two of the coolest chicks I know, and ones I'm proud to call friends. Sorry for making you cry the other night at dinner, G. But the fact is… You two have *changed my life*. I bloody love the both of you.

Kelly and Joanne at Have Book Will Read. My God. Those two arranged the most rockin' blog tour Facebook has ever seen, and I'm still in awe that they managed to pull it off. And then, just one short week later, they got to work arranging a cover reveal for RW3. Crazy ladies! I am so happy to have had the chance to hang with you in person in London, and can't wait to do it again. Sorry for keeping you out so late. Not really. ;)

A few blogs that deserve special mention:
If These Boobs Could Talk, The REAL Housewives of Romance (thanks for the most asstastic teaser pics!), Miss Construed, Gigi's Book Blog, Worth the Read, The Best "Read" Wine Book Blog, Kimberly Faye Reads, I Love YA Fiction, Sugar and Spice, Romantic Reading Escapes: All that sharing hasn't gone unnoticed. Thanks for the cheerleading and pimpin'.

The rest of the blogs from the tour and the cover reveal: Thanks so much for your involvement.

Any other blogs that have kindly read and reviewed my books in the past: Thank you. I still get giddy with each and every green light, every new review.

Super-readers: Kay Miles, Linda Della Volpe, Happy Driggs, and newcomer Kari Matthes. Praise Jesus.

Critique Partner, Stevie Kisner: You always give it to me straight. You make me laugh; you let me vent. You're letting me edit your next book, so clearly you've lost your mind. But I love you much, beeyotch. I still owe you that drink.

Editor, Casey Moore Smith: What to say here? Your flailing red pen slashed through this puppy like the sorcerer's apprentice wielding his magic wand, bringing your specific brand of enchantment—yet again—to one of my stories. I hope you know you have a job for life. Xoxo

My high school girlfriends: I'm sitting in my bedroom right now, writing this book instead of being with you at our 'reunion'. I'm thinking I owe you all a slumber party to make up for it. My house, this Saturday, seven o'clock? I'll buy the boxes of wine. You bring the Twinkies. Again, special mention to Dana for another beautiful cover.

Thanks to Z for the guy stories. After twenty-five years, I finally got that glimpse into the boys' locker room. And now I need bleach for my eyes.

The rest of my Forever Friends and my entire family: Hugs, kisses, and much thanks.

My sister, Diana: I already dedicated the book to you AND named a character after you. 'Nuff said. ♥

Mom and Dad: I love you. Thanks, as always, for the support.

Dad O and Barb: Thanks again for the use of your house. Your fish are alive, your appliances are intact. I win. Xoxo

Brother-in-law Joe: I didn't use your photo for the cover, and I still feel badly about it. But here's a plug for YOUR book to make up for it: https://www.facebook.com/WeirdHollywood
and your website: joeartistwriter.com

Lastly…

Michael: I know, I know. I owe you pretty huge after this one. I've been neglectful to everyone these past few months, but you've suffered the brunt of it. Thank you for understanding. ♥

The Two Most Incredible Kids on the Planet: Pack your bags, monkeys. We're going to Disneyland! (And Mom's leaving the laptop AT HOME.) You've earned it. Xoxoxo

About the Author:

T. Torrest is a fiction writer from the U.S. She has written many books, but prays that only a handful of them will ever see the light of day. Her stories are geared toward readers of any age that know how to enjoy a good laugh and a dreamy romance.

Ms. Torrest was a child of the eighties, but has since traded in her Rubik's cube for a laptop and her Catholic school uniform for a comfy pair of yoga pants. She's a pop-culture junkie, a movie aficionado, and an enthusiast of talking about herself in the third person. A lifelong Jersey girl, she currently resides there with her husband and two sons.

She also really digs it when she hears from readers, and is known to use words like "dig" in a non-sarcastic way. You can find out more about her books at her website: www.ttorrest.com

A Note from the Author:

Wow. I just want to thank you for holding this book in your hands right now. When I first put "Remember When" out to the masses, I never dreamed it would become such a beloved story. But so many of you have gone out of your way to let me know how much that book touched you and how you fell in love with the characters. Your kind words have meant so much and gotten me through many a moment of writer's block!

If you haven't already done so, please come "like" the TTorrest Author Page on Facebook.
We have lots of fun discussing books, movies… and the eighties!

You can also follow me on Goodreads: T Torrest

I love hearing from readers and am curious about your book club discussions.

If you'd like to drop me a personal message, my email is:
ttorrest@optonline.net
I always do my best to write back!

And lastly, as always, if you enjoyed reading this book, I ask you to tell your friends, loan it out, and please, please leave a review (without spoilers!).

TALK ABOUT IT. On Facebook, on Goodreads… any time you're asked about a funny read, a swoony romance, or an awesome book boyfriend.

Word of mouth is *truly* the only way we indie authors survive.

And now… a special thank you surprise.

(Surprises are good.)

YOU AND ME AND EVERYONE WE KNOW

Trip

St. Nicetius Class of '91 15th Reunion
November 25, 2006

The green and white crepe streamers are twisted around the room and there's a spinning disco ball suspended from the ceiling. Every wall is plastered with a million pictures from our yearbook, and between the big hair and the stupid neckties in all the shots, it looks like John Hughes' brain has exploded. But I gotta say, the sight of all these cheesy decorations is actually kind of... comforting. A reminder of where—and when—it all began.

I glance beside me and grin at the girl who was supposed to be on my arm all along.

Finally.

I give Layla a kiss just because she's looking at me with those expectant eyes of hers, smiling like she's hiding some big secret. Well, I've got a secret of my own.

I take a peek over her shoulder to look for Pick. When I find him in the crowd, I give the "go" signal and he gives me a thumbs up. Lisa's standing next to him with her hands clasped together, practically jumping up and down at having seen our exchange. She knows what's coming.

I grab Layla's hand and drag her over to the stage, with the intention of asking the DJ if I can borrow his microphone.

But before I can do it, I feel a tug against my arm and stop dead in my tracks. Layla is resisting my pull, which, let me tell you, doesn't happen too often. *Heh heh.*

She's got this mysterious little smirk playing at her lips, and I'm curious to know why, but right now all I want to do is kiss that smile right off her face.

So I do.

After a few seconds, she breaks away, raising her eyebrows at me. "You're famous."

I glare at her in confusion, and my expression must look pretty funny, because it makes her laugh.

Not that I mind. It's probably my favorite sound in the world.

I wrap my arms tighter around her waist and say, "Yeah, no kidding. Big news flash there, Lay."

She slides a hand to the back of my hair. Christ. It's something she's done a million times, but that little move never fails to kill me. I close my eyes and lean my head into her hand as she says, "What I meant is that so much of your life is public, all the time." She brushes her face against my jaw and whispers the next part against my ear, "Some moments can be private."

I pull back and look at her, amazed at this woman in my arms.

She knows, dammit.

She knows what I'm planning to do. No way she could possibly know *how* I'm planning to do it, but she seems pretty sure of herself that she's nailed down the *when*. As in, right now. And shit. She's right.

What she doesn't know is that I've got Slanker Knox behind that curtain, waiting to play a cover of "Paradise City" the second I pop the question. They didn't come cheap. But seriously, who cares about the cost? You can't put a pricetag on awesome. Hell, if G N' R were still together, I'd have forked over whatever they were asking just to get them here tonight. Barring that, Slanker Knox is one heck of a second choice. I figure for something as huge as this, it's either go big or go home. What girl doesn't want fanfare like that?

I look down at the girl in question. She's calm, staring right back at me, her lips quirked into a slight smile. Her brown eyes are full of patience, as though she's waiting for me to work it all out.

And suddenly, I do.

This girl. This girl in my arms. Jesus. She never stops surprising me.

I give her a stunned smile and a squeeze of her hand, then send her off to say goodbye to our friends while I head backstage and talk to the band. I offer my apologies to the lead singer JT, explain what's going on, and tell them they can either pack it in for the night or play a set. Either way, they know they're getting paid. And knowing these guys, I'm sure they'll choose Option B, whether I was paying them or not.

You're welcome, Class of '91.

I reclaim my girl and we head out for the *TRU*.

* * *

I'm sweating. I'm actually nervous and sweating about this.

Dammit. Why did I let her talk me into this? I'm used to putting on the show. I was all set and ready to put on the performance of a lifetime back there at the reunion, and now I'm waiting for this damn elevator to bring us forty-fucking-nine floors up to our room so I can do it privately.

Penthouses are overrated.

Layla's no help. She just keeps smiling and squeezing my hand. Like that's supposed to ease my mind? Christ.

I get it. Fine, okay. She wants *me* right now for this. Not *him*.

Fair enough.

No surprises. No theatrics.

Just us.

Fine.

The elevator *dings!* as the doors open directly into our suite...

And what's the first thing I see?

A very familiar flash of turquoise, right there in the middle of the room, greeting me like some old, long-lost friend.

Ho. Ly. Shit. No freaking way did she really do this.

I turn to Layla, who's about to bust out of her skin, smiling so wide I think she's gonna pull a cheek muscle. "Layla. Effing. Warren."

She starts cracking up as I make a lunging dive inside The Tent.

That's right. Our fucking *tent*. Where it all started.

Where it's going to start again.

She throws some music on the stereo while I whip off my shoes, and then joins me in *our fucking tent*. I lie down on my side and prop a hand under my head as Layla drops down cross-legged onto the floor.

"How the hell did you manage this one?" I ask, staring dumbstruck at the gorgeous woman settling in next to me.

She smiles out, "We'll have to find a way to thank Jeffrey properly tomorrow."

"Jeffrey? Jesus. I would've paid good money to see him trying to set this thing up. He doesn't really strike me as the outdoorsy type."

"Yeah, well neither do *you*, Chester. Yet here we are."

I slide a hand up her knee and kiss it, right there on that spot of exposed skin. "Here we are."

She smiles and swipes a hand over my ear. Always screwing with my hair.

And yeah. Here we are. In the very hotel that brought me to New Jersey in the first place. They'd barely broken ground on the thing when I first met Layla. Turned out, our relationship was being built right along with it.

It sure as hell took us long enough to figure that out.

I'm not waiting anymore.

My hand moves on its own to pull the ring out of my pocket. It's been burning a hole against my chest all night, and having it out in the open like this actually brings some relief. For that reason alone, I'm suddenly struck with a strange calm about this whole thing.

I loop it around my knuckle and hold it up between us, looking right into the eyes of the most beautiful woman I've ever met in my life.

"Marry me."

She doesn't gasp. She doesn't cry. She doesn't even look at the ring.

Her eyes are still locked on mine, seeing right through me like no one but her ever has.

My Layla.

For a quick second, I get the impression that she's actually *grappling* with the 'yes' I assumed would be a foregone conclusion. Before I know it, I find myself pleading my case. "You and me, Lay. I want forever. Tell me you do, too. *Be mine.*"

Her face turns almost sympathetic, and I feel my heart drop clear out of my body. All the ridiculous arguments and stupid miscommunications race through my head like a worn-out rerun. All that lost time we wasted when we should have been together instead.

I don't believe it. *She's actually going to say 'no.'*

Panic burns in my stomach, slowly rising until it forms a solid lump in my throat. She's trying to find a way to let me down easy. She doesn't know how to say it. She—

"It's too late, Trip."

Fuuuck!

Before I can ask, before I can *beg*, her lips quirk into a sly grin as she adds, "You already made me yours years ago. Sixteen of them, to be exact. That lovely little bauble is just a technicality as far as I'm concerned." She points to the "lovely little bauble" in question; the monstrous blue sapphire that's bigger than this freaking tent.

I want to laugh. I want to cry. I want to strangle her.

My voice sounds hoarse, like it's not even my own as I ask, "Is that a yes, then?"

She smiles—God, that gorgeous grin of hers—and smoothes a hand across my jaw, leaning down to kiss me. I throw an arm around her middle and bring her body underneath mine to kiss her back.

When we finally come up for air, her gaze travels over to my hand next to her head. "Can I see it?" she asks, almost shyly. Her question is a softball, practically begging for an off-color joke, but this is kind of a big moment. I'm not going to screw this memory up for us.

So, instead, I hold my pointed finger up between us, revealing the vintage platinum ring I found weeks ago. I knew it was perfect the first second I saw it. Kind of like how I felt when I first saw *her*.

Layla's mouth drops as she tilts her head from side to side in order to watch the light dance through the sapphire from different angles, alternating awe-struck looks between the ring and me.

I am Superman.

"Trip... It's... It's *gorgeous!*" Her eyes are glossing over with unshed tears, and I'm trying to stop my hands from shaking as I take the thing off my finger and go to slip it onto hers. She pulls her hand back, though, and before I can ask her why, she says, "I think it's only fair that I tell you something first."

I pause, every muscle in my body tensing. I stare at her empty finger and feel my heart take another plunge. *What the hell?*

I start to roll off her but she tightens her arms around my shoulders, looks me right in the eye, and just lets out with it. "I have something I want to give you."

She reaches over to a pocket of the tent and roots through the thing, coming up with a small, flat box.

"You got me a present?" I ask, incredulous.

"Well, I knew you'd gotten me something, so I wanted to have something to give you back."

I'd spent weeks planning the perfect proposal with Lisa's input. All along I should have remembered that Layla was way more intuitive than we'd given her credit for. So much for surprises.

At least for her.

Because when I unwrap the box and pull off the lid, I realize the surprises are all on me tonight.

I'm looking at this white stick thing... with two little pink lines in the window.

It takes me a few seconds, but I finally comprehend what I'm looking at. "Lay?" I ask, and my voice is cracking like a twelve-year-old boy's, "Is this...? Are you...?"

She grabs my hand and meets my eyes. I can see the tears streaming down her cheeks as she finishes my question. "Having your baby? Yes."

Holy shit!

"Holy shit! You're… we're… Lay!" I can't even form a complete sentence, much less find a way to tell her how amazing she is. How much I love her. So, I don't bother saying anything at all. I grab her and crush my lips to hers, this woman who owns me, this woman who's carrying our baby inside her.

Holy shit! Our baby!

We're having a baby.

My *fiancée* and I are having a baby.

"Looks like you'll *have* to marry me now, Chester."

There are no words. I'm struck dumb by this incredible woman in my arms. This infuriating woman I've loved since we were kids. This woman I'll love forever. And "have to" doesn't even cover it. Yeah, I'll have to marry her. Only because I'll wind up in a rubber room if I don't.

I slide the ring onto her finger and pull her to me, molding her body to every inch of mine. My hands roam, trying to discern any changes to the curves and dips I know so well, envisioning what they'll look like as she grows a piece of me inside her.

"Lay?" I ask in a rarely-heard, serious tone. I can tell by the look in her eyes that she knows I've got something really important to say. I swipe a strand of her hair behind her ear and duck my face next to her head to ask softly, "Did you really just give me a present that you *peed* on?"

She pauses for just a moment, and I bite my lip, the both of us fighting the hilarity that's threatening to erupt. We find out soon enough that it's a losing battle. She tries to shove my body off of her, but I'm not going anywhere. She settles for a slap on my shoulder instead, her giggles bursting between us. "Nice, Chester. Real nice."

All I can do is grin and plant one on her. I don't think I'll ever get tired of kissing her through our laughter. I pull back and look into the beautiful face of this beautiful woman who's stuck with me for life. "I am *so* in love with you, Lay."

Her eyes are glistening with tears, her gorgeous smile shooting straight through my heart, the heart that she has owned—and will continue to own—forever. She slides her hands around my neck and looks me right in the eyes before answering back.

"I know."

NOW IT'S THE END.

Made in the USA
Middletown, DE
25 May 2016